A RAGE OF WOLVES

"Do you have any idea what you have gotten us into?" Mayelna demanded. "Do you even know what you are doing?"

"Of course I know what I am doing!" Velmeran replied hotly. "Three entire ships agree."

"What are you trying to prove? That you can attack a whole Union planet for vengeance?"

"No, not for vengeance. For me, Mayelna!" Velmeran declared so fiercely that Mayelna was driven back by his wrath. "For every Starwolf alive today and who will live in days to come! I am a warrior, a Starwolf, and I want that to mean something. I want my kind to be able to go where they want without fear of being shot. I want my people to have worlds of their own, to write their own music and their own stories and build their own monuments. I want this war to end *now*.

"Let me do what I can ... what I must. Help me, if you dare, mother, because I need all the help I can get. But if you are afraid, then get out of my way."

THE STARWOLVES

THORARINN GUNNARSSON

POPULAR LIBRARY

An Imprint of Warner Books, Inc.

A Warner Communications Company

POPULAR LIBRARY EDITION

Popular Library®, the fanciful P design, and Questar® are
registered trademarks of Warner Books, Inc.

Cover illustration by John Harris

Popular Library books are published by
Warner Books, Inc.
666 Fifth Avenue
New York, N.Y. 10103

Ⓦ A Warner Communications Company

Printed in the United States of America

First Printing: January, 1988

10 9 8 7 6 5 4 3 2

1

Valthyrra Methryn slipped smoothly out of starflight to cruise at a speed that was just sublight, paralleling the freighter lane, just far enough out to avoid being seen. She was as vast and black as space itself, three kilometers long and more than one across the short wings of her arrowhead shape. Flaring main drives were tucked protectively beneath her wings; her upper hull was a smooth, armored shell that she could turn toward enemy fire. She moved like a warship, with the smooth, graceful control of a big ship with more than enough power for its size. She was beautiful and frightening to behold.

By design, the Methryn was a destroyer of immense size, all engines and weapons and very little crew. She could turn and accelerate like a ship a fraction her size, while the cannons in her shock bumper were more than a match for a fleet of heavy cruisers. On the underside of her tapered nose was a cannon that could turn an entire planet into dust.

By definition the Methryn was a carrier, existing to provide for her handful of fighters. Tucked up against her belly, insignificant against her total bulk, were a pair of bays which housed ninety fighters, a fifth of what she could allow. In truth, for all her speed and power, the

1

Methryn had not seen actual battle in more than half a century. Her fighters ran down and captured her prey, and defended her against the occasional warship daring and foolish enough to take her to task for her discreet piracies. She carried a crew of barely two thousand, existing only to tend her fighters and their own needs. Valthyrra Methryn took care of herself, and she was more than capable of that. There were only twenty-two like her in known space.

For now, Valthyrra Methryn settled in to wait. Company freighters, still running in starflight toward the system only two light-days ahead, would never see her cruising barely five thousand kilometers to one side of their lane. In starflight, their scanners were confined to a narrow cone immediately ahead, and were effective only in avoiding collisions. The first indication that they had wandered into a trap came when nine swift fighters descended upon their tail. Valthyrra had learned patience during her long career and this laying in wait did not bother her. That was not the case with her young pilots.

For Velmeran, this was a time he dreaded as much as the run itself. He was the youngest pack leader on the ship; at twenty-five, a leader when most were still just students. Seven of the eight pilots in his pack were indeed the youngest on the ship, most having never flown with a pack when he had received them four months earlier. His last pilot was too old to fly a transport, let alone a fighter. His was a pack that should not have been, all students thrown together and expected to fight. It badly needed strong leadership, but that was something Velmeran not only lacked but feared.

At times like this, Velmeran was led to wonder if the Commander hated him. Of course, he had always been on the best of terms with the Commander, and he knew that she thought well of him. He had the ability, he had to admit, but neither the experience nor the inclination to make the most of those abilities. He also knew that the Commander would have never done this to him. This was all Valthyrra's idea, because she believed in him too much.

The lift lurched to an uncertain stop, and Velmeran smiled to himself in anticipation of revenge. Valthyrra would soon be in need of a complete overhaul, an involved process that took half a year in airdock and resulted in partial dismemberment of the unfortunate ship. Valthyrra disliked being dismantled almost as much as she disliked being confined in dock.

Velmeran entered the wide bridge from the left wing. Bridge crewmembers in white armored suits sat at their stations or hurried about their duties. Consherra glanced up at him from the helm console on that side of the raised middle bridge, and an instant later Valthyrra quickly rotated her camera pod around and focused both lenses on him before turning her attention back to the Commander's console on the upper bridge. Velmeran frowned. The three of them together, Commander, helm and ship herself, was entirely too much motherly attention, and it only seemed to him like an accusation of his inability to make a pack of students fly like veterans.

He hurried—as well as his armor would allow—up the steps to the upper bridge. Consherra was scrupulously bent to her screen, and his disposition was soured all the more to find the Commander in exactly the same position. Valthyrra was all but peering over her shoulder, her boom extended well back into the recess of the upper bridge. Velmeran wondered whose idea this was. Valthyrra and Mayelna were a pair; they were schemers, and seemed to take turns dreaming up ideas. The ship was audacious enough to be pleased with herself. The Commander simply had no conscience.

"This one is yours, Meran," the Commander remarked without looking up.

"So I had heard," Velmeran replied evenly.

"I am sorry to have to send you out again so soon," Mayelna continued absently. "Opportunities come rarely, and it is rarer still when we can afford to make our own opportunities."

Velmeran shrugged both sets of arms, an exaggerated gesture. "Did I complain?"

"We can catch a bulk freighter in this lane," Valthyrra explained with bad timing. "A big, slow ship, all holds heavy with cargo. Something your students should be able to take without trouble."

Mayelna glanced up in annoyance. "They are not students."

"I cannot imagine what else they may be!" Velmeran exclaimed in disgust. "In our last two runs, we wrecked one cargo and allowed the other to escape. Escape! A Starwolf pack never misses its prey, never!"

"You put your least experienced pilots on a ship that was too fast for them," Mayelna pointed out. "Let your pilots make a run or two, for the practice. Then you get on that ship's tail and bring her out of starflight for them to work over in their own good time. They only get frustrated if they run too long without success . . . you lost your last two ships to that."

Valthyrra glanced from the Commander to Velmeran and back again so quickly that her lenses hardly had time to focus.

"Try to be patient," Mayelna continued when he did not answer. "That is a large part of your problem. You are—you always have been—too good of a pilot to understand the limitations of those who lack your talent, and too young to understand that. Be patient and work with them. If they think that you believe in them, then they will learn to trust in their own abilities."

Velmeran began to say something, then paused and turned away. Valthyrra lifted her pod in alarm, and even Mayelna sat up straight.

"Velmeran, what about Keth?" the Commander asked quickly.

He stopped and turned slowly. "I have no one to replace him. Not this late."

"You will have to tell him," Mayelna insisted. "Before your pack goes out again. Or I will."

"But Keth is the only experienced pilot I have," Velmeran protested weakly. "He is still better than most of the others."

"But that is the point," the Commander insisted. "The others will continue to improve. Keth will only get worse."

"Do you suppose that I do not know what happens out there?" Valthyrra asked. "Keth hesitates in his runs, and he cuts his turns wide. He tries to show off, but he only gets in the way. Pilots who refuse to retire usually end up running into something, like their target, or one of their own. Or me."

Velmeran did not reply at once, but stood looking down. At last he nodded reluctantly. "Very well. But we cannot fly short. Let him fly this last time, and I will tell him when we come back. Just give me an experienced replacement."

Mayelna looked up at him skeptically.

Velmeran shrugged and turned to walk away. "Do what you want, then. You will anyway."

She nodded. "Granted. By the way, Baressa's pack will fly watch for you."

Velmeran stopped short and stared in utter astonishment. This was the insult added to injury. "Baressa?"

"She is under strict orders not to offer so much as a word of advice."

Velmeran, with a final gesture of hopelessness, turned away a last time.

Mayelna turned back to her monitors, but Valthyrra made no secret of watching him go. Several of the others, Consherra in particular, watched him just as closely. Valthyrra swung her boom back around to the Commander's console.

"Is he still your choice?" Mayelna asked without looking up.

The pod itself nodded in agreement. "More than ever."

Mayelna looked up sharply. "He is a good pilot, I will

grant you that. But that does not make him a good leader."

"No, the two are not related," she agreed. "But I still believe that when he learns to lose his fear of being a leader, then he will make a very good one."

Mayelna leaned back in her chair, crossing her arms defiantly. "How can you know that better than me? I am his mother. . . ."

"And I have been a carrier for nearly twenty thousand years," Valthyrra replied firmly. "I should know who I want to command on my bridge. He will prove himself soon enough."

The landing bay was dark and silent, empty except for the nine fighters seated in their racks just inside the forward bay door. They were starships in their own right, large for single-seat fighters, with main drives tucked under down-swept wings and a large star drive in their tail. In color they were a dull, nonreflective black—even their cockpit windows deeply tinted—like swift shadows against the darkness of space. They were sleek and powerful, built for speed and maneuverability, and there was nothing, neither piloted nor computer-driven, that could outfly them.

For now they sat poised for flight, landing gear retracted, ready to leap from their racks into battle. They lacked only their pilots, who were as finely crafted by genetic engineering for their specific task as the ships themselves. The wolf-pack pilots had been made with the accelerated reflexes needed to fly their ships at tremendous speed, the strength and endurance for harsh accelerations and heightened senses to feel the locations of the ships about them. Together, a Starwolf pilot and ship made the most deadly and efficient war machine known.

Velmeran completed his inspection of his ship and climbed to the rack's boarding platform, using the overhead supports to lift himself into the outthrust cockpit. He often came alone to the bay to be with his ship when his thoughts troubled him. The ship was the other half of his life; being with it reminded him why he flew with the packs, catching company freighters for the carrier he served. Too often he found the same answer. This had been decided for him a very long time ago. He could have no plans of his own because, like this ship, he was too specialized for his task to do anything else.

He thought then, as he often did, of the first time he had sat in the cockpit of a wolf-pack fighter. It had been his mother's ship, sitting on its stiltlike landing gear centermost of its pack of nine, just in from a hunt. The pilots were always exhausted then, barely able to walk for fatigue and the dreamlike concentration of flight. But she had been alive and alert, eager to say to him the things she had to tell. She had stood for a long time, watching him without expression, and the intensity of that stare had demanded his full attention.

"Listen well, Meran," she had said suddenly. "The Commander is old and very sick, and I will likely be called to take over his duties at any time. After that I will never fly with the packs again, and so I wanted to say this to you now.

"Fifty thousand years ago we owned these stars we now haunt. But then the Union came like a sickness from within, a group of fringe worlds who thought that they would be happier and wealthier if they could run everything for themselves. And we fought them, back in the days when we were the old Terran fleet. But all of our bases were swallowed up, and our little ships were destroyed. We withdrew for a time to the one base that the Union never found, and tried to think of how so very few could fight something so large.

"Our friends, the Aldessan of Valtrys, did what they could. They gave us these big carriers, self-contained worlds, and these fast little ships that can run down anything. And they made us better, so that we can fly these ships. The Union learned very quickly to leave us alone. They always think in terms of cost and profit, and it costs too much to fight us. They prefer to pay us ransom in the company freighters we take.

"But it was a trap of our own making. They cannot defeat us without destroying themselves, and we cannot defeat them with the few carriers we have. We survive the only way we can, preying upon their freighters and protecting the fringe worlds. Four-fifths of the colonies are fringe worlds, not a part of the Union but dominated by it, and the companies steal away their lives and sell them back with transport charges attached. If we do any real good, it is in the fact that we keep the Union humble and the companies from making slaves of the minor worlds."

She had paused a moment to run a hand lovingly over the sleek hull of the fighter. Watching her, he had realized that these little ships were more than just toys or machines to the pilots, but a part of themselves. And Mayelna had been there to say farewell to her own, knowing that she would be going up to the bridge to stay in a matter of hours.

"Someday you will most likely fly one of these ships," she had continued. "I almost wish that you will not. It is a terrible life, and often a short one. But you are a Starwolf and made to fly, and you will have only half a life if you do not. You will know what it is like to become one with this machine. To outthink and outreact your on-board computer and never need to look at scan because you can feel in the back of your mind the singing of the crystal engines of all the ships about you. The fear for your own life, the remorse and guilt for what you must do as a warrior, the sorrow for those you will lose along the way. All the heavy prices you must pay, and still it is worth it all. Because this is what you exist for. One day you will understand."

He had listened, and he remembered every word. But he had not understood. He had known only a growing, impatient desire to have one of those sleek little ships for his own.

* * *

Now Velmeran understood only too well. He had been content as a mere pilot. Now he was pack leader. With that came the responsibility for eight lives beyond his own, the greater responsibility to defend his ship, and the fear of failure in those duties. He dared not fail. With that also came the relentless need to know that he was doing the right thing whenever he led his pack into battle, that there really was some justification for the death and destruction, the lives that were risked and sometimes lost; and above all else he needed to know, for his own satisfaction, that he was not just a machine made for war, with no life or will of his own.

He had no answers to any of those questions, but still he took his pack out and fought. Perhaps that in itself was answer enough, but he did not yet have the experience to understand what it meant.

Velmeran paused when he saw his reflection in the black monitor screen that dominated the upper part of the fighter's console. The Starwolves, the Kelvessan, were a race apart, vaguely human in appearance but not derived from human stock. They were small in size, disproportionately long of limb with powerful arms and legs that looked to have been matched to a body several sizes too small. Far more than just an extra set of arms and unnatural strength separated Kelvessan from men.

Indeed, as he peered at his reflection, he thought that he could never pass as human. His eyes, outsized for good light sensitivity, were more than twice as large as they should have been. His ears, equally outsized and set farther back on his head, had been tapered to a delicate point for purely aesthetic reasons. He also thought that his nose was about half the size it should have been, and his mouth was too wide. And he had always been told that a Starwolf's shaggy mop of brown hair, remarkably thick and soft, was natural padding against helmet and collar.

Other, more extensive refinements were not visible. His bones were not calcium but precipitates of iron, and quite as hard as iron bars of equal thickness. His cartilage and tendons could withstand tons of stress and his nervous-system was electrical rather than electrochemical, allowing reflexes that were thousands of times faster than those of humans. His strength was tremendous, to allow him to not just withstand but function under forces that would kill an ordinary man. He was a machine, the living control center for an equally remarkable starship.

But was there also a person within that carefully engineered machine? He certainly was not human. He accepted that. But if not human, then what was he? He was a Kelvessa, a Starwolf. His only hope was that those simple words described something more than just a fighting machine.

The Vinthra military complex was by far the largest free-orbiting station in the Rane Sector, an immense, imposing structure that sprawled across several kilometers of space. Over a thousand ships, from tiny couriers to the vast, threatening hulks of battleships and heavy carriers, could be docked and serviced there, while another fifty could slip into its airdocks for extensive repairs. Between the firepower of the ships stationed there and the shields and cannons of the planetary defense system, not even a Starwolf carrier could approach this world in open hostility. For this was Vinthra, and Vannkarn, its port, housed the government and military command for this entire sector.

A single ship moved swiftly toward the station, braking gently with its forward engines. Its lines were those of a Union destroyer, sleek and powerful, with a slender hexagonal hull and armor plates concealing its drives. Now it was the private yacht of the High Councilor of the Rane Sector, a fact that was proven as other, sometimes larger ships moved quietly out of its way. Its path was centered upon a single portion of that vast station, a set of moorings near the shuttle bays set aside for diplomatic vessels.

A single figure stood at the window of the carpeted and paneled corridor that adjoined those mooring berths.

He was a tall man, at two meters a giant by modern standards, lean and well-muscled. Although no longer young, he was far from being old. Indeed he was well thought of as handsome in a rugged way that was now rare in his diminished race. And yet there was a sense of darkness about him, a ruthless, mercenary quality reflected in the hard, measuring glare of his black eyes. His physical presence was far more threatening than his rank, so that those who crossed that section of corridor passed through quietly.

A muted vibration ran through that portion of the station as the incoming ship nudged cautiously into its moorings. Attendants assembled quickly but quietly to service that ship as soon as its one, infinitely important passenger was discharged. A last metallic clang announced the opening of the ship, and a moment later the inner doors of the airlock rolled back. A pair of guards with rifles stepped out to take positions to either side, followed a moment later by an older man pursued by the automated carrier that bore his luggage. He was a tall man as well, not as tall as the Sector Commander—even allowing for his slightly bent back— but still far taller than anyone else within sight. And like the Sector Commander, he was clearly of older, purer Terran stock, his features rougher and more clearly defined than the norm. But there the resemblance ended. He wore no uniform but rich if subtle civilian dress, with an unruly mane of long white hair and deep blue eyes that were alert and held a glint of skeptical humor, as if he was amused with his own pretensions.

"Hello, Don!" he exclaimed when he saw the one who awaited him. "How nice of you to come all this way up here to meet me."

"Richart couldn't make it," Commander Trace said tightly, but with no regret. "But how did it go?"

"Well enough. But not here," the Councilor said, with a subtle gesture for him to remain silent.

Donalt Trace nodded in agreement. "I understand. I have a shuttle waiting."

"Your ship?" Councilor Lake asked. He knew that Trace would have flown himself in a launch borrowed from the pool. If so, there was little chance that anyone would overhear, accidentally or otherwise, what they had to discuss.

"I had one called up for servicing this morning—and then I chose another at random," he explained as they started toward the shuttle bay.

The Councilor laughed. "Don, you are the suspicious type!"

"I learned from you, Uncle Jon," Commander Trace replied.

The shuttle was indeed a small one, hardly large enough to seat six. An in-system fighter would not have been much smaller. Donalt Trace slipped the tiny shuttle out of the bay and shifted easily into their designated path of descent. Since the military station was on the opposite side of Vinthra from the port, they had to make a fairly quick descent in only half an orbit. That added somewhat to the roughness of the ride, since they would be braking most of the way down. But Councilor Lake had anticipated this, and two glasses of his favorite wine beforehand helped smooth the bumps somewhat.

"Well, they bought it," Lake said, leaning back in a seat that was too small.

Commander Trace made a derisive sound. "They bought it, after the problem became so bad that it could no longer be ignored. Then they accept your theories and plans? All of it?"

"Nearly all of it," Lake replied, grinning. "They certainly bought more of it than I thought they would. You will get your weapons, Don. Even the big, expensive one. And I get my plan of genetic population control. The only thing we don't get is a Union Fleet Commander. A High Council of Sector Commanders, yes. But the sectors are by no means ready to give up their old political and military autonomy. We will cooperate for the good of all, but we live or die by our own efforts."

"But that was the most important part!" Trace protested. "We cannot fight the Starwolves separately. They have a unified command. . . ."

"We assume."

"Jon, you know they do. They will fight together, when there is need. They just seldom have to, since a single carrier can take on anything an entire sector can throw at it."

"And there are more carriers in the Wolf Fleet than we have sectors," the Councilor added. "Obviously we cannot fight them, one on one or all together, not the way we have been going about it. We have to find new ways to fight them. That's why I consider that a small loss. You have only one carrier to worry about, and her name is Methryn. You find a way to destroy her, and then we can go after the rest."

Which was much easier said than done, Councilor Lake reflected. And just the beginning of his own problems. The human race was dying, or at least degenerating to the point that it could no longer care for itself. The genetic message that made a human was deteriorating; random, detrimental mutations were not only occurring at an alarming rate but were being passed into the common genetic pool. There was no determining the exact cause, although the Councilor preferred to believe that mankind had been too long removed from the laws of natural selection that had guided its evolution.

People were smaller than they had been in the first days of space flight, slighter of build and gentler of mood and feature. Unfortunately, people were also less intelligent than they had been, less able to reason and remember. Mental deficiency and imbalance claimed a fourth of the population, and another fourth was genetically sterile. It was a problem that had been a very long time coming, but it had finally become so, bad that the High Council could no longer ignore it. For in another thousand years the machinery of the Union, of human civilization itself, would grind to a halt for want of maintenance. That might seem like a very long time, but for a problem fifty thousand years in the making, it was already too late.

Still, Councilor Lake wanted to save what he could. And if stern measures were taken now, a large part of the Union could be saved. The only solution was to enforce the sterilization of large segments of the population, intervening where nature had failed. The general population would not take such controls lightly. The military would be needed to enforce order, especially on those worlds that bore little love or loyalty for the Union from the start. And for that, the problem that the Starwolves represented would have to be eliminated. Or at least reduced to a manageable level.

That was Donalt Trace's responsibility as Commander of the Sector Fleet. Never before had the Union been able to fight the Starwolves effectively. They had technology that the Union did not and now would never have, ships that were faster and pilots that were better. The Union's only advantage lay in its seemingly inexhaustible resources, its ability to replace ships, supplies and personnel as fast as they were lost. But the old resources were disappearing, and new ways had to be found to fight and win.

It was up to Donalt Trace to find those answers. He had been selected for that task at an early age. Every aspect of his training, all of his education in strategy and military concepts, had been selected and guided by the elder Lake, just as the Councilor had selected and trained his grandson Richart to be his replacement. But there was that element in Trace that was unpredictable, a blind, self-righteous confidence in his own abilities and his hatred for his enemy. Councilor Lake was aware that his weapon was flawed, but he had no choice. The fact remained that if Don could not do this, no one could.

"Then everything is ready here?" Lake asked, roused

from his reflections when the shuttle began to buck as it slipped into the upper air.

"The trap is laid," Trace assured him. "I don't give this old ploy a chance of working, but it will put the Starwolves off their guard."

2

Valthyrra Methryn found her prey after five hours of waiting. It was, as she had anticipated, a medium bulk freighter. Bulk freighters were about as big as they came and generally ships of the inner lanes, while smaller ships of three hundred meters or less ran the fringe. The packs caught one of the largest bulk freighters, wallowing monsters of nearly six hundred meters, perhaps once a year.

This was a bulk freighter of just over five hundred meters, and just the right size for a pack of students. Designed to move heavy cargoes inexpensively, she was too underpowered to ship a full load, and too slow and barely maneuverable under ordinary speeds. The difficult part of this task was that the pack was not trying to destroy the ship but disable it with a minimum of damage, and without touching the holds at all, so that her cargo and most of her parts could be salvaged. Bringing down a freighter intact required some very delicate shooting.

Velmeran was in a more hopeful mood once he knew what they would be hunting. But as always, it seemed, his timing was bad to the end; the call had caught him when he had just removed his armor. He was still securing the suit as the lift carried him down to the bay while a flight deck crewmember, already in her white armor trimmed in black,

16

assisted him. He was still setting the controls when the lift door snapped open.

The others were already at their ships, either in their cockpits or waiting nearby as crewmembers made final adjustments. Vayelryn was already in her ship, strapped in and helmeted; he hoped that her eagerness would be reflected in her flying. She was the slowest, shakiest pilot of the lot; he had moved her to the far right of the pack formation in the hope that she would not run into anyone if she rode on the outside.

The twins Ferryn and Tregloran comprised the middle part of the pack's right wing; Velmeran kept them together, since they seemed to work best that way. They were his best pilots, perhaps because they had more ambition than the rest. But Tregloran was also his greatest embarrassment; in the last month he had once landed gear-up, although with no damage to his tough little ship, and he had been the one who had ripped open the hold of that first freighter. His problem was that he was entirely too eager. Ferryn's problem was that she spent too much time watching out for her brother, and not enough watching her own business.

Of the rest Velmeran had few worries. Merkollyn and the other two girls, tall Gyllan and tiny Steena, would make good, reliable pilots. Delvon would also be a good pilot once he lost his fear that he would lose control in a tight turn.

Velmeran found Tregloran and Ferryn between their ships, either conspiring or consoling each other. They looked up guiltily when they saw him watching them, and all but shook inside their shells when he started in their direction. Velmeran put on his charm, hoping that he radiated mature affection and concern as befitted their teacher and pack leader. It was a difficult task, considering that he was only five years older than they.

"Treg, you run in first and go after her star drive," he said. "Ferryn, I want you be ready to go in second. You can have four turns each."

"Us, Captain?" Tregloran asked. "Is this punishment for last time?"

"This is what you are here to learn," Velmeran insisted. "Take your time and set up your shots carefully—I am sure you can do it. Consider it practice, for you are under no stress to bring this ship down. Although the one who does take her gets first choice of anything on board . . . within reason."

"Fair enough!" Tregloran exclaimed, as if that was all the encouragement he needed to fly like a hundred-year veteran. Velmeran sent the younger pilots to their ships and then hurried to his own. But at the last moment he discovered the seeds of another plan, a way to solve his remaining problem, and paused at Keth's fighter.

The older pilot was already in his cockpit, arguing with his attending crewmember about the condition of some system on board his ship. He saw Velmeran and waved the frustrated crewmember away.

"I was just thinking that you and I should hold back," Velmeran called up to him. "I am giving this one to the twins for practice. Valthyrra says that this is a big, slow ship, so they should have no problem. They need the confidence as much as the practice."

"Oh, right!" Keth agreed enthusiastically; the bait had been taken. He was pleased and flattered to be in on this little conspiracy, never realizing that Velmeran only looked upon it as a chance to keep him out of the way.

Velmeran hurried on to his own ship, aware that he was taking too long, and feeling guilty for his deception when he realized that this would be Keth's last time out. Most pilots were wise enough to retire in grace and honor before they were asked. Keth was too proud, even if it was a false pride. He climbed the boarding platform of his fighter, lifting himself with all four arms by the overhead supports and lowering himself into the cockpit. He immediately powered up the on-board systems and got a clear check. The conversion generator purred gently, cycling its tremendous power back into itself.

"Do you know what Keth was complaining about?" he asked Benthoran as the bay crew arrived to secure his straps.

"No, but I can imagine," the older crewmember said, frowning. "His fighter is as worn out as he is. Maintenance said that only a new ship would cure that, but Valthyrra put his request on hold."

"Of course," Velmeran agreed. "Save a new ship for someone who can use it."

"Are you going?" Valthyrra demanded suddenly over ship's com.

"Yes, M'Lady!" he replied, and held still as Benthoran slipped the helmet over his head and closed the clips. He sealed the canopy and powered up the main drives as the crew chief quickly withdrew the overhead supports and the boarding platform. All of his fighters indicated ready, and Velmeran relayed pack ready to flight control. The forward doors were already going up, and Valthyrra gave them the count while it was still rising. A row of red lights above the wide door began to flash, beginning at either end and moving quickly to the large green light in the center.

Engines flaring, the nine little ships leaped out of their racks and thundered out of the bay. They slipped casually into V formation and they hurtled down the length of the Methryn's hull and shot out beneath her tapered nose. Once clear, the ship at the tip of each wing moved to the center of the pack, one above and one below. A moment later a second pack emerged from beneath the carrier, moving into formation as it closed rapidly to a position just behind the first.

Velmeran shifted power from the main drives to the star drive, and the two packs moved unhesitantly with him into starflight. They accelerated rapidly to overtake the freighter, setting a course to intercept the big ship. Velmeran could feel the slow, heavy drone of her star drive distinctly. Pilots depended more upon their inner senses than on scan, and visual was of no use at the speeds they flew. The packs flew wing to wing even in starflight, at speeds when Union pilots liked to put kilometers between each other, and yet with an accuracy that no automatic system could match.

They overtook the freighter in seconds, still unaware of her pursuers. Velmeran oriented by feel on the steady, rapid pulsing of the giant star drive. He could also sense the fighters about him, like nine high voices holding a single sustained note, and a second set of nine close behind. Far behind he could still hear the gentle hum of the Methryn's main drives. Starwolves could identify the size and type of ships by the frequency of their drives. Union ships pulsed low and heavy, phasing lower as the size of the drive increased; their warships phased more rapidly, forcing more power out of a crystal engine at the expense of slowly burning it out. Starwolf ships sang in clear, sustained tones; they knew how to get a great deal more power out of an engine without tearing it up.

The pack moved in close behind the freighter and matched her speed, breaking formation. Tregloran had first chance; he dove in with frightening speed and locked on the freighter's tail with surprising ease. But his prey was aware of him now; she executed a series of slow but elaborate turns and dodges, but he was still waiting when she righted herself and fired everything he had. That unfortunately included his tail cannon, and Velmeran had to jump to save his left wing. Several of his bolts caught the star drive too far near its outer edge and discharged into the flare.

Ferryn dropped into place immediately and tried to follow up on her brother's attack, but the freighter resumed her evasions. Ferryn held back until her chance came, then rushed forward. She fired too soon; her first bolts were deflected by the freighter's shields while her later shots were too near the center of the star drive and dissipated in the backwash of far greater energy.

Tregloran, greatly daring, began his run almost on his sister's tail, this time catching the freighter before she had time to evade. Velmeran doubted that he could make that work, for such tactics, while he might have observed their like from experienced pilots, were beyond his limited skill. But luck was with him that run, or else the promised reward inspired him to performance beyond what he would give for duty, ship or pack leader. A bolt slipped past on just the fringe of the star drive's flare, striking the immense crystal within centimeters of its outer edge. The drive flare intensified and exploded in a sudden, sustained flash as the damaged crystal melted from the core.

The freighter dropped out of starflight with an abruptness that almost twisted her apart, and the pack was upon her instantly. They saw her now for the first time; she was long and fat, her forward cabin extended forward of the holds, with generator and drives in a blocklike module behind. Now the fighters began their strafing runs at her bridge, as the freighter did her best to run sublight under her main drives.

It did not take long. A final shot found her bridge and discharged. With the main computer gone, the freighter quietly shut down her drives and major systems, leaving only lighting and atmosphere as she drifted in silence. Velmeran came in alone and sat just twenty meters off the ruined bridge while the short-range scanners of his ship probed for any sign of life. There was none, nor were any major systems in operation.

Now the capture ships moved in. Long and slender of body, almost all generator and drive systems, they approached the lifeless bulk of the freighter cautiously from behind. The pair moved in slowly, one to either side of the ship's ruined drive section. Three pairs of long, sturdy mechanical arms unfolded from their slender bellies to press their flat locking plates against the freighter's hull. Those locked down magnetically, and the capture ships pulled themselves close against the larger vessel's hull. Firing their main drives simultaneously, they slowly brought the drifting hulk around on a new course, back to where the Methryn waited patiently.

Velmeran thought that he had reason to be pleased, for

his pack had flown well. They had run down and captured a fairly large freighter, nearly as big as they came, her damage limited to her star drive and bridge. He knew that her holds were full by the way she had slid through her turns; freighters were generally built to the specifications of an empty ship and running with cargo, as they were meant, actually strained their capacities. This run had been a victory for him as much as it had for his students. He was beginning to overcome self-doubt and indecision, and to look forward with hope to greater successes. Victory had a very sweet taste, and it was very addictive.

At that moment disaster was snatched from the jaws of victory.

Velmeran was instantly aware of a vague presence far behind him, at the very limit of his senses. It was remote and indistinct, like a very low, distant throbbing beneath the high voices of the ships about him. But, as each second passed, it grew louder and more certain. All too soon he had absolutely no doubt.

"I feel ships behind us!" he announced over com. "Cut loose that freighter and get out fast. This may be a trap."

The two capture ships cut acceleration and released their hold, leaving the freighter to drift as they shot away. The packs did not wait; Velmeran brought his around in a tight circle, turning back to meet this new threat, and Baressa's pack followed closely. The Starwolves were fearful of traps, for too often freighters exploded under attack or soon after capture. Sometimes their cargoes were volatile, but more often the freighters themselves were decoys and loaded with explosives. Such a trap had destroyed most of Velmeran's first pack, leaving only himself, Keth and Steena.

Valthyrra Methryn and her crew were just as quick to react. The Methryn, waiting just outside the system, fired her main drives and began to move in at her best sublight speed. Every fighter, transport and capture ship was made ready. Damage-control crews stood by while the bridge crew waited at their stations, ready to take control of their parts of the giant ship should Valthyrra have to shift her attention elsewhere.

"Velmeran, what is it?" Mayelna demanded over com. She had to take over the supervision of the packs, since Valthyrra was preoccupied with preparing herself for battle.

"Ships," he answered simply.

She looked up as Valthyrra's camera pod moved toward her. "I can just make them out, sixty-five units from our present location and approaching rapidly. I count two carriers and three battleships, with about twenty escorts ranging from stingships to destroyers."

"And that freighter?" Mayelna asked.

"It never exploded," the ship explained. "No trap. My guess is that the attack run proceeded too far into system and was observed. The local commander is either trying to scare us away, or else he believes in his good luck."

"We do not scare," Mayelna said coldly.

"No, not from this," the ship agreed. "I already have a pack in each bay. They will go as soon as they have pilots."

Mayelna bent over the com controls in the arm of her chair. "Help is coming. Can you and Baressa distract them for about five minutes?"

"They are already on their way," Valthyrra reported, amused.

"We are closing to attack," Velmeran answered. "Tell Valthyrra to keep herself clear."

Indeed he had long since led both packs into low starflight speeds, rushing into the depths of the system ahead to intercept the approaching ships as far from the Methryn as they could. The small fleet was coming toward them at about the same speed; for Union pilots, taking a ship into starflight within the confines of a planetary system was an act of either desperation or daring. Baressa had never said a word, so Velmeran assumed that she was following his lead. He was surprised by that; Baressa was not easily impressed.

Velmeran had somewhat impressed himself with his decisiveness, daring to lead a pack of students against a fleet. But there was really no choice as he saw it. He had two clear duties when the Methryn came under attack: to protect his carrier against her enemies, in spite of the fact that Valthyrra could take care of herself, and to protect the reputation of the Starwolves. Fear was the most effective weapon his kind possessed; the Union lived in fear of the black carriers and would more often run than fight. But that reputation had to be carefully maintained. The Starwolves had to answer every challenge and win every battle, pay back every hurt twice over, and they could never afford the luxury of a judicious retreat.

The two groups closed quickly, for starflight reduced planetary distances to small jumps. The packs split to circle around to either side and strike from opposite directions. The Unioners had to drop sublight to fight. They could not defend themselves effectively in starflight, and they certainly could not attack. They would drop to low sublight speeds, increasing their enemy's advantage but at least allowing their own fighters to attack and give their cannons a chance to track the quick wolf ships.

Without warning the fleet went sublight, braking hard, and the packs cut in sharply to strike from either side. The two carriers had already opened their immense bays and were expelling fighters at a furious pace. The three battleships and eight destroyers moved to the outside, prepared to distract their attackers with their own cannons. Stingships made ready their own attacks, while tenders and escorts could do little else but try to look small.

Their skill and innate sense of timing was such that the two packs struck the fleet from opposite sides at exactly the same moment. Now their advantage became most apparent. They could easily withstand the stresses of quick turns and accelerations hundreds of times as great as ordinary humans could endure, so that they could dodge in and out among the larger ships faster than the defenders, or even their automatic systems, could track.

Velmeran went first for the stingships, the greatest threat, in his opinion, to his students. These powerful little ships were all engine, faster even than fighters and possessing a pair of cannons with the range and power of the main battery of a destroyer. Most of his pilots were impressed with the larger targets, and were busy ripping up the big cannons on the battleships and destroyers. Baressa had sent her more experienced pilots after the fighters, even shooting into the bays to prevent the rest from launching. Keth and Treg had gone after the smaller gunships.

Velmeran had cut in at the rear of the fleet and was making his way up its scattered length, seeking out and removing the more subtle threats. Wolf ships were moving in and out too fast for him to identify most by the pitch of their engines, although he did see that Tregloran had disabled a destroyer and was following it to its end. Velmeran would have liked to have seen what the younger pilot did with his target, but in the next instant he had to jump to avoid flying headlong into the forward battery of a battleship. He barely had time to fire twice into her bridge before he shot past, well aware that bolts from her cannons were passing him within meters. That served as a quick lesson in failing to pay attention; he could end up the first casualty for worrying about his students.

By the time that he had turned back, he saw that he had done better with the battleship than he anticipated. While his bolts had missed her main computers, they had still destroyed the bridge. The immense ship was flying blind, her engines flaring and completely out of control. Her automatic systems continued to fight, but slower than normal, and she was firing at anything that moved. Tenders that had been moving to assist her were forced to retreat quickly when her cannons destroyed two of them.

Velmeran fell in with two others who were going after her drives. They took out four of her six main drives and were setting up for another run only to shear away suddenly. The ship's damaged computers had kept her generators running at full, still trying to feed engines that were no longer in operation. Major circuits overloaded and burned out and a series of explosions began to rip apart the aft of the giant warship. A moment later her generators exploded with force enough to vaporize the entire ship, as well as the tenders and escorts still trying to get clear. Only the wolf ships had been quick enough to escape.

The remainder of the fleet was quick to react. All of the larger ships suddenly paused, their engines stilled, as they pivoted thirty-five degrees from their previous course. Then they refired their engines and shot off in this new direction. That move caught more than half of the Starwolves by surprise and they suddenly found themselves left behind, separated from the fleet but surrounded by Union fighters and stingships.

But it came too late. Only the stingships had the power and speed to be effective, but just two of those ships remained. The Union fighters were too slow and too lightly shielded, their guns too weak. The Starwolves turned to pursue the fleeing warships, destroying everything in their path. The fighters were left behind instantly but the stingships accelerated quickly, hoping to keep the wolf ships in range long enough for a few shots. But two of the black fighters had held back, and now fell in behind the stingships. The hunters became the hunted, and the chase did not last long.

Free of its own fighters, the Union fleet now ran at several times its former speed, its ships spacing out to twist and evade. Time was beginning to work to the Starwolves' advantage. All of the Union ships had suffered some damage, their stingships were gone, and their fighters were left behind. But the Starwolves' numbers were still intact, their ships were undamaged, and their pilots were still fairly fresh. Moreover, they were expecting the support of eight more packs at any moment.

One of the two remaining battleships suddenly faltered and began to fall behind, having lost its main computer control. Velmeran held back to watch, for the ship was not heavily damaged and could have been restarted. But her crew had had enough. Launches and transports began to leave her after a long moment, and even a few escape modules popped out of their tiny bays. That left a nearly intact battleship to drift, which the Starwolves could recover at their convenience.

Velmeran accelerated quickly after the remainder of the fleet, with Keth and Steena close behind him. Keth had been hard pressed to keep up this pace. But he had disabled that last battleship, if more by chance than actual skill. Now he felt young and quick again, encouraged by his success. He moved rapidly through the fleet, firing into the tail of a destroyer as he bore down on the remaining battleship. He was coming up close behind one of the carriers, but he ignored her as he sighted on his real target. The destroyer he had just strafed exploded and he glanced back, wondering if he had been responsible for that.

He turned back to his intended prey, only to see that the carrier had turned abruptly across his path. He was streaking down the length of her hull on a course that would cause him to strike her just forward of her bays, in the crew section just behind the bridge. Already it was too late to turn away. Just ahead he saw a large airlock with double doors nearly as wide as his own ship. This was one of the main crew ports; a wide corridor would run right through the width of the ship, emerging on an identical lock on the opposite side. If he kept up his speed, and his shields held, he could poke a hole right through this carrier.

Keth threw full power to his engines and dove straight toward those double doors. His fighter struck with a jarring impact, crashing through both outer and inner lock doors. For an instant longer the shields continued to hold, forcing a path for the fighter by crushing back the walls and ceiling of the corridor. But the stress was too great, and the shields suddenly failed explosively. The wings and fins of the fighter were ripped off in that same instant, but its main body was thrown forward to slide down the length of the corridor. The walls continued to press on it, breaking its momentum, grinding slowly to a stop that left it firmly wedged in the passage.

Keth released his tight grip on the controls and sat back, breathing heavily. He would have made it if his engines had not failed, for the doors of the second airlock were only five meters from the nose of his ship. If he could restart his generator, he could shoot out those doors and use his engines to squeeze on through. He removed his helmet and the upper straps of his seat so that he could bend over the screen and small keyboard on his on-board computer, ordering a systems check.

The screen began with a four-way schematic of the fighter, then began to subtract from those sketches to allow for missing parts. The computer considered the extent of the damage and announced its verdict: FAILURE: ALL MAIN SYSTEMS. But he had expected that, and began to work his way past all the safeties and lock-outs and tried to restart the generator. There was no response except that the computer investigated the damage again, thinking about it a long time before it reached a conclusion: GENERATOR INOPERATIVE: FAILURE ALL MAIN SYSTEMS. To prove its point, it quickly sketched out the schematic for the generator and main power channels. Keth knew enough about the mechanics to see that this ship was better off scrap.

That left him one last chance. He quickly locked down his helmet and powered up his suit, then released the canopy. He could still abandon his ship, jump overboard out of the lock just ahead, and call for someone to pick him up. But the canopy rose only a short distance before it jammed against the ceiling overhead. Ordinarily he would have been able to rip that canopy from its hinges, but not while he was trapped within the confined cockpit. His genetically bred strength was defeated by poor leverage.

"Meran, can you hear me?" he asked over com, rather apologetically. "I seem to be in considerable trouble."

Velmeran heard, and instantly knew that something

was wrong. He moved free of the battle to pace the fleet a short distance out. "I hear you, Keth. What is it?"

"I seem to be stuck inside one of the carriers," he explained. "She turned in front of me. I tried to punch a hole through a main corridor. But I did not quite make it, and now my generator is wrecked. I was hoping that you would be able to disable this ship."

"We will do what we can," Velmeran assured him. "Which ship?"

"I am in the lead carrier."

"I hear you. Baressa?"

"I am on it," Baressa responded immediately.

"Right. Valthyrra, where are those other packs?"

"I cannot get enough pilots to their ships to launch a pack from either bay," Valthyrra responded. "The first two should be leaving in the next two minutes. Can you hold out another five or so?"

"No! You had better bring yourself in, so that you can deliver them to the scene. And charge your cannons."

"Coming!" Valthyrra replied, and she did not sound at all unhappy.

By that time Velmeran, Baressa and a third ship were moving up on the lead carrier, intent upon clipping all six of her main drive engines. An instant later it seemed that every Union ship in the fleet was firing at them, so that they were forced to break off their attack and move away. That was when Velmeran realized just how much trouble they were in. The Union fleet had captured a live Starwolf. Whatever else they had come to do was quickly forgotten; their only goal now was to protect that carrier long enough for her to escape.

And they were quick to seize their chance. The lead carrier suddenly broke free of the fleet, so abruptly that she left her escorts and tenders behind. She reversed course almost a full half-turn and began to accelerate rapidly back into the system, building swiftly to light speed. Three wolf fighters broke from the fleet to chase her, but they were only just beginning to close when she went into starflight.

"She just jumped!" Velmeran warned. "Valthyrra, put a drone on that ship."

"On it!" Valthyrra promised. One of her smaller forward bays began to open. A small machine shot through the bay doors as soon as they opened enough to allow it to pass. The drone paused a moment as it oriented on its target, then disappeared into starflight with a blinding flash of its tiny engine.

The drone was a fail-safe, for Velmeran did not intend for that carrier to escape. The giant ship continued to accelerate into higher starflight speeds, faster than he had thought Union ships could run. But she was mostly bays, and those were empty. Nor was she retreating back to the main base, a move that would not have kept her safe. She was running out of system.

"Velmeran, she is casting something loose!" Baressa warned.

She had been in a position to see the small bay door swing out. The three fighters scattered, and a moment later a launch was ejected from its small bay. Without acceleration dampers to drain off the energy of its tremendous speed, the little ship was vaporized almost the instant it left the carrier, and it radiated the energy of its acceleration in a tremendous destructive flash. But the trick had failed, for the three fighters were back on the warship's tail immediately.

Velmeran was moving in for a shot at her star drive when he again sensed the droning of many drives at low starflight speeds. He paused a moment, realizing that the Union base had launched another fleet nearly the size of the first, moving quickly to reenforce the remains of the first. It was a trick to make him let go of that carrier, a trick he could not refuse. He could not leave two packs to fight that without their pack leaders.

"Valthyrra, are those packs out yet?" he demanded.

"Just leaving," her reply came.

"There is another fleet closing in."

"So I see," Valthyrra agreed. "Three battleships and twelve destroyers. And forty stingships."

Velmeran cut his com link and swore every oath he had ever heard, including the really good ones he had learned from his mother. But the matter was decided for him; he reversed course, and the two fighters joined him.

"Keth, there is a drone on your ship," Velmeran called back while he could. "We will come to get you."

"Do not worry about me," the older pilot replied. "They want me alive, so I am in no danger. You just keep those kids out of trouble. Tell the Commander that I'm sorry."

Their com link faded as the carrier moved out of range, screaming out of the system at her best speed. The tiny drone followed it at a discreet distance, silent and unobserved.

3

The odds were worse than ever, just three fighters against fifteen warships and two score stingships. Velmeran had no idea who the third member of his group was; he hoped that it was one of Baressa's pilots and not his own. He had to overtake that second fleet and stop it short; if it caught up with the first group, his students, now tired and quickly reaching the limits of their endurance, would be outnumbered and vulnerable. There were enough stingships with this second group to be effective, especially against pilots who might be growing inattentive and careless.

"Valthyrra Methryn, do you have packs out yet?" he asked a final time.

"Two packs just moved into starflight and can reenforce your pilots in perhaps two minutes," Valthyrra responded. "Another two packs can be there within another minute."

"Listen. I am going to try to get this second group of warships out of starflight before they join the first," Velmeran explained quickly. "We will have a greater advantage if we can keep them apart. Send these two packs to reenforce me. Send the next two to relieve the packs already in battle."

"Anything you say," she agreed. "Meran, that first group is driving directly at me."

"Do you prefer to reenforce the pilots there and stop it?"

"No, I can fend for myself if anything comes through. I need the practice. Barthan. Shayrn. Take your packs and reenforce Velmeran's position."

"We are on it," Barthan agreed.

On board the Methryn, Valthyrra moved the standby alert up to full battle alert. Crewmembers looked up apprehensively from their stations or paused in her corridors, awaiting orders. The Methryn had not gone into battle in many long years, for most not even in their lifetimes. They had played out this alert in test runs so often that the reality was something of a shock. But the ship was to be protected at any cost and no one dared to cross a Starwolf carrier. And yet for some, those who tended the machines or sorted supplies or taught the young, it was the first time in many years that they had felt like real Starwolves.

"All crewmembers stand by," Valthyrra announced through her maze of corridors and many decks. "This is a class one battle alert. All on-duty personnel to their posts. All damage control parties stand by. All nonactive personnel will remove to the inner sections."

"That second fleet just left starflight to fight," Velmeran reported. "We need reenforcements. Baressa and I are up to our . . . necks in stingships."

"You can have two packs in two minutes," she assured him. "Can you hold on?"

"Do we have any choice?"

"No," Valthyrra said. "We will have matters well in hand shortly."

Velmeran paid her excuses little mind. He was getting tired of excuses, and at the moment he was too busy to care. He had not exaggerated; three fighters among all those stingships were simply too few targets for too many guns. Stingship cannons were powerful but slow to fix on target. By keeping close in, they were not allowed the time they needed to get off a good shot. Indeed, the stingships had to be careful to avoid shooting or even ramming each other.

The two packs had been left to their own designs for several minutes now, and they were finally bringing their own part to an end. Of the original fleet there remained only a battleship and two destroyers as well as several tenders and transports, themselves no threat but a considerable nuisance. The Methryn was still closing, now so close that her viewscreens were picking up cannon flashes. The battleship suddenly cut from the main group, driving directly at the Methryn, while the rest continued at a right angle to her approach.

"Go clear up whatever might be left," Valthyrra told the pilots when she saw them circle back to give chase. "I will take care of this one."

Mayelna glanced up from her screens. "Do you know what you are doing?"

"I should certainly hope so!" the ship replied indignantly as she swung her boom around to the helm and weapons stations on the middle bridge. "Cargin, I will operate the cannons. Consherra, stand by with your hands on the manual controls in the event something happens." She glanced around. "Do I know what I am doing? Do you think me a tottering wreck?"

"You are getting a little old," Mayelna commented as she sat back to watch, seemingly disinterested.

"Old?" Valthyrra asked incredulously. "Now I feel obliged, just to prove that I am still a very alert and capable fighting ship. Indeed!"

"Then shut up and do it."

Valthyrra quickly launched the two packs that stood ready in her bays and immediately brought in her carrier arms to remove the empty racks to make way for another pack. At the same time she prepared a single cannon for only one shot.

"Watch your controls. Consherra, stand ready," she

warned, and glanced up at her main screens. "Ramming speed!"

Mayelna rolled her eyes and sighed heavily.

The Methryn fired one bolt directly into the nose of the approaching warship. In spite of the distance that remained between them, it caught the battleship dead center on her bridge, slightly below where her own viewscreens would have been. Content, Valthyrra cut speed and waited. Nothing seemed to happen at first. But with her main computer destroyed, the various systems aboard the smaller ship began to shut down, leaving her to drift helplessly. The crew might have restarted her easily enough, but they had already learned the futility in that. They began to evacuate her in launches and transports, leaving the ship itself like a token of appeasement to their conquerors.

"Simple, but effective," Valthyrra remarked smugly as the first launch cleared its bay.

"Why, you greedy old fool!" Mayelna exclaimed. "You want to capture as many of those ships as you can so that you can sell them back at a profit."

"Not me!" Valthyrra insisted, rotating her cameras around. "First you question my abilities, and then my motives. Actually, I want those ships so that I can sell them to non-Union colonies."

"Valthyrra?" Velmeran called in suddenly. "Those two packs have arrived and have matters well in hand. Baressa and I are on our way back to our own packs."

"Very good," Valthyrra acknowledged. "Two more packs will join you about as soon as you can get there. The rest will close up matters with that second fleet."

"Fair enough."

"You close up things out there," Valthyrra added quickly, ignoring Mayelna's look of protest. "But go ahead and get your pack out of the fight as soon as possible. You have done more than you should already."

"No problem."

"And why did you do that?" the Commander demanded as Valthyrra extended her camera well back into the upper bridge for privacy.

"Velmeran has had things well under control from the first; he should be allowed to finish," she said firmly. "Besides, he is going to want answers to a great many questions the moment he comes on board. And the fact is that I do not have all the answers myself. The battle is nearly over, but the trouble has just started."

Velmeran and Baressa were the first to lead their packs in, even though it was some time after the fighting stopped before they found the opportunity to do so. Chance had cast Velmeran in the role of leader, which everyone but he seemed to recognize and yet no one questioned. Although the Commander had remained silent, Valthyrra was deferring to his judgment. No one dared to question the situation. The other pilots had been late when they were needed, and had failed in their duty. They were in no position to protest.

The end of the battle saw the beginning of a process that was longer, more complicated and potentially as dangerous. Every usable part of the two wrecked fleets had to be collected, secured and brought in. Damaged ships were drifting over an area from the fourth to the seventh planet of the system, and to complicate matters, the survivors of the Union fleets were still in the early stages of what promised to be a very slow retreat. Hundreds of launches, escape modules and a fair number of tenders were heading back to base as best they could. Predictably, nothing moved out of the station to assist them.

The Starwolves had fared well enough for what had proven to be a major battle. Aside from their one captured fighter and pilot, they had no damage and no injuries—except for their wounded pride. Having been taught a harsh lesson, they carefully scanned each ship, fragment of ship and piece of machinery before it was brought back to the Methryn. Disabled but intact ships were the largest item, more than the Methryn could possibly carry away. A carrier, four of the six battleships and nine destroyers—as well as the freighter—were in good enough condition to be saved as they were, refitted with spare drives and other parts from ships that had not survived.

Even so, the task of salvage would not take long. Usable ships were identified and carried out of the way. Drives and generators were simply cut free of the wrecks and welded together in stacks for storage in the smaller bays (the ships themselves went last into the Methryn's two main bays). A final concern was the fair number of captives, nearly a thousand in all, who were found trapped or stranded in disabled ships. Every drifting stingship had a crew of five who had no means of escape. The Starwolves ordinarily collected ransom of stray crewmembers, but this was simply too much and the Methryn was in a hurry. The captives were loaded into three stripped destroyers and given a firm push in-system by the capture ships.

Velmeran could see the captured freighter being edged into the right holding bay as he began his approach. She was even larger than the battleships, and yet she looked insignificant againt the Methryn's vast, sleek shape. Nearly four hours had passed since he had led his pack out of the bay, although most of that time had been spent just drifting through the wreckage, alert for trouble. But that was still too long in the fighters. His pilots needed to go home. But there would be no rest for him, not until he did whatever was needed to free his missing packmember.

"Welcome back, Pack Leader Velmeran," Valthyrra said with odd formality as he began his final approach. "Please allow me to extend both my appreciation and gratitude for the skill and efficiency that you and your pilots have demonstrated. I can imagine how tired you must be, but I might suggest that you had better be alert for the difficulties ahead."

Velmeran did indeed sit up straight. Valthyrra's warnings did not come much plainer than that. "Oh? Does one of my difficulties have a name?"

"Yes, and she would throw my circuit breakers if she were to hear me mention it aloud."

"My regards to the Commander."

"You guessed it!"

Velmeran turned a final time and moved in beneath the Methryn's tail, just beneath her star drives, braking gently with his forward engines to match speed with the larger ship. The packs came in according to how they flew in formation; the leader first, always in the middle, then the others moving alternately outward one step down the wing. He brought his ship through the wide, low slot of the bay door, blinking in the sudden light of the bay, bringing his fighter to the forward portion of the flight deck before gently setting down. Bay personnel rushed forward before he could get the engines and generator completely shut down.

Fighters were generally put into their racks immediately, for any unsecured fighter could be thrown across the bay like a projectile if the ship made a sudden turn. The rack was dropped down and slid into place behind, and the carrier arms lifted the fighter up and set it into place. Benthoran pushed the boarding ramp into place and climbed up to assist Velmeran, who had managed to do little except open his cockpit and pull off his helmet. The crew chief began unstrapping him, while another crew-member went to work on the other side.

"Welcome back, Captain," Benthoran said. "All well?"

"Nearly. We lost Keth," Velmeran said, then noticed the startled looks from both. "We misplaced him. He rammed a carrier and got stuck inside her, and she escaped out of system."

"Old fool!" Benthoran muttered as he snapped down the overhead supports.

Velmeran did not answer as he lifted himself out of the cockpit. He stood for a moment holding the frame of the rack for support, wishing that he had as many legs as arms, and paused, noticing for the first time the figure in white armor waiting in front of his fighter. He straightened and descended the steps with all the grace he could muster, hoping he would not fall. He was saved from embarrassment by Steena, whose arrival gave him an excuse to stand and watch.

"Play no games with me, Pack Leader Velmeran," Consherra said as she came to assist him.

"And what are you doing here?" he asked. "Am I in that much trouble?"

"You are not in trouble," Consherra said firmly. "Indeed, you are about the only one who is not."

"I did lose Keth," he pointed out.

"Keth is a problem of his own making."

Velmeran did not reply, for he was beginning to grow concerned about the incoming fighter. It was Tregloran's, to judge by its engine pitch, and he seemed destined to repeat a past mistake, for he was coming in quickly with his landing gear up.

"Treg, remember your landing gear," Velmeran said to himself. But Tregloran continued his approach, heedless of crewmembers waving their arms. He entered the bay and moved unerringly to his place in line. Then he hovered, a long moment suspended out of time, and his landing gear folded down. The little ship settled to the deck with almost contemptuous gentleness, hardly flexing its struts.

"At least I am spared that disaster," Velmeran remarked as he continued on toward the lift, leaving Consherra to hurry after him. "Now, you tell me what happened to the support we needed. And no excuses."

"Excuses?" Consherra asked. "Is that why you think I am here?"

"Why are you here?" he asked in return. "Either Valthyrra or Mayelna sent you."

"Valthyrra did suggest that I come, although I was happy to do it," she said, somewhat defensively. "I am here to help you, so you listen to me. Mayelna has called an immediate council to decide what we should do about Keth. We have no time to lose and you had better know how matters stand before we get there. No one is going to blame you for losing Keth. Right now, the big question is why eight packs were fifteen minutes getting clear."

"Fifteen minutes!"

"Yes, fifteen. I am sure that it seemed like an hour to you, since things were rather busy at your end. But that is still three times longer than it was supposed to take. To put it simply, no one took matters seriously until it was too late. Valthyrra put out an attack alert at your first warning. But most of the pilots took their time getting to the bays and quite a few, including five pack leaders, ignored the alert until it was repeated for the third time."

"How could they..."

"As I understand it, too many people got the idea that the freighter you were chasing turned out to be a battleship, and that your students were frightened. They thought that Baressa's pack could handle the matter, and that the alert would pass before they got to the bays. The pack leaders kept calling up to the bridge, asking if they really had to bestir themselves. Valthyrra roasted their ears with a few choice words, put every pilot and crewmember not in armor on probation and threatened suspension for everyone not at their ships or stations in five minutes."

"Then it was not just the pilots?" Velmeran asked.

"No, but it was the worst among the pilots," Consherra said, pausing a moment to press the call button for the lift. "Valthyrra remarked that she has had trouble getting her packs out before, for a variety of reasons, but never laziness. She said that perhaps we do not fight often enough."

"That sounds like something Valthyrra would say," Velmeran remarked. The lift doors snapped open and they stepped inside. "She may be right."

"You, at least, have nothing to worry about," Consherra repeated as she set the controls for their destination. "You have managed to impress all the powers that be... even the Commander, although she is not likely to admit it."

"Do not make me out to be the hero of this battle," Velmeran exclaimed. "I did nothing special."

"You most certainly did."

"Then I was too busy to notice."

"That is exactly the point," Consherra insisted. "You led the attack. You made all the important decisions, while we were all too busy trying to figure out what was going on. Baressa was senior pack leader out there, by more than a hundred years, and she deferred to your leadership."

Velmeran did not know how to answer that, for it suddenly occurred to him that she was right. Then a very different thought came to mind. "This has not been Mayelna's day."

Consherra frowned. "Your mother is taking this hard. We all knew that Keth was too old to fly. Mayelna is nearly as old herself, and she has been thinking for some time about naming her Commander-designate."

Velmeran considered that and nodded thoughtfully. "And the Commander-designate has to be named from among the pack leaders. And I doubt that there is anyone she would choose, especially after today."

"That is the problem," Consherra explained. "That decision belongs to Valthyrra, not her. And Valthyrra has already indicated her choice. But Mayelna has delayed in naming the new Commander-designate."

"Mayelna disapproves of Valthyrra's choice?" Velmeran asked, and shrugged. "Who would suit her?"

The Council Room behind the bridge was nearly empty, since most of the pack leaders and officers were away. Mayelna sat at the head of the oval table at the bottom of the audience pit, watching the screen mounted in the table before her. Valthyrra was trying to peer over her shoulder, although her angle of attack made that difficult. She was operating a camera boom mounted overhead, above the very center of the table, but not so long or mobile as the main camera boom on the bridge. Of the major officers, only Cargin, the weapons director, Veyndayk of cargo and salvage and the engineering officer Tresha were present. The gallery was empty of onlookers; this was not a safe place to be just now, for those who had any choice.

Velmeran and Consherra descended the steps to the council floor, moving carefully because of their armor. Valthyrra looked up immediately, and after a moment Mayelna put the monitor on hold and glanced up. Velmeran did not much like the way she looked him up and down as if checking for dents in his armor. Apparently satisfied with her inspection, she sat back.

"Welcome back, Meran," she said. "I feel obliged to tell you that you did very well, especially under the circumstances."

"Even if so much trouble came of it?" he asked.

"Even so. Her Worship is so pleased with herself that she is likely to burst the seams in her hull, and Veyndayk is dreaming of the loot we are going to collect on pillage. And while I am hardly pleased by it, I am glad to know that we have personnel problems . . ."

"Laziness!" Valthyrra inserted.

". . . in time to do something about it." She paused and bent over the com unit mounted into the table. "I want all pack leaders in the Council Room in ten minutes."

"Ah . . . Commander, we really do not believe that we should leave our packs just now, under the circumstances." A hesitant reply came after a long moment.

"I do not doubt that you would want to be anywhere but here just now, under the circumstances," Mayelna replied. "But if you do not want to be suspended, then you had better stop questioning orders. I want to see you here in five minutes. Your packs will be just fine without you."

Velmeran tried not to look startled, but it was the first time that he had heard anyone threatened with suspension. And he could tell that she meant it, if only to prove that she could and would. "Has it really come to that?"

"We shall see, I suppose," Mayelna replied simply, although she looked troubled. "The crew of this ship is beginning to forget that we are a military force, not a gang of thieves and pirates. And yet this is the type of behavior that I would expect from pirates."

"Perhaps there have not been enough reminders lately," Valthyrra suggested. "We never attack anything but freighters. Starwolves used to spend more time breaking Union invasions and trade monopolies."

"That may be changing, if this is any indication," Mayelna said. "Perhaps this was more misunderstanding and circumstance than laziness and insubordination. I hope so, because personnel problems will endanger this ship if the Union is becoming more aggressive. If things do not change quickly, then I am going to inquire about changing out packs with five or six other ships."

This time Velmeran could not help looking surprised; even Valthyrra's glass eyes seemed to widen. A change-out of five packs meant half the pilots, which meant that she was dissatisfied with nearly the entire group. At least he was safe. No ship would take a pack whose members could put together all their years to make the age of only one experienced pilot.

"Tresha, is there any reason why we cannot reopen the upper level of each bay?" Mayelna asked.

"Not that I know of," the engineer answered.

"Do we have crewmembers for it?"

"We have an overabundance of crewmembers in too many areas," Valthyrra replied. "By shifting some to new duties, we can easily run the upper decks. When those bays were closed five thousand years ago, I did not have enough crew for it. I kept ten packs in those days simply by using pilots who would be rejected now. Do you know that I once flew with only nine hundred crewmembers?"

Mayelna glanced up at the camera pod in mild annoyance, and continued. "It might seem superfluous, most of the time. But four functional decks would mean that we could ready and launch twice as many packs at a time."

"Is the Union really getting more aggressive?" Cargin asked.

"We lost nearly an entire pack two years ago," Valthyrra replied. "There were three such incidents in the four months prior to that, and eleven since. Twenty-one ships have been lost from our carriers in the last two years. We did not lose that in the quarter century prior to that. This trap was the most that the Union has thrown against a carrier in fifty years."

"But was it a trap?" Velmeran asked. When he saw that everyone was looking at him, he continued. "An intentional trap, I mean. Their perimeter scanners showed a freighter under attack. The Station Commander sent out half of his fleet, perhaps just in the hope of chasing us off. It might be that they never meant to close for battle, but they underestimated our speed and we were on them before they realized. Then, when he knew that he had a Starwolf stuck inside one of his ships, he sent out the rest to distract us."

"It has happened before," Valthyrra agreed.

"That is easier to believe than to think that this was planned," Velmeran insisted. "They could not know that an old fool would try to poke a hole through the hull of a carrier, and this attack makes no sense otherwise."

"Now that is the other part that I do not understand," Mayelna said as she crossed both sets of arms and leaned back in her chair. "If Keth had time to locate a hatch, then he had time to turn away."

"On the contrary, I understand it only too well," Valthyrra said. "It was my reason for wanting him retired. Your race, the Kelvessan, was genetically engineered for two main reasons. Hypermetabolism gives you the swift reflexes needed to fly the wolf ships and the strength to withstand accelerations far beyond what your buffer shields can compensate for, far beyond what any true human could endure.

"Older pilots generally do not fail because they get too slow, but because the elaborate structural supports in their joints and internal organs begin to give out. Keth had been fighting hard for some time, harder than he had fought in years, and I do not doubt that his pain was growing with each turn. Yes, he had time to turn from that carrier. His reflexes were also quick enough to find an alternative to the pain such a turn would have caused. Older pilots do have a tendency to run into their targets."

She rotated her camera pod around so quickly that the others glanced up as well. Pilots were entering, mostly Velmeran's own pack members, moving almost fearfully to seats in the lower portion of the gallery. Baressa had arrived sometime before and had quietly taken her seat at the table.

"The question, of course, is what happens now," Mayelna continued. "Keth surely deserves what he might get. But it remains a matter of duty and protection of our reputation to get him back."

"Keth is my responsibility. . . ." Velmeran began to protest.

"I would permit it if I could," Valthyrra said, ignoring Mayelna's hostile stare. "But your pack does not have the experience for such a task, and you are shorthanded besides. I have already taken the liberty of locating and contacting a special tactics team."

Mayelna nodded in silent approval.

"We will contact Thenderra Delvon in about forty hours for the transfer of the special tactics team," Valthyrra continued. "Another sixty hours will be needed to trace the carrier to its projected destination. We might still be needed for such matters as creating diversions and discouraging pursuit, so I want this ship and all packs battle-ready with time to spare."

"It is just that simple?" Velmeran asked.

"Neither the Commander nor myself has any intention of allowing you to go after Keth by yourself," Valthyrra said firmly. "You are perhaps the best pilot we have, but this requires more. You were trained for the packs, and you are very good at what you do. Leave this to those who have been trained for it."

She paused and looked up. The other eight pack leaders had arrived, waiting fearfully at the outer door.

They had come as a group, apparently in the mistaken belief that there was safety in numbers. Valthyrra glanced back. "If you will excuse us, the Commander and I have some armored butts to chew. Veyndayk, please continue the salvage operations as quickly as possible."

Everyone at the table or in the gallery rose to leave. Consherra fell in beside Velmeran, even though she was second in command and might have stayed. Tregloran, with the rest of the pack behind him, waited on the steps, refusing to leave without their pack leader. Velmeran could not guess what was foremost in their thoughts—their concern for their lost member or their astonishment at what they had done.

"I am sorry, Captain," Tregloran said. "We would have gotten her, if we had not been forced to turn back."

Velmeran stared at him in surprise. "Treg, was that you flying with Baressa and me?"

"Of course," the younger pilot answered. "I saw you go after her, and I thought that small help was better than none."

"Hardly small help," Velmeran said. "Not when we were flying wing to wing in a herd of stingships. You earned your pay today."

"And a bonus," Consherra added. "Double bonuses, in fact, for your entire pack and Baressa's, while everyone else will get only a stern lecture on tardiness. As for yourself, you are wanted in the left holding bay immediately."

"Me? What did I do?" Tregloran asked nervously, looking alarmed and surprisingly guilty.

"You were the one who plugged that freighter?" she asked, and he nodded. "Well, she is a real freighter and full of cargo. Since you brought her out of starflight, you get first pick of her goods."

With a cry of delight, Tregloran tried to force his way through his packmates on the steps ahead of him. When that proved impossible, he was reduced to trying to hurry them on ahead. Fortunately for his patience, the others were nearly as eager as himself to get to that bay. This was the first big ship that they had brought down by themselves, a minor accomplishment compared to fighting a fleet of Union warships, by themselves and outnumbered. Now they remembered, and wanted to get to the bay to see what they had caught. Velmeran smiled, and decided that he would very much like to go with them.

"So the students have fought with the big boys now," Consherra remarked as she walked beside him. "Perhaps they are no longer students."

"They still have much to learn," Velmeran said. "But they are learning."

"So, I believe, are we all," Consherra added, then looked over at him. "Meran, do not take it so hard. You did what you had to do, and you did it very well. That is real trouble."

She indicated the council table, where Valthyrra and the Commander were busily bombarding the erring pack leaders with a variety of threats and dire promises. But Velmeran lacked the courage to stay and listen. Despite everyone's assurances, his own conscience was not clear. He had lost a pack member, a life that was his responsibility. Ultimately he had only himself to blame for his failure to solve a problem that he had known existed.

4

Tregloran's recent run of luck nearly failed him, for the big freighter contained mostly clothes, tons upon tons of clothes being shipped to the port ahead for redistribution to the colonies and fringe worlds. All worthless to Starwolves, who needed an extra set of sleeves. He did find a few things that he took for use by the entire pack, and Veyndayk allowed him a small fortune in jewelry.

Tregloran might have sold the jewelry in their next port to purchase something he could use, but he decided to put most of it into keeping. Wealth meant little to Starwolves. There were practical limitations to what they could have; whether it would fit into their cabins, or withstand the stresses of shipboard accelerations, or whether it even had any practical use in their lives. Jewelry they used as a type of universal currency, since they could not wear it (gold interfered with their high-speed nervous systems). They certainly were not poor, as Union propaganda tried to make them out to be. Piracy was their weapon against Union trade tyranny. They did not have to depend upon it for a living.

Velmeran stayed to watch as the captured ships were brought in and stored in the bays. He was interested in them, for he and his students had fought these ships and yet it was the first clear look that he had of them. They had seemed big enough outside, but when four were packed inside one of the Methryn's bays they looked small and pitifully inadequate. After a time the damage, the shot-out turrets and wrecked bridges, began to bother him. Starwolves were well-trained to think of themselves as fighting machines; in the name of duty they seldom considered the consequences of their acts. Looking at these ships up close, however, it was too easy to remember that people had been inside their battered hulls. Not his own kind, perhaps, but even humans were people.

After a time Velmeran retreated to a forward observation deck. The Methryn had few windows, and none at all in her armored hull sections. She had only two pairs of observation decks, directly over the fighter bays, the forward windows showing the holding bays and the rear windows allowing crewmembers to view incoming fighters, and a fifth platform in her bow directly above her shock bumper.

The crews were all hard at work securing and cataloging salvage and the pilots were standing by their fighters, with two packs still out. Velmeran was seated alone, except for an automated floor-cleaning machine that sat idle a short distance away.

"I thought that you might be here," Mayelna said suddenly, and he turned to find her approaching from the entrance to his right.

"Valthyrra told you I was here," Velmeran said in return.

Mayelna smiled. "Valthyrra Methryn sees all and knows all . . . at least everything that passes within her own thick shell. Do you suppose that we tickle her insides?"

"I imagine that the feeling is one of nausea," he replied glumly, and immediately wished that he had not. It sounded a little poutish, even to him. If he could not even evoke self-pity, then he certainly could expect no sympathy from the Commander.

Mayelna sat down on the bench beside him. "Why are you still in armor? Meran, what is wrong?"

Velmeran glanced down, frowning. "Mayelna, what is right? I have done my best to make pilots out of that pack of children, and then I lose my most experienced member. I wonder if there is something more, something that I have yet to learn about leading."

"Yes, I suppose that there is something you have yet to learn. The knowledge of what you can and cannot do, the confidence to act when you must, and the courage to seek help when you need it." She paused a moment and looked at him. "Your pilots are no longer students, not after today, even if they still have much to learn themselves. And Keth is a problem of his own making. He should have had sense enough to retire, or I should have told him. But not you. There are too many years between the two of you for you to have been able to tell him that, and I doubt that he would have listened."

"I still feel responsible for him."

Mayelna nodded. "I know. I would be concerned if you did not. You know, we had thought to give your pack to Keth, after your old pack was nearly destroyed. We knew that he would have to retire very soon, but by then he would have the students half-trained and you would be more ready to become pack leader. But Valthyrra said no. She said that he has no sense of responsibility toward others, that he is too self-centered and showed off more and more as his abilities began to fail. She was right, as always. Keth would have been too busy with himself to have taught those students a fourth of what they have learned from you. And if he had led that pack out today, I do not doubt that he would have lost half of them."

A short distance away, the cleaning automaton quietly, carefully moved its camera around for a better view of the pair.

"Our pilots are no better than the people who teach them, and who lead them," Mayelna continued. "And a person who does not really care will never be his best at what he does. After today, I wish that many more of my pilots had your devotion and sense of duty. Perhaps Valthyrra is right. Perhaps we do not fight often enough."

"Why?" Velmeran asked suddenly, looking up. "Why do we fight? Why should we fight, except to satisfy a need that was probably bred into us anyway?"

Mayelna frowned. "I do not suppose that you want another history lesson."

"No, you gave me that fifteen years ago," he answered. "We judge the Union unfit, and we seek to destroy it. Why? Are we the keepers of humanity's conscience, when we are not even human ourselves? Why should we continue to fight when we cannot win. And what would we do if we did win?"

Mayelna nodded slowly, almost sadly. "Very few of us question the reason for our own existence. Valthyrra considers it an encouraging sign if you do, and I do see the wisdom in that."

She sat, deep in thought, for so long that the automaton turned its camera slightly to focus in on her, and even Velmeran began to wonder. At last she sighed heavily and shook her head. "I cannot tell you. There is an answer, but you must find it for yourself. Your own reason . . . not just to fight, but to work toward the day that the fighting may end. My whole life, as pack leader and then Commander, has been to do what I can to shape the future that I would like to see. But I will not live to see the end of this war. For today, I am satisfied to know that matters would be worse without our contribution, that the colonies would all be slave camps for the fat inner worlds." She turned to look at him. "Nor do I believe that you really question the value of what you do. You are too good of a pilot to be filled with doubt, for that doubt would always be holding you back."

The automaton turned its camera back to Velmeran and adjusted its focus. He shook his head. "No, I suppose not. But that still does not make it any easier to accept the fact that I have no choice."

"Do you want to leave this ship?" Mayelna asked so suddenly that both Velmeran and the automaton looked at her in surprise.

"No," Velmeran said without hesitation. "Flying with the packs means everything to me. I suppose all I really want is the chance to have decided that for myself."

Mayelna nodded. "Meran, every one of us desires, more than anything else, to fly with the packs. But only one in twenty is good enough. All the rest must serve those fighters and the ship that carries them, and they can only dream of what you have. I flew with the packs for nearly three hundred years and I had to give it up, not because I want to command this ship but because I was needed. You have what you want most. Would you be willing to give it up, even if you were needed somewhere else?"

Velmeran considered that and shook his head. "No. At least not yet."

"I know," Mayelna said gently. "I will not tell you to accept what you are and make the most of it. Soon, I hope, you will find that it fulfills your needs as well, and you will be happy."

"I suppose that you're right," Velmeran agreed. "I am not dissatisfied with what I have, but perhaps with what I am. Sometimes I feel like a machine, genetically programmed to seek and destroy."

"Valthyrra Methryn is a machine," Mayelna pointed out. "She was built a fighting ship, and that is all she can be. Compared to her, you have all the choices you could want to be whatever you want. But she is happy with what she is, and I could hardly deny that she has both life and free will, as much as anyone."

"Yes, that is true," Velmeran agreed. The automaton dipped its camera, almost a gesture of relief. Velmeran saw that movement, and looked at the machine in mystification. "I might be mistaken, but it seems to me that cleaning unit is taking an unusual interest in us."

The unit glanced up with a startled look, only to see Mayelna peering at it intently. The machine executed a quick turn and made a hasty retreat across the observation deck as fast as its padded magnetic tracks would carry it.

"Valthyrra Methryn, you nosy machine!" Mayelna declared, leaping up in wrath.

Velmeran laughed. "Valthyrra Methryn knows all and sees all, however she can contrive it."

"You would think that I would know all her tricks too well by now," Mayelna said, watching the machine until it disappeared out the opposite door. She turned back to Velmeran. "I would not be foolish enough to ask you not to worry, but I do wish that you would not worry so much."

Mayelna returned to the bridge in time for their departure. Valthyrra had estimated forty hours to making their meeting with the Delvon. The Methryn could have made that jump in far less time. But she was fat with plunder and she was not about to risk having something break loose and damage itself, or her. She had even cast out her transports and capture ships to fly under their own power, so that she could stuff their holds with salvaged engines.

Mayelna paused for a moment in the right wing of the bridge. Tresha saw her and left her place at the forward console, indicating for her assistant to watch the screens.

"Commander, all systems are functioning well with recommended tolerances," the engineering officer reported. "This ship is in good order and battle-ready."

"Especially considering her age," Mayelna added. "You do not fool me! 'All systems functioning within recommended tolerances.' Indeed! You mean to imply that Her Worship could be better."

"I do not mean to imply that the ship is in need of repairs, nor unfit for battle," Tresha insisted. "But we should give serious thought to a complete overhaul in the next two or three years, especially if she means to fight hard and often."

"That has occurred to me already," Mayelna said. "If I can . . ."

"All crewmembers stand by," Valthyrra announced

suddenly. Everyone paused as they stood or sat and glanced up at the camera pod, but Valthyrra was staring unfocused at the main viewscreen, her attention on her scanners. "All crewmembers stand by. This is a class one battle alert. All on-duty personnel to their posts. All pilots to the bays. All damage-control parties stand by. All nonactive personnel will remove to the inner sections." She paused to switch channels. "All free transports and capture ships are to scatter immediately. Do not attack or approach any ships."

All the bridge crewmembers were already hurrying to their stations. Mayelna climbed the steps to her own station on the upper bridge, just behind Consherra. After all her words on laxness and inefficiency, she was only too aware that she was the only one on the bridge not in armor.

"What is it?" she asked as she lifted herself into her seat by the bars on her overhead console, not waiting for the seat to roll back.

The camera pod moved into the upper bridge, although it continued to face forward, watching the viewscreens. "A freighter."

Mayelna glanced up. "A freighter?"

"Well . . . yes, a freighter," Valthyrra said. "Just now dropping out of starflight to enter the system at high sublight speeds."

"You find that odd?" the Commander prompted, knowing already that there must be more.

"Well, it is a medium bulk freighter, nearly identical to the one now in my hold," she explained. "My scanners indicate that it is empty of both cargo and crew, although there is something in its hold that reminds me, by its power output levels, of a fairly large total conversion bomb being powered up for detonation."

"Another trap?" Mayelna asked.

"No, the same one, twelve hours late," Valthyrra replied cryptically. She turned her camera pod abruptly to face Mayelna. "This is the bait that we were meant to take. Circumstance, or poor planning on their part, put an identical freighter on this same lane twelve hours earlier. The bomb was meant to destroy our packs and perhaps even damage or disable me. That fleet was meant to take care of anything that was left. They saw us chasing what they took to be their own bait and launched their fleet before they were aware of their mistake."

Valthyrra moved her camera pod forward to the middle bridge. "Consherra, take direct manual control. That ship has turned and is driving at us. It is under remote control from the station now, and they will try to get it close enough to detonate. Keep at least fifty thousand kilometers between us, but evade the thing so as to keep it running in circles. Cargin, keep a cannon on that ship but hold your fire until I say."

"What about yourself?" Mayelna asked.

"I am going to try to match frequencies and get that freighter under my control."

"You do not have to pass control to me for that!" Consherra protested, already fighting her manual controls.

"I know," Valthyrra agreed. "You need the practice. Do not let that thing get close enough to blow me up, or I will likely never let you fly this ship again."

The ship closed at speeds no real freighter could have achieved under the burden of a full hold. Linked now to the station deep within the system, it was engaged in a suicidal attack, driving hard at the larger ship in the hope of getting near enough for the total conversion device it carried to be effective. And Valthyrra judged that distance to be twenty-five thousand kilometers, although such a thing could be hard to predict.

Consherra faced the difficult task of maintaining the proper distance, and playing dodge with that little ship at three-quarters light speed made that distance uncomfortably tight. But the Methryn was feeling her full eighteen million tons, and she was shipping nearly two million extra tons besides. The ships circled each other like two fierce predators; the freighter kept turning back to dart at its target, and Consherra would use the Methryn's superior acceleration and maneuverability to circle around behind it.

"Just a little longer," Valthyrra gently assured her. "Hold it steady."

"I am!" Consherra snapped, fighting the controls as the freighter rushed in yet again. "I only have four hands!"

"Is there some point to this?" Mayelna asked impatiently. "You cannot possibly want the thing. Where would you put it?"

"No, I do not want it," Valthyrra replied, the servos in her boom humming against the strain of their tight turn. "The conversion device is already powered up, so that ship is not safe to approach. I just want to prove a point."

A moment later the freighter broke off its suicidal attack. It seemed to pause for a moment, then turned in-system and accelerated to low starflight speeds. Valthyrra Methryn held her camera pod at a decidedly smug angle.

"Where is it going?" Mayelna asked, as mystified as the rest. "Did they call off the attack?"

"No, I have control of it," the ship said. "I am teaching them a lesson, a taste of their own medicine. Turn about is foul play, but fair is fair to equal share and all's the same in love and war. I am returning the favor . . . and the bomb."

"What the deuce are you babbling about?" Mayelna demanded. "Do you mean to say that you are going to destroy their station with their own bomb?"

"That, or at least scare them badly."

Valthyrra refused to explain, and the members of her bridge crew could only watch the scan of the system schematics on her forward viewscreen as the giant freighter hurtled inward toward the military station and the world it circled. No one could believe that she intended to destroy not only the station but the planet itself, for Starwolves would never reduce themselves to such barbarity. And they were quite correct. Valthyrra waited until the final moment before detonating the conversion device just short of target, doing no damage but lighting up all space in that general area. They could well imagine every loyal Unioner, beginning with the Station Commander, shaking with fright in that fierce glare.

"All stations secure. Resume normal duties. Prepare for immediate transfer to starflight," Valthyrra announced with total lack of concern. She turned her camera pod to look at Consherra. "You have the coordinates. Please recheck those figures a final time and execute the transfer to starflight. Your speed will be fifty. You have the helm."

Valthyrra left the astonished first officer at her post, moving her camera pod up into the upper bridge. Mayelna sat back in her seat, both sets of arms folded on her chest. "Are you quite finished?"

"For now," Valthyrra replied. "What do you think?"

"About your aggressive new policy?" the Commander asked. "You know that I do not agree with you completely, or you would not ask. I prefer that we be a little more cautious. Our pilots—none of our pilots—are used to real warfare. They are used to slow ships that do not fight back."

"Pilots like Velmeran and his pack?" Valthyrra asked. "If the performance of the entire ship is to be hampered by your hesitancy to send your son into battle, then he must transfer out. I can arrange for Thenderra Delvon to give us a pack in exchange."

Mayelna frowned. "You do know how to fight dirty. I would not part with Velmeran for anything . . . and I say that as his Commander. He is just not ready. He has not yet decided what he believes."

"He talks undecided, but he acts like he knows exactly what he believes in, and what must be done. You said something to that effect yourself."

"While you were eavesdropping through a vacuum cleaner," Mayelna said accusingly, and sat back in silence. She rubbed her nose and pulled her ear at regular intervals, thinking furiously. But, try as she could, she could come up with no good excuse. "It is not just Velmeran. I feel responsible for every pilot on board this ship. I would not send them out to something they are not ready for."

"Of course," Valthyrra was quick to assure her. "Every person on this ship is like a child to me. I am, after all, a mother ship."

"But this is what we were made for. And we will be as ready for it as we possibly can be." Mayelna paused and glanced up at the camera pod. "That means you as well. We are going to have to give serious thought to an overhaul."

"Ah, me . . . well, yes," Valthyrra agreed weakly, although her lenses appeared unfocused.

The lift door snapped open and Consherra, head down, stepped forward. She immediately struck something large and black and bounced off with a sound like a Class D freighter slamming into dock about three times faster than was good for it. A head-on impact between two armored Kelvessan can be the closest approximation of the meeting of the immovable object and the irresistible force. Consherra was the smaller of the two and thereby lost the contest, the weight of her armor, nearly equal to her own, got the better of her balance and threatened to send her over backward. Four strong arms caught her, preventing a certain fall.

"Are you all right?" Velmeran asked.

"Fine. Fine," she answered as she swatted his hands away and pushed him back inside the lift. "Can we get out of here before anyone comes to look?"

"I was hoping to find out what happened," Velmeran said, confused by this hasty retreat.

"I know that," she replied irritably as she typed in the coordinates for the area of her own cabin.

"So explain," Velmeran said. "I already know the general history. What about the interesting little details?"

Consherra laughed. "The little details do seem to be the most interesting these days. Then listen well, and forget who told you. Valthyrra took matters into her own hands. In fact, she rather blatantly avoided telling Mayelna what she was doing until it was done."

Velmeran nodded thoughtfully. "Valthyrra Methryn is ready for a fight, but the Commander is hesitant. That is obvious enough. But why?"

"Simple enough," Consherra said, just a little pleased with herself. "I know how those two operate, but I also know that Valthyrra is the smarter of the two. Mayelna feels that it is her duty to protect the crew of this ship, even above fulfilling the purpose of our existence. Valthyrra is less cautious because she has a better understanding of how things stand. She knows the real worth of this crew. She knows that she and Mayelna will quickly work out a compromise of aggression and restraint."

Velmeran shrugged. "I knew that."

Consherra looked at him in astonishment and opened her mouth to demand an explanation, but the lift door opened at that moment. She started to step out, then deciding that she did not want to give Velmeran a chance to escape, took him by the arm and brought him with her. Not releasing her hold on him, she led the way quickly to her cabin and pulled him inside.

"What do you mean, you knew that?" she demanded almost before he was inside.

Velmeran shrugged again. "When you have been an object of special interest and contention between those two for as long as I have, you get to know their tactics. Mayelna is bright, more so than you might think, but she is not very subtle. Valthyrra is the mistress of subtlety, with the lessons of eighteen thousand years of sneakiness behind her. If you will consider, then you would know that Valthyrra almost always gets her way."

"If you know so much, then what were you trying to discover by going up to the bridge?"

"Just confirming my suspicions," he replied. "What does it matter to you anyway?"

"Do I have to have a reason?" Consherra asked in return.

"I was wondering," Velmeran said. "You are no gossip, and yet you seem to make a point of informing me of how matters stand on the bridge. I have to endure quite enough motherly ministrations from Fidgit and Fanny without you joining in."

"Motherly ministrations?" Consherra demanded, and drew herself up proudly. "One of the biggest questions on the upper bridge of late has been the matter of the appointment of the Commander-designate. That person has to be one of the pack leaders. You are in very high standing just now, and very likely to get it. And as second in command, this is of considerable importance to me."

She paused and stood glaring at him, as if awaiting some anticipated reaction. But Velmeran did not seem to be particularly impressed. He stood calmly, arms crossed, staring back at her. A long, tense moment of silence followed, broken suddenly by the sound of Consherra's suit cycling on.

Velmeran smiled. "Now look, you have yourself all heated up. Your thermostat must be wired to your temper. But you worry needlessly. We might be on the bridge together in a hundred years or so, but just now I am neither old enough nor respected enough to be accepted as Commander-designate."

"It is entirely Valthyrra's choice. . . ."

"And Valthyrra is old enough to know better. A Commander must be respected to be effective, and I do not have the respect of the pilots and officers of this ship. If Valthyrra has indicated any favor toward me, then it is only a game she is playing to get what she really wants."

"She is waiting for something," Consherra insisted.

"She is trying hard to encourage me to be a good pack leader, and that is all," Velmeran said. "And just now I am finding it hard enough to be that. Please do not complicate my life any more than it already is."

"Keth and I had been working on the same ship, so I was lucky enough to be near when it happened," Tregloran explained to an appreciative audience of younger pack members, nearly a score in all, gathered close about the table where he sat with members of his own pack.

Velmeran, sitting alone several tables over, did his best not to listen. But Kelvessan have ears like sonic dragons, one of the many gifts of their genetic perfection. And just now his ears had a will of their own, tracing that particular conversation to its source like scanners. At least he was pleased with the younger pilot's honesty; Treg made it clear that he was much more an observer to these events than a participant. Unfortunately, Velmeran also noticed that his own role was more prominent than he remembered.

Then he noticed, to his dismay, that he was not the only one eavesdropping on this tale. The dining hall was about as full as he had ever seen it, and everyone, perhaps three hundred people in all, was listening attentively to Tregloran as he unwittingly recited his story for the entire group. Velmeran felt a moment of panic. His real desire was to silence his young pack member on some pretext, but that would be too blatant. Instead he thought it time for a hasty retreat.

"But there was no way that they were going to fool the Captain," Tregloran continued blissfully. "He was on her tail the moment that carrier broke from the rest. And Baressa was right behind him."

Velmeran rose quietly and began to slip away, unobserved. He edged out the door, thinking that he had made his escape, only to find a small delegation of his fellow pack leaders. Then he knew he was in trouble. Barthan, young and cynical—for a Kelvessa—was the obvious leader of this group, with the older Traln a close second. He was surprised to see Shayrn rounding out this group of malcontents; she had always been supportive of him in the past.

"Off to save a world, Captain?" Barthan inquired, radiating sarcastic displeasure. "We want to have a word with you. We would like to know what you thought you were doing out there."

"My duty," Velmeran replied evenly. "And I would like to know what you thought you were doing while I was out there."

"That is beside the point. . . ."

"Is it?" Velmeran demanded. "My pack and I did your duty as well as our own. If you believe that you are better than I am, then you tell me why you were not there when you were needed."

"So we made a mistake," Barthan snapped impatiently. "Well, you made a bigger one when you decided that you could give us orders."

"You are not a senior pack leader," Traln added. "In fact, you are the most junior pack leader on this ship. Baressa was senior, and she was out there with you. Why was she not giving the orders?"

"Perhaps because Baressa is smart enough to recognize a superior leader when it counts," Baressa answered for herself, seeming to appear out of the very air behind the three disgruntled pack leaders. She walked around them to stand beside Velmeran, obviously casting her support with him. "All this talk about junior and senior pack leaders is foolish. A few extra years of sitting in a fighter or wearing a rank does not make you better than anyone else. A good leader comes that way, ready-made, and you know it because you listen when he or she gives an order. And from now on I listen to him."

Shayrn was so moved by that endorsement that she abandoned her previous group, edging around to stand close to Baressa. Even Traln looked doubtful. Only Barthan remained unconvinced.

"You could be Commander-designate if we pushed it," he reminded her.

"I know that," she agreed. "But if Valthyrra says that he is the one, then I believe her. You will see. Or else you will find yourself another ship."

"I will not take orders from him," Barthan insisted.

"Yes, you will," she said with icy firmness. "If Valthyrra or the Commander indicates that he can, then you are going to listen. Refusing his orders under those circumstances is the same as refusing their own. You know that. You would lose your rank, and you might find yourself without a ship, if Valthyrra turns you out, because no one else will take you in. If you do not like the way things are, then get out while it is your idea."

"But things do not have to be that way," Barthan argued with equal force. "If we stand together on this . . ."

"You still do not understand," Baressa interrupted him, her tone cold enough to be intimidating. "Management wants it this way, and I agree. Too many of the senior pack leaders—which you are not—stand with him in this matter. You cannot gather enough support to have your own way, so you had better shut up before you get yourself in trouble."

"I believe that I have had enough of your game," Shayrn agreed.

"Traln, you need to take your young friend aside and make a few matters clear to him," Baressa continued. "I thought that you, at least, were old enough to know better."

With that she took Velmeran by the arm and led him down the broad corridor toward the pilots' apartments. The younger pilot was too stunned to know what to think. He could only recall that Baressa had been his stern teacher only a few years before. For her to champion him so firmly left him speechless.

"Barthan is a fool and he always will be," she complained aloud, more to herself. "Rank and seniority are all-important to him, now that he has a measure of his own, and he would like to forget that the only pack leader he is senior to is you. I guess that means a lot to him, since he does not have a fourth of your talent or quick wits. You threaten him, you might say, not that I am offering that as an excuse. And I certainly do not want you worrying about trouble from him. Traln is our other resident fool, but he just needed to have things spelled out for him. He will keep Barthan under control now."

She paused, noticing that Velmeran was staring at her, and smiled. "I would not have you intimidated by me, either. It was one thing for me to be a little strict with you when I was teaching you how to run a pack. The time for teaching is past, but there are still some things that I can do to help you. And if I am standing firmly behind you, the other pack leaders will too. Seven of them, at least. That seems like a good percentage to me, certainly at this point."

"Help me what?" Velmeran asked.

Baressa paused and regarded him closely. "You are no fool, Meran. And you are certainly no coward. Now you tell me what I am talking about."

"I think that you mean to make me Commander-designate," he answered cautiously, afraid that she would scorn him if he guessed wrong. Up until Consherra's very blatant hints, he had always thought of Baressa as filling that role, officially or not.

She nodded firmly. "So you do understand. I know that it was understood that I was the only candidate for that position. And I would have taken it for the same reason that your mother did, because I was needed. But I do not want it."

"And you think I do?" Velmeran asked.

"No, but you will take it. You are better than I am," she replied as she turned to leave.

"But I am not ready to command this ship!" he protested.

Baressa paused to glance back at him. "You will be."

5

In Donalt Trace's experience there was nothing so boring and pointless as a formal dinner party. These were the battles that young Richart Lake had been brought up to fight; in his opinion, he could do more good for trade and commerce by fighting Starwolves, subduing unaffiliated fringe worlds and chastising the colonies. He had to admit that the old Councilor and his grandson did fight and win major battles armed with only hors d'oeuvres and wineglasses, hammering out sweet deals for Farstell Trade or alliances between the allegedly unified sectors. The only thing he failed to understand was why he was expected to have any part of it.

Tonight he had retreated into a dark corner. Councilor Lake's suite was spacious, occupying two-thirds of an entire level of the Sector Residence. He preferred the cavernous halls and chambers of the Lake Mansion, some distance down the coast from Vannkarn, where it was easy to lose one's self without committing the social felony of simply disappearing. Quarters were too close in this apartment, but for the moment he was left alone, a glass of warm, flat wine in his hand, as he watched young Richart, seemingly a boyish figure surrounded by the old fools he was deftly maneuvering into trade agreements that were not to their best advantage.

Just then he saw the Councilor's personal servant approaching in a very purposeful manner and used that as an excuse to remove himself, suspecting that there must be some message. Only an attack of Starwolves would get him out of this entirely, and he knew that he would never be so lucky, but any respite would be welcome.

"A courier is in," Javarns explained. "There is a messenger who wishes to speak with you, sir."

"Here?"

The older man nodded. "He is waiting in the hall, sir."

"Thank you, Javarns," Trace said, handing him the half-empty glass. "I will speak with him outside."

The messenger was indeed waiting for him in the hallway just outside the suite's double doors, shifting nervously as he eyed the armed guard who had escorted him up. He was a young officer, no doubt captain and crew of the courier that had brought him (couriers were really stingships, their sophisticated attack systems removed to make room for a pocket-sized cabin and a tiny hold). One of Trace's greatest regrets was that the Union lacked an effective long-range achronic transceiver such as the Starwolves possessed, their own being barely good enough for in-system use.

"So?" he asked impatiently. "Are you out of Tallin?"

"Yes, sir!" The young officer snapped to attention and presented him the locked metal folder bearing the report. The Sector Commander only stared at it and shrugged.

"I have no time right now. You were there?" he asked, and the messenger nodded. "So you tell me, quick and simple, what happened. Did it work?"

"No, sir," the officer explained. "Apparently there was some malfunction in the decoy ship. It evaded but did not respond to contact from the station. It certainly did not explode."

Trace shrugged again. "Doesn't sound like my ship, if

it evaded. The one we sent out wasn't that smart. I suppose we got whipped in the process?"

"Yes, sir. We lost all the system fleet," the messenger reported in a quiet voice, then brightened. "We did take a prisoner."

"A prisoner?" the Sector Commander asked himself, and glanced up. "Did you say a prisoner?"

"Yes, sir. A Starwolf rammed a carrier and became trapped inside, alive and well. Being empty, she was quick enough to whip around and break from the battle, and we covered her escape. Her pursuit gave up just as she was heading out of system."

"At least her captain had sense enough to take her out of system," Trace mused. "Do you know where they were bound?"

"No, sir. They refused to say over com, for fear it would be overheard. They did promise another courier as soon as they arrived."

"That was all they could do, I suppose," he told himself, then glanced down at the messenger. "Put that report on my desk and leave the key with me now. Then wait in port until I dismiss you. I might have a message for you to take back."

The messenger saluted smartly and turned to leave. Trace returned to the apartment, closing the door quietly. A prisoner? A live Starwolf? He had never heard of such a thing happening before. As soon as he entered the dining room, he found that Councilor Lake, with his uncanny talent for sensing trouble, was already moving to intercept him. Richart, the well-trained apprentice, appeared a moment later from another direction. Trace turned abruptly to the bar, seizing that as their excuse for a few quiet words.

"Courier from Tallin?" the elder Lake inquired quietly as he inspected the stock of wine on hand. "So how did it go?"

"They took the bait, but the conversion device failed to detonate for some reason. We lost the system fleet as a result," he reported quickly, then grinned. "We did take a prisoner."

The Councilor stared at him, wide-eyed. "A what?"

Donalt quickly explained all that he had been told. The elder Lake obviously did not know what to make of it, seeming to weigh whether it was good news or not. Richart, however, had no such trouble deciding, his boyish face uncharacteristically solemn. Since Trace expected only some advantage to come of it, he was somewhat dismayed by their cautious reactions.

"Have you ever heard of our taking a Starwolf prisoner before?" he asked.

"No, I haven't," Lake admitted, still distracted by his own thoughts. "We have managed to acquire a body from time to time, which is how we know as much about them as we do. But we've never had a live body before."

"Why not?"

"Mostly because the Starwolves would rip this sector apart to find him."

"But what can they do about it, if they have no idea where we have him?" the Sector Commander demanded. "That is the trick, isn't it? We just need to keep him in hiding until we're finished with him. We did it before, with the Vardon's memory cell. We kept it hidden for thousands of years."

"That is a completely different case," Lake replied, brushing that impatiently aside. "For one thing, they weren't even aware it existed until we finally put it on public display here in Vannkarn. And the memory cell is also an imperishable good; you can bet that they plan to come for it in their own good time. But a prisoner is altogether something else. They know that we have him, where we got him, and they are going to do whatever they must to get him back."

"You think they can trace him?" Richart asked.

"I am willing to bet on it," the Councilor said firmly. "They have technology we can only dream about. For all we know, their scanners can track a ship across stellar distances. And just as likely, they can follow its trail of energy-emission residue. How should I know?"

"Here comes trouble," Richart said suddenly, having spied one of their distinguished guests approaching. "Let me distract him for a moment."

With that he shot off like a missile to intercept his intended target. Trace stared after him for a moment, surprised at such a magnanimous gesture on his part. Trace had always held the younger Lake in mild contempt. He was small for one of old Terran stock, hardly any taller than most modern humans, stocky and plump. His boyish looks had now followed him into his thirties; he was cherub-cheeked, with curly brown hair and the eternally amused look in his eyes that he had inherited from his grandfather. But Donalt did not let personal dislike interfere with his judgment. Richart was an administrative genius exceeding even his formidable grandfather.

"You want this prisoner, don't you?" Lake asked.

"Of course I do."

"Why?" the Councilor asked, eyeing him shrewdly. "Prestige?"

"Hardly!" Trace declared, somewhat indignant. "It has occurred to me that, with a live subject to study, we might finally discover how Starwolves were made. So that we can make our own."

"Ah, I see," Lake said thoughtfully. "The ultimate weapon to use against a Starwolf is another Starwolf."

"Of course," Trace agreed. "That is the premise behind our Tracer missiles. But we already know that anything mechanical we build will never equal the real thing. Therefore we need the real thing."

The Councilor nodded thoughtfully. "All right, then. If you can keep him, and I emphasize the 'if,' then you will have all the help we can muster in probing their secrets. But that is sort of out of your hands right now, I'm afraid. They will have to get their prisoner situated somewhere long enough for you to issue some orders on his handling. Right now we don't even know where he is."

* * *

Boulder was essentially just that, a big rock in the middle of open space, not large enough to be a real planet, barely large enough to have served some planet for a moon, and with no sun to warm it. How such a piece of basalt had ever happened to end up in the middle of nowhere was uncertain, so it must have been drifting about for quite some time. To the Starwolves, however, it was a valuable piece of property indeed. It was just big enough to have the gravity to hold a carrier in stationary orbit twenty kilometers out. It had a hole in it just large enough for a damaged carrier to back into, the guns of its forward battery facing out, and, best of all, the Union had no idea it existed.

ne ship was already waiting, not the carrier Delvon but one of the immense Starwolf freighters. Although the size and general shape was the same, the freighters had less than half the mass. They were not fighting ships, being only lightly armored, and more than half their main hull was devoted to several cavernous holds. The Union knew nothing of these ships, for they never showed themselves.

"Hello, who is there?" Valthyrra called out as she approached. There were, of course, official rules and procedures for recognition, but the Starwolf ships tended to be more informal, since they were all old friends.

"This is Fyrdenna Lesdryn," the freighter responded. "Hello, Valthyrra. Long time, no see."

"Hello, Feery. You look well. But what are you doing here, if I may ask the obvious?"

"Thenderra transferred your call to me, and I was closer to Boulder at the time than any of you. I'm on my way home, in fact, but I have plenty of room for all the junk you have to give."

"You may have it with my gratitude, and especially Thenderra's," Valthyrra said. "She did not sound at all happy to have to take it off my hands."

"I should say not! My bridge crew is still laughing at

the sight of you popping out of starflight with your transports and capture ships following you like a brood!" Fyrdenna exclaimed, then became serious. "Still, you do have more than Lyerrana Vyesden gave me."

"Lyerrana?" Valthyrra prompted, unsure whether she should have heard this. The entire bridge crew paused to listen, since she was putting this over audio.

"You were too far to one side to have caught the news on achronic," the freighter continued. "Lyerrana was making her usual rounds of the outer fringe when she came upon a Union invasion of a nonaffiliated world. Balgan by name. It seems that they were just starting to make a profit, and the Union decided that it wanted that profit for its own trade companies."

"The old story."

"Yes, and Lyerrana said that she has been expecting it for the past twenty years. But this was strange. It was only a small invasion force, a battleship, three carriers and four troop transports. A force like that usually just runs when they see Starwolves coming, but instead they turned and fought like they had never heard of us. She caught the battleship and two of the carriers—I have them in my hold right now—and sent the survivors heading for home in the transports. Then she sent for me to haul home the spoils so that she could stay and watch the system. I almost believe that she will indeed have another load by the time I get this home."

"I heard that there is a new Sector Commander in my haunts," Valthyrra mused. "But that is not even an adjoining sector."

"I can understand an invasion," Fyrdenna continued. "But what happened to you defies explanation."

"Oh, it did turn out to be a trap," Valthyrra said, and quickly explained the details. Then she had to pause, since the channel was echoing with the laughter of the Lesdryn's entire bridge crew.

Fyrdenna was laughing with the rest. "Wonderful! It was your good fortune to spring the trap in halves."

"Oh, there was no mistaking that ship," Valthyrra insisted. "They had it phasing so hard that it would have burned itself out in twenty minutes of hard running. I got control of it and sent it on with my compliments. I popped it right over their heads, just to give them a good scare."

"The Union is getting mean, and I fear that we have some hard battles yet ahead of us," Fyrdenna said. "I am beginning to wish that I had been built a fighting ship. I would envy you, if I were not so thoroughly pleased with myself. Now park yourself and start off-loading. Thenderra cannot be four hours behind me."

The two ships met far enough out from Boulder to avoid the bother of its feeble gravity. They drifted together bellies facing, upside down in respect to each other, with just enough room between them for the Lesdryn's handlers to shift the load. The Methryn opened every hold and bay she had, and her own capture ships came in to haul away the intact ships as they were freed from her holding bays. These were set in a row between the two larger vessels, for the Lesdryn's handlers to look at and decide how best to pack them in her own vast bays. Her largest bay had folding racks for transporting a large number of ships, but this constituted a respectable fleet by Union standards. Some of the destroyers might have to be secured in other bays.

"Bless my buttons, what a haul!" Fyrdenna exclaimed. "You must have come away with just about everything they threw at you. My compliments to your pilots. They must be the best."

"Thank you," Valthyrra replied graciously. "But the truth is, I had only two packs out during most of the battle. They had things well under control before I could get anything else out."

"You ironclad hulk of a bragging bitch!" Mayelna muttered under her breath without looking up from her screen, privately glad that Velmeran had not been present to hear all this. Valthyrra heard that, however, and quickly cut the audio, keeping the conversation private at least on her end.

"Do you want this credited to your account?" Fyrdenna asked.

"Just make sure that they knew where it all came from," Valthyrra replied. "I am going to be coming in for a complete overhaul before long."

"Oh, ho! Valthyrra Methryn is getting old!"

"We are all getting old, my dear. Some of us simply do not show it. By the way, do you know if Home Base might have any plans for these ships? Balgan might be in the market for a few, if they are getting that rich."

"Balgan will get all they can afford, certainly," Fyrdenna said. "Our prices are always low, and our rates reasonable. This wealth of star drives will put a great many other ships in service as well. The trouble is that we still do not have a fourth of the ships available for delivery that are needed. Things should be improving, though, if I continue fetching home loads like this. And that seems promising, with things heating up all over."

"Of course, half of our carriers will be wanting overhauls in the next few years," Valthyrra pointed out.

"No problem!" Fyrdenna insisted. "How long has it been since you were home? Our support worlds have been prospering, and they are all behind us. Home Base is expanding. There is going to be a new construction airdock, and more carriers. There is even talk of a final push to defeat the Union."

"The rest I can believe, but not that," Valthyrra said doubtfully. "We lost too much when we lost Terra, and that was a long time before you or I came out of the construction bay. We will have to get back what we lost before we can seriously consider making an end to this war."

"So?" Fyrdenna asked. "You send your crack pilots into Vannkarn after the Vardon's memory cell, and we will have Terra back in a year to two."

Valthyrra hesitated in her response, since the idea had definite appeal. Of all the big wolf ships, the Vardon had been the last to know the location of Terra. She had been destroyed when Valthyrra had still been very young; one of her memory cells, the big information storage units of her computer mind, had been found by the Union centuries later. Their attempts to access that wealth of information had proven futile, and at last the unit had been placed on display in Vannkarn, the capital of the Rane Sector. The Starwolves had long believed that they would one day get it back and find the way to Terra, where the big carriers had first been built. Perhaps that time would be soon, Valthyrra thought, if a certain pack leader could be trained to the task.

Thenderra Delvon arrived slighty ahead of schedule, coming out of starflight at Boulder barely an hour after the Methryn. Valthyrra Methryn turned immediately and accelerated; she had given up every spare ton of cargo to the Lesdryn and now felt light and quick and just a little mean. The second carrier fell in behind her and began to close quickly. Two small ships shot out from beneath her, a transport and a single fighter, both as black as space itself. The two little ships shot along a straight line toward the Methryn, slowing to match her speed as they dropped down slightly to pass below her star drives as they approached her left landing bay.

Only a small group had gathered in the bay to welcome them. Most of the crewmembers had to remain at their posts, with an immediate jump to starflight coming. And none of the pilots, even the pack leaders, had dared to show themselves in the past two days. Out of sight was not necessarily out of mind, but it was a good deal safer.

Mayelna, in white armor, led the delegation. Consherra waited nearby, wearing the white tunic and pants that were the general uniform of an officer. Valthyrra was present in the form of a probe, a special type of remote, a simple streamlined shape barely a meter long, with folding wings and a retractable neck with a pair of cameras inside a protective cowling. Despite its small size it could outfly and outshoot a Union fighter and yet hover motionless on projected fields, and it even had a pair of arms folded inside of narrow bays along its underside. Velmeran, uninvited but not unwelcome, wore the black armor of a pilot.

Side by side, the two ships entered the bay. Flying with an easy precision that would have put most pilots to shame, they moved to the front of the bay and landed gently. A rack was immediately lowered behind the fighter and locked into place. Benthoran had the boarding platform folded down just in time to assist the pilot out of the cockpit.

It was then that Velmeran saw that the pilot, who he assumed to be the pack leader, was female. There was no guessing her age, since Kelvessan did not change in appearance from early adulthood to old age three hundred years later. But there was something about her that made him think that, however long she had lived, she had seen and done quite a lot in that time. She looked to him very capable and very dangerous. And his first reaction was one of shame, that this was the type of leader he could only pretend to be.

She was joined by three others from the transport, one male and one female in black armor, and another male in regular clothes who carried both of his left arms in a sling. That, at least, was some indication that this group did fight. The pilot was clearly the leader, for the others waited for her, and she went first as they approached the waiting group from the Methryn. She stopped before Valthyrra's remote and bowed her head in respect.

"Valthyrra Methryn, I am pack leader Dveyella of special tactics. This is my second, Baress." She indicated the injured member first, then the armored male and female. "Threl and Marlena."

Valthyrra dipped the probe's camera pod in response. "I welcome you. This is Commander Mayelna, First Officer Consherra and pack leader Velmeran. We are grateful for your assistance. . . ."

Dveyella held up a hand to interrupt. "Please, before we go any farther, I must tell you that my pack is temporarily shorthanded. Baress, the only other fighter pilot I have, is recovering from a recent accident and will not be able to fly for at least another week. His fighter was hit and damaged, so that his field drive controls failed on approach. . . ."

"I bounced twice," Baress admitted guiltily. "Once off the Delvon's lower hull and again off the side of her landing bay. Thenderra was so mad she almost begrudged sending out a capture ship to get me."

"I can imagine," Valthyrra remarked softly.

"Then you cannot fight?" Mayelna asked impatiently.

"I thought I made this plain when you contacted us," Dveyella said with some surprise. "I said that we could fight if you could loan us a good pilot to take the place of Baress. Valthyrra indicated that we could have Velmeran, that he is the best you have."

Velmeran's surprise was nearly as great as Mayelna's. Both were greatly astonished that Valthyrra would go so far to have her own way, surprised that she had managed to trick them both, and surprised at themselves for not expecting it. Velmeran at least was spared Mayelna's indignation, since he obviously had no prior knowledge of this. But he quickly decided that if fate, or a conniving computer, was going to give him the opportunity, then he was going to seize it. For herself, Valthyrra was glad that probes were practically indestructible.

"The best pilot you have is good enough for me . . . assuming that he has the endurance," Dveyella continued after a moment of profound silence. "Most people cannot maintain hypermetabolism long enough to work in special tactics."

"I can recommend no one else," Valthyrra declared.

Dveyella crossed her arms as she looked Velmeran up and down very closely. "What about strength? I am strong enough myself, but I do like to have a second who can assist in matters of . . . lifting and removing obstacles."

Valthyrra turned her pod to look at Velmeran. "Do not fail me now."

"Do you have something in mind?" Velmeran asked.

He was not worried, for he was sure that Valthyrra knew his strength.

Indeed she did. The fighter was quickly unracked and Velmeran approached it quickly and confidently. It was, of course, no secret that he proposed to lift the nose of the little ship. That was no small task, for a Starwolf fighter was twenty meters of heavy machinery, dense plastics and spun carbon filaments. A great deal of its weight was in the very back; in order to tilt it back on its rear struts, all he had to lift was about six tons. But he did that easily with only his upper arms.

"He is stronger than I am," Baress admitted quietly to his captain.

That was saying a lot, and Dveyella did not answer. Among their own kind, size and sex were not good indications of strength. Baress was about the strongest person she had ever met, and she was herself just a little stronger still. But Velmeran was even stronger. There was no longer any question about whether she would allow him to go. Indeed, Valthyrra Methryn might have a hard time getting him back.

"Suits me," she admitted casually. "Commander?"

"It seems to have already been decided," Mayelna answered slowly, still loath to agree. "If you are going to run our errands for us, then we should at least offer you any help we have to give. I had meant to have Velmeran's pack standing ready to help you get clear. . . ."

"Velmeran's pack is shorthanded," Valthyrra pointed out, as if some automatic relay had failed to note that the argument was over. She turned her camera pod to Dveyella. "My drone reports that the Union carrier is approaching its predicted port. I should have all the information I can get for you coming within the next few hours."

"If you would care to shed that armor, my first officer will show you to your rooms," Mayelna said, her behavior improving quickly as her good humor returned. "If Valthyrra has your luggage ready."

"Coming!" Valthyrra announced. A remote, a small

flat-topped freight carrier, emerged from the other side of the transport, piled with boxes and bags as it rolled off toward the lift. Mayelna quickly took Velmeran by the arm and led him on ahead of the others. Consherra flinched when she saw that; Mayelna might not be able to stop this —indeed she had not really even tried—but she would certainly lecture him long and hard until it was done, and then start over by pointing out his mistakes. She did not notice Dveyella until the pilot fell in beside her.

"I seem to have walked into the middle of something."

"Oh, do not let those two bother you," Consherra assured her. "Unfortunately, this is an old argument. Can you keep a secret?"

"Better than you."

Consherra smiled. "I am hoping that the end justifies the means. To put it simply, Valthyrra wants Velmeran for Commander-designate, and Mayelna refuses to name him. Velmeran gained quite a beginning of a reputation as a capable leader during our last battle. Now Valthyrra is obviously contriving to help him win as much favor as she can, so that Mayelna will have no reason not to approve the appointment."

"Ah, I see. Well, I have no objection to my part in this game, so long as Velmeran delivers as promised."

"Do you doubt?"

"If I doubted, he would not be going," Dveyella replied casually, although she obviously meant it. "But why should your Commander question his abilities?"

"It has nothing to do with his abilities," Consherra replied. "Commander Mayelna is his mother."

"Oh!" Dveyella exclaimed with a look of both comprehension and horrified dismay.

As soon as she was settled into her cabin, Dveyella asked Velmeran to meet her as soon as he could, in full armor, on a high observation platform in the left holding bay. She did not tell him what she had in mind, but he could guess easily enough; she meant to teach him what she could of the special tricks he would need to know for this mission. Velmeran found her already waiting on the platform, leaning with her upper set of arms on the rail, her lower arms braced wide as she stared down into the depths of the vast bay.

"You know, we Kelvessan are truly amazing fighting machines in our own right," she began almost absently. "I have been told that we can be over a hundred times stronger than an ordinary human of the same size, and our reflexes are thousands of times faster. And yet most of us know little of just how much we can do. For the purposes of today's exercise, Valthyrra Methryn has consented to turn off the buffer fields in this bay. Let me begin with a simple demonstration."

With that she casually leaped over the railing. Velmeran was not caught by surprise; he had figured out what she intended to do, and watched with interest. The static field that took the place of gravity was only a fair substitute for the real thing. It seemed like one standard gravity only to stationary objects, but decreased as objects moved faster relative to the motion of the ship. An ordinary human could have easily taken a fall of five meters. But Dveyella was jumping nearly the entire height of the bay, almost one hundred and fifty meters. As easily as she landed, it might have been only two.

Velmeran followed without waiting to be asked. The long fall was not so bad as he had anticipated, for it gave him time to prepare for his landing. Since he had the strength to kick open an airlock, he wisely allowed his legs to catch him. He landed almost gently, just slightly off-balanced by the top-heavy burden of his armor.

"Very good," Dveyella remarked. "That is about the most that you should ever try to jump under one real standard gravity. Remember that it is not how far you jump, but how hard you hit that limits you. Higher gravity decreases the height you can jump."

"What is the most I should be able to take?"

"Oh, you should be able to survive an impact speed of three hundred kilometers per hour or more," she said, looking him over. "And by survive, I mean that you should be able to pick yourself up and continue on without pain. You can endure more, but it will hurt. We do have our limits, one of them being our suits. Do you know that we can actually take more stress than our armor? Well, what goes down must often come back up."

Dveyella indicated a docking tube about fifteen meters to Velmeran's left and thirty straight up. She jumped from where she stood. Her body rigid and her arms spread wide for balance, she seemed almost to be flying for the long moment that she was in the air. She caught hold of the edge of the tube and flipped herself atop in a graceful move. Velmeran, knowing that he lacked the experience for anything that elaborate, made a much simpler leap from almost directly below the tube. He overshot by nearly ten meters, but arched gently over to land in the very middle of the tube.

"Well, you made it on your first try," Dveyella remarked. "Most people need a little practice to be able to jump that far. You seem to have a natural talent for this."

"Talent has less to do with it than common sense," Velmeran answered as he peered over the edge. "The easiest way is always the surest."

"Words to live by," Dveyella agreed. "That is why I jumped at an angle, showing you one of my fanciest tricks from the start. Most people would have tried to do it the hard way, and they learn their limitations very quickly."

"I prefer to face my limitations from the cautious side. I like surprises as well as anyone, but a limitation becomes a failing when it catches you by surprise."

Dveyella laughed. "That is the lecture that I was supposed to be giving you. Is there anything you do not know?"

"I just indicated that there is," Velmeran said. "All this business is new to me. Is it very likely that we will have to fight?"

Dveyella shrugged and sat down on the machinery that joined the docking tube to the wall. "That depends upon how chance works for us. Sometimes everything goes as smoothly as you could want. Other times everything seems to go wrong. Usually it falls somewhere in between."

"What about my armor and my fighter?" he asked. "Will they be good enough for what I need?"

"I have already requested a new suit for both of us," Dveyella said, glancing down at the burnt scoring on her lower right arm that could only be bolt flash from a deflected hit. "There is really nothing better than ordinary flight armor, since anything sturdier would also be heavier. Our fighters are exactly the same, since we use the same auxiliary guns and other accessories as we need. Your fighter will be good enough, as long as she is in prime condition. How long have you had her?"

Velmeran shrugged. "As long as I have been flying."

Dveyella only sat and stared at him.

"She has never taken a hit or had a major breakdown in any component," he continued, somewhat defensively. "I consider her as good as the day she was built."

Dveyella could only assume that either the ship must be getting shabby or else he had not been using it all that long. She suspected the latter, and now she was sure of it. "Velmeran, how old are you?"

"Twenty-five."

"And you already lead a pack?"

"Because I am about the best pilot on this ship."

Dveyella laughed. "At least you believe in being straightforward about it!"

Velmeran only shrugged. "I have no false vanity. I cannot take credit for being what I was designed to be. My mother was the best pilot that this ship has seen for some time."

"And your father?" Dveyella asked.

He shrugged again. "Mayelna has never seen fit to enlighten me. But I do not doubt that my father was . . .

worthy, considering how discriminating she can be. Do not worry about me. I know what I can do and what I cannot do."

Dveyella shook her head slowly. "I still cannot help but think that I have been flying twice as long as you have been alive. But Valthyrra Methryn does recommend you highly."

"Valthyrra Methryn seems to have plans for me," Velmeran remarked as he chose a sturdy connecting rod to sit on.

"Valthyrra obviously thinks a great deal of you, and I trust what the ships think. They have been around so long, and have seen so many people come and go, that they can tell," Dveyella said, keeping her real thoughts to herself. She wondered how much he really knew about the plans that Valthyrra had for him; somehow she suspected that he knew more about what was going on than anyone thought. This was the most interesting ship that she had been on in years. "And do not think that you would fly in my pack if I did not trust you."

"How did you come to lead a special tactics team?" Velmeran asked.

"By being as good as they say you are," she explained. "I was asked to fill a vacant place—just like you —and I was asked to stay. After fifty years I am now the senior member of the pack."

"They all died?"

Dveyella shook her head. "Some, but mostly they retire back to the regular packs. Marlena plans to go soon, so I might keep you if you do well enough, and if you want. Have you thought about it?"

Velmeran considered that a moment, and shook his head slowly. "No, I have not. I have a pack. . . . I might not be the best leader, but I have a responsibility to my pack." But then he paused as a new thought occurred to him. "Maybe that is what Valthyrra has in mind for me, though."

"Why would you think that?"

"I have been a source of dissension lately," he explained. "After our last battle, part of the crew has come to look upon me as something of a hero, while others—a few others—only resent me. Valthyrra and the Commander have problems enough without me in the middle of it."

"I have been told something about pilots who refused to go out until they were certain that the trouble was real," Dveyella said. "Would it surprise you to hear that this is not the first time in recent months?"

"No, I suppose not."

"I also heard that you were indeed something of a hero. . . ."

"According to Consherra!" Velmeran said accusingly.

"By Consherra, yes," she agreed reluctantly. "The pilots think otherwise?"

"My opportunity for heroism arose because I was out there alone, unsupported by pilots who did not want to trouble themselves until they were sure that they were needed," Velmeran explained hotly. "Two packs against a system fleet, and it was mostly over before the Methryn could get a single fighter out. Management is by no means prepared to allow them to forget it. You can surely see how that could cause resentment."

"Envy is the seed of resentment."

"Witticisms do not run the starship," Velmeran said. "This comes as a good opportunity to get rid of me gracefully. I can leave the hero, to a task more suited to my abilities."

"You think they want to be rid of you?" Dveyella asked in amazement. "The Commander is your own mother."

"And you might recall that she did not protest strongly," he reminded her. "Mayelna is a good Commander, but she works hard at it. She learned long ago the flaw in our standards of advancement, that being a good pilot does not necessarily make one a good leader."

"Valthyrra Methryn has something in mind for you, and I doubt that she would willingly let you go," Dveyella said. She rose slowly and shifted her shoulders to settle her armor into position, then turned back to Velmeran. "Perhaps you would be the most use here. We will go get Keth, and you can see for yourself what you think."

6

The Union carrier did not turn toward a new destination but dropped out of starflight and rushed into port so fast that it barely slowed itself for orbit. It was followed, discreetly and silently, by a machine hardly larger than a transport's star drive. The drone was fast and very maneuverable, and it had scanners and sensors of such range and sensitivity that the Union could only dream about. It also had the intelligence to perform its tasks efficiently, as well as judge new situations and act accordingly.

The drone watched patiently as the carrier settled into orbit, then it moved quickly, evading detection as it probed the planet to its very core. At last the little machine assembled all the information it had gathered into a neat package, opened an achronic channel and transferred it all back to the Methryn. Valthyrra quickly analyzed the information and was delighted with what she found. She quickly called Dveyella and the members of her pack to a meeting in one of the smaller conference rooms. The Commander left Consherra to watch the bridge, much to the first officer's dissatisfaction.

"My drone reported that the carrier reached its destination a short time ago," Valthyrra began. "It orbited just long enough to discharge a passenger and the remains of a fighter by way of a freight shuttle before moving on to the station to secure for repairs. The planet is called Bineck, fourth planet of a system by the same name, so called after the captain of the ship that first discovered it . . . a common enough ploy by otherwise unknown and unremarkable Union officers to stake a claim for immortality."

"If we can dispense with the trivialities," Mayelna remarked in her best patience-under-adversity voice.

"They seem to have decided upon stealth rather than security to hide their prize," the ship continued. She activated the viewscreen at the back of the small table where the group sat, turning her camera on its short boom to watch also. She quickly drew out the schematic for the system in question, showing the path of the carrier's approach, before moving on to the planet itself, drawing in features as she described them.

"The planet is uninhabited and uncolonized. The Union maintains a small orbital base, and there is also a major base on the planet itself, mostly a supply and refitting station for small ships. There are no facilities for larger ships, so they are dealing with the carrier as best they can. There are about fifty fighters at the station and some two hundred more at the base. There are also forty stingships and fifteen destroyers at the station. The carrier is in no condition to fight, and she is so tied up with cables and gantries that they could not have her free in time anyway."

"What about the carrier's fighters?" Dveyella asked.

"She lost those the last time we met," Valthyrra replied, and continued. "The extinct natives were great builders in stone. Even though they never developed a higher technology, they built fortresslike cities, kilometers across and so far down that the drone had to scan with deep-probe. Archeologists finished with these cities long ago and the Union has been using them ever since as long-term storage shelters. The native race died out about ten thousand years ago, long before the Union expanded into this area. We knew of them but never made contact. They were gone before we knew of their difficulties."

"Radiation traces?" Dveyella asked.

"No, the catastrophe was a natural one. A sudden, naturally mutated virus stripped the planet of vegetation in a quarter of a year's time. It was a type of super-virus, immense in size and complexity, that turned sugars into alcohols. Even grains stored in the deepest levels of the cities were ruined. The animal life either starved or died eating planet life that was infused with toxic alcohols . . . or from simply ingesting too much alcohol of any type."

"Quite an interesting little bug," Velmeran remarked. "Did the Union clear it properly?"

"They seeded a virus-chaser and imposed a full standard century of quarantine, but we had already eradicated it nine thousand years before. You do not leave nasty little things like that lying around for fools to blunder into. Which was a good thing, since survey teams came and went for half a planet year before they finally figured things out."

"But the Union is able to use these ruins, even after ten thousand years?" Dveyella asked.

"Ruins might not be an accurate word, since very little is ruined. These people built to last. And I will grant that the Union had to do a great deal of cleaning and a few repairs to make those cities fit for storage caches."

Valthyrra quickly pulled a file picture of a curious alien creature, short and powerful of build, with four long legs on a short main body and a pair of long arms attached to a small, vertical upper torso. Its eyes and ears were immense. "The natives were nocturnal cave dwellers. The cities they built are indeed more like caves, with few outer doors and no windows, and walls so thick that the temperature does not vary much throughout the year even in the levels aboveground. And most of the cities are well below the surface. They would come out on the surface—by night—to farm, but they would not dwell there by choice."

"The point of all this history and archeology is that

Keth is being kept in one of the supply caches, not in the main base. He is under very little guard, and is in fact very easy to get at. There is nothing remarkable about the cell he is in, just an ordinary storage room like millions of other rooms in the eighty-seven major cities across the planet, but he is on a level so deep that Union technology could not possibly scan for him.

"So they stuck him in a hole as quickly as they could and are trying to pretend that nothing has happened, ready to feign bewilderment to any Starwolf that might descend upon them. But they made two mistakes. They do not know that we were aware of Keth's location from the moment they put him into safekeeping. And they have that half-wrecked carrier tied up at the station for repairs, right in plain sight. I can excuse the first, but hardly the second."

"Can you show me where they have Keth?" Dveyella asked.

"Simple enough," Valthyrra said as she began to display graphics on the viewscreen, beginning with a map of the planet. "Because of the great size of the major cities, the Union has always assumed that the native population was between two and five million each. We know, from actual observation, that few populations ever exceeded fifty thousand. Because of their naturally stable temperatures, these cities are to be found from the tropics to just within the arctic regions . . . just as long as a major crop could be grown in the region. The only exceptions are a few that were more dependent upon coastal fishing. They lived long lives, nearly as long as that of your own kind. They built to last, and they were very careful in their building."

Valthyrra paused to rotate her map of the planet, moving in on a single city. "The place where they have Keth is on the far northern coast of the larger continent, one of those fishing centers on the edge of the arctic sea. The city itself is just a few kilometers inland in a fold between ridges of a rather rugged band of mountains. The city is a fairly large one, for its coastal cliffs had caves enough for a vast fleet." The image focused on a section of the city. "Keth is here, in the southwest corner. You can land your ships here on this wide ledge on the ridge overlooking the city, no more than a kilometer from the southwest entrance."

Valthyrra indicated the ledge and drew out a careful map down from the heights to the entrance and on into the interior of the city. "After entering, you will proceed a short distance to the main stairs leading down. Here you will descend twelve levels to the very bottom. That is a deceptively far distance down, nearly half a kilometer, since there is considerable space between levels. Fortunately there is a freight elevator installed in the stairwell itself. The remains of the fighter are stacked together in shielded boxes not far from the entrance, beside a landing pad used by freight transports."

"So what we have is a round trip of three kilometers or more, one of which is an elevator ride," Dveyella commented to herself before looking up at the hovering camera pod. "How much time do we have?"

"The nearest fighters are at the main base on the other continent, and much farther to the south." Valthyrra indicated the two locations on her map projection. "That is just over nine thousand kilometers. The fighters will undoubtedly go subballistic to make the best time. Count on no more than thirty minutes, but be prepared if they only give you twenty."

Dveyella nodded thoughtfully. "And we can enter through the polar magnetic corridor and fly in low?"

"Yes, that is what makes this easy. There is not much in the way of surveillance equipment, since there has never been any need. The Union has always disdained radar because of its limited effective range due to its speed-of-light time lag, and the planet has a strong enough magnetic field to deflect achronic sensors and scanners."

"And what of guards?"

"There are no living personnel at the complex, although there are perhaps a hundred automatons walking the halls." She quickly drew up the schematics for a curious machine. Its heavy, rounded upper body was carried on four spindly legs, with guns sprouting like antlers from its head and upper back and a long whip of an antenna like an upraised tail. "They are all of the new Shepherd design, smarter and quicker than the old Prowler sentry model."

"I am familiar with the design," Dveyella said. "What do you want done with the wreckage of the fighter? We cannot leave it, and I would rather take it with us than try to destroy it. Our fighters are too well-built; it would take quite an explosion to blow it to worthless bits, especially if it is in shielded containers."

"Do you propose that we should haul it out on our backs?" Velmeran asked. "Is that why you wanted to know if I was strong?"

"No, hardly," Dveyella said, smiling. It was a ridiculous thought, even though they could lift twelve tons between them. "Our transport has an oversized cargo door and heavy-duty handling arms. We can get those boxes on our way out."

Threl nodded in agreement. "All I have to do is set us down beside it, and Marlena can snatch them up in half a minute."

"There is surveillance equipment, visual and infrared scanners, at the complex. That is why you cannot come in for that fighter until you are ready to depart. Most of the planet's security is designed to guard the world as a whole and keep anything from approaching too closely in the first place. That is why you will not have to worry about automatic cannons tracking you. There are none."

"Unfortunately, that is also why your packs are going to have to stay well back," Dveyella added. "If they see fighters coming in, they are going to be on their guard."

"That is true as well," Valthyrra agreed. "But my drone will be watching you closely, and I can time matters close enough so that my packs will be there to support you on your way out."

Dveyella nodded. "Our problem with fighters is going to be inside the atmosphere, since we have to keep our speed down to their level. Outside it is going to be stingships and destroyers. Out transport is good, but it is still no fighter and it will be the most vulnerable to stingships. We have to keep them off her tail."

"I will have nine packs there to help you by then," Valthyrra said. Then, seeing Velmeran's look of dismay, she turned her camera pod to stare at him. "Nine packs, not ten. I will not allow your children to launch. Short one, perhaps. . . ."

"But not without me, no," Velmeran agreed. "They already know that they will not be going out, and they have been taking it fairly well. But Treg wants to go with me so badly he is positively begging. I wonder if it would not be easier to simply lock him in his cabin until this is over."

Mayelna laughed aloud. "Now perhaps you will be able to appreciate how hard it is for me to try to tell you no!"

Velmeran sealed the last closure of his new suit and opened the chestplate, flipping down the hinged mirror so that he could see to set the controls. The visual display was cleverly designed; the monitor displayed normally for an assistant's use and, at the touch of a button, backward and upside down so that the wearer could see it in the mirror. He quickly set the controls and the cooling unit cycled on strongly but silently. The one flaw in the Kelvessan's impressive design was that they generated a great deal of heat even when they were inactive, and reached dangerously excessive levels during hypermetabolism. Outside the cool environment of their own ships, they depended upon their suits for comfort or even life in temperatures that ordinary humans found normal.

Valthyrra might not have been able to improve upon the construction of the suit, but she made a vast improvement in the fit. The armor itself fit much closer about the suit inside, and was no longer free to shift and turn during swift or difficult movements. She had made suits for both himself and Dveyella to very precise measurements, so precise that they would have to be careful of both gaining or losing weight. And that was a problem in itself, for Starwolves had to eat enormously to maintain their powerful metabolisms.

"Now this is the way it was supposed to be!" Dveyella declared as she lifted both sets of arms high over her head and shifted her shoulders back and forth. "It feels as if you have articulated the backplate."

"I have," Valthyrra said, hovering near in the form of a probe. "Both the front- and backplates are split down the middle and joined by a continuous hinge, with the protective plastic coating molded in one piece over the top. All of our suits are built that way, although it seems that no other ships have adopted the design."

"Can you give me plans for that design?" she asked.

"Of course," Valthyrra said, and turned to Velmeran. "I have also made you a pair of special guns to carry in the belt of that new suit. More powerful than anything I have in reserve. They will not pierce the armor of those automated sentries, but their high-output generators will allow you to shoot more rapidly. Up to four times a second."

"You will not find better than that," Dveyella said. "Take them."

"I will," Velmeran agreed. "Where are they?"

"Down in one of the shops," Valthyrra said, pausing a moment as her camera pod quickly scanned the room. Consherra stood quietly in the doorway, and the machine focused on her. "Consherra, my dear, do you recall the place?"

"Of course," the first officer replied, and gestured for Velmeran to follow her. "Come along, killer."

"Meet me in the landing bay as soon as you can," Dveyella said quickly.

"I will not be long," Velmeran promised as he followed reluctantly. He knew that Consherra was by no means pleased with him, and he expected a lecture. Dveyella was much better company, and prettier too.

Velmeran surprised himself with that last thought, since he seldom entertained such notions and never seriously. It was true; Dveyella was prettier, but not by much. She was also more interesting because she told him about the things he liked to hear. Consherra was intelligent, knowledgeable and even witty, but she seemed to think that her most pressing duty was to attend to the lecturing and nagging that she thought Mayelna missed. It was easy enough for him to see how he would like Dveyella. What surprised him was that he compared her with Consherra, when he had never given the Methryn's helm any thought in the first place.

"So, you actually mean to go through with this," Consherra said disapprovingly, staring straight ahead as she marched down the silent corridor at a brisk pace.

"It seems to me a little late to back out now," Velmeran said. "Even if I wanted to. The thought had not occurred to me."

"Velmeran, you have never done this before!" she exclaimed as she stopped before the lift door and hit the call button so hard she nearly broke it.

Velmeran only shrugged. "No one is born experienced."

"And is that any reason why you have to do it? What good does it do you?"

"None, perhaps," Velmeran replied. "Or perhaps a great deal. Dveyella has said that she might like to keep me."

Consherra stared in disbelief. "Would you really go, give up your pack to be a new student in another?"

"I would, if I like it well enough," he said. "Valthyrra made me a pack leader. You would have me command this ship. But my one and only talent is for flying, and Dveyella is willing to allow me to fly like I never will on this ship. She appreciates me for what I can do, not for what she would make of me. Can you understand that?"

"Unfortunately, that makes perfect sense," Consherra agreed meekly. "But is that what you want?"

Velmeran considered that for a moment before he replied. "I cannot yet say. I have two futures before me, and I will decide upon the one that will allow me to do the most good. But I will have to look at them both before I will know which one."

"I have the answer to that question," she said firmly.

"I am sure you do. And Dveyella has a completely different answer. So it remains for me to decide. And you are not helping matters."

"Me?"

"Yes, you. Dveyella is nicer than you."

The lift doors opened and Velmeran entered quickly. Consherra only stood and stared in disbelief, unable under the circumstances to indulge her temper. Before she could decide what to do, the door closed in her face.

"Dveyella indeed! What does she have that I do not?" she demanded of the closed door. In her fury she paced in a complete circle, returning to stand before the lift doors. "You will come back to me yet, Velmeran! You have no idea of where you are supposed to be going!"

Valthyrra Methryn pushed the best pace she could, cutting her jump from Boulder to Bineck to only thirty-six hours. She wanted to catch up with Keth before the Union had the opportunity to move him to some more secure location. But that also meant that she did not have time to service all her fighters as she would have liked, so that more than half of the packs had to go out again in the shape they were in, fresh from the last battle.

The pilots had their own way of preparing themselves for the coming battle, spending their last few hours enjoying a precelebration. A party, small, quiet and private, helped to distract them from worrying excessively about what lay ahead. And Kelvessan were, by natural inclination, excessive worriers. Velmeran, as the only member of the assault force who was also a permanent resident of the ship, acted as host. His pack, like all others, was housed together in a suite of nine apartments that opened upon a large common room that included all the comforts the pilots were given in return for their hazardous duty. The walls were paneled, with wooden beams to support a ceiling that did not look metal. The floor was carpeted, although showing some wear since the Methryn's last overhaul, with comfortable loungers and a large sofa bolted into place. There was audio and video equipment for their entertainment, and shelves with a wealth of books secured behind locking glass doors.

Aside from the members of Velmeran's pack and Dveyella's team, there were only two other guests. Baressa had come looking for Velmeran in time to receive a special invitation. The other guest was Consherra, uninvited and unexpected, refusing to say how she even knew of this little celebration. That was not so hard to figure out, since she led a procession of three automated carts overflowing with food . . . and all automatons were under Valthyrra's command. But no one questioned her right to attend, once they saw that food.

"This is a nice place you have," Dveyella mentioned as she sat alone with Velmeran in one corner. Velmeran lifted his head to glance around the room, as if seeing it for the first time in his life. When not involved in business, he was about the most innocent, unassuming person she had ever met. Already she had seen that he seemed unable to take a compliment for what it was; he always weighed it and then himself in comparison, to see if it was deserved.

"You have a nice group of pilots in your pack," she said, deciding to try again.

"Do you think so?" Velmeran asked, somewhat concerned.

"Yes, of course," she insisted. "They are young and innocent. That is very refreshing to a pack of battle-weary veterans like ourselves."

"Young and innocent?" Velmeran asked, laughing to

himself. "Does that include Baressa and Consherra? You see in them two of the sharpest tempers on this ship."

"Baressa?" she asked in disbelief. Baressa was busy in the opposite corner conferring with Baress, having discovered that they shared the same name. They appeared to have more in common than just names, to judge by the undue interest she had in his injuries and his tale of how they happened.

"Actually, I cannot imagine why Baressa is acting so silly," Velmeran said, mystified. In his years as a student, he had always looked upon her as what a pack leader should be. He was shocked and annoyed to see her acting like a . . . a person!

"I can understand," Dveyella said suggestively. "In fact, I feel like acting a little like that myself right now."

"Well, I hope I never do!" Velmeran declared. Dveyella sighed softly. If they stayed together, she was either going to have to grow him up or become very blunt.

"Eat!" Consherra ordered, seeming to appear from nowhere to force a large hot roll with cheese into Velmeran's hands. "Valthyrra says that we will be coming into system in about four hours."

Dveyella shrugged. "I guess that we did not get started in time to have any real fun. Some things might have to wait until later."

"I certainly hope so," Consherra muttered coldly.

Dveyella glanced up at her sharply, at first in surprise, but then with an appraising look that became shrewd.

"Yes, I do like to take my time," she responded in an insinuating voice. "But not too long. I—for one—believe in taking advantage of my opportunities."

"Well, you certainly impress me as the type," Consherra remarked cattily.

Velmeran chewed his roll, blissfully unaware of the battle that raged over his head.

"Well, Meran, I certainly envy you," Baressa said as she and Baress approached at that moment. "Not many pilots get a chance to do the things that you will. You should learn a few things that the regular pilots never know."

"You will have to share your secrets when you come back," Consherra agreed guardedly.

"If he comes back," Dveyella corrected her.

"What do you mean?" Baressa asked anxiously, misunderstanding her.

"I mean that if he works out as well as I expect, I might not be willing to let him go again," she explained. "I will still be shorthanded even when Baress comes back to work."

No one was more surprised to hear her say that than Velmeran himself. He had already known that he had two futures for the choosing, but he considered that choice a purely personal and private one. He certainly did not consider it to be a matter of contention between two and possibly three factions aboard this ship.

"Velmeran, is this what you want?" Baressa asked gently, startling him out of his own thoughts. He was surprised by her apparent concern for his desires.

"Yes, I want it," he admitted slowly. "But I also want . . . what we talked about. I do not know which."

"But you think you will be able to decide after you fly with Dveyella's pack this first time?" she inquired with the same gentleness, as if all she wanted was what pleased him most.

"No, I doubt it," he admitted frankly. "That will only make it harder for me to decide. And yet I also know that I am not going to be able to decide until I do."

Baressa considered that and nodded thoughtfully. "Do what you feel you must, and have faith that you have made the right choice."

She turned to leave, but Consherra, nearly speechless with indignation, blocked her path.

"What are you doing?" the first officer demanded. "You said that you were going to talk to him."

"And so I did," Baressa answered impatiently as she

forced her way past. "But I said nothing about coercing him to do what you want of him."

"You know how much we need him," Consherra insisted.

"Of course. But I also . . ."

But I also believe that he will, in the end, do what is expected of him. Or so Velmeran finished for her in his mind, after her soft voice was lost beneath the music that his students were playing rather loudly, or perhaps, he realized, his conscience was only too willing to supply that answer, because he knew it to be true. Doing what he wanted might satisfy his desires, but doing what was expected of him, what he took to be his duty, satisfied his needs. And ultimately he wanted the future that would allow him to accomplish the most.

"Is this your room?" Dveyella asked suddenly, glancing at the door to her right.

"Yes, it is. Would you like to see?" Velmeran was quick to seize upon that as a chance to escape the others, if not his own thoughts.

As Dveyella followed him into the cabin, she happened to see Consherra, still conferring hotly with the others, staring at her in sudden alarm. Resisting the temptation to stick out her tongue, she ducked into the room quickly, stepping away from the door so that it would close.

As pack leader, Velmeran had the largest room in the suite. As always, the small bed folded into the wall; Kelvessan did not sleep unless driven to the point of exhaustion. There were two large reclining chairs and a fairly large desk with a terminal for access to the ship's computers. As outside, the floor was carpeted and portions of the wood were trimmed with real wood. There were two suit racks near the bed, one holding his old armor while the other displayed the new. A small kitchen area was partially removed from the rest of the room by cabinets, a welcome luxury for a people who had to eat tremendously, while a bathroom and closets filled the wall adjacent to the bed.

That was all standard, and Dveyella had seen its like on many ships. What did interest her were the things that he had done to make it his home. Curtains closed off an entire blank wall to the left of the door, suggesting that a large window lay beyond rather than a metal bulkhead. He had also brought in his own audio equipment, and enclosed shelves that contained his generous selection of books. A drawing table was mounted near the desk, so that she wondered if he had done the handful of paintings that hung about the room. One showed nine girls, obviously human, in some manner of archaic armor, each one bearing a spear, their golden capes flowing in the wind as they rode flying horses through a dark, stormy sky. Another depicted a dragon seated atop a mound of gold, glaring menacingly at a tiny figure that was so nearly invisible as to be just a vague shadow. Velmeran apparently liked fanciful subjects.

"Do you like it?" Velmeran asked.

"Yes, very much," she agreed. "It reminds me of why I wish that I had a home of my own."

"And something that I would have to give up, if I went with you," he reflected thoughtfully.

Dveyella turned to look at him. "Could you really leave, with so many people counting on you to become Commander-designate?"

"I really do not know," Velmeran said, indicating for her to take one of the two large chairs. "I know that Mayelna plans to retire in twenty years, more or less. And that is a little soon for me. I think that I might be ready to command this ship in twenty years. And yet . . ."

"Yes? What would you like most?" Dveyella prompted him when he hesitated.

"I want to fly—I have to fly—for a time yet to come," he explained haltingly. "I would prefer to be Baressa's Commander-designate when she takes command of the Methryn after Mayelna retires. I would be her present age before she is ready to retire. But that would be asking too much."

"Not at all," Dveyella insisted. "In fact, that sounds

very good to me. This is what we should do. You fly with me this time. Then, if things work out and it is still what you want, we will get together with Baressa and Valthyrra and work out a deal."

"Do you think that they would agree to that?"

"I imagine so, as long as you are willing to return when Mayelna retires."

Velmeran nodded thoughtfully. "Fair enough. But is that fair to you, that I should fly with you only twenty years?"

Dveyella shrugged, unconcerned. "Twenty more years and I will be more than willing to retire from special tactics myself. Then we will return."

Velmeran glanced up at her. "We?"

"The Methryn seems like a good ship to retire to," she said quickly, reluctant to be too forward out of fear of frightening the boy. But that plan suited her very well indeed. She could have him entirely to herself, away from the Methryn and Consherra, for twenty years—or until he grew up. The only remaining question was why she thought she needed him so much in the first place.

Sector Commander Trace handed tne message file to Councilor Lake and leaned back against the edge of his desk as he considered the problem. In his possession was one Starwolf, old but undamaged from his impact with a carrier, as well as one fighter that had not fared as well. A damaged fighter was unimportant; Union technicians could understand and appreciate Starwolf technology, but they could not reproduce it. They could build fighters that were a rough approximation of the black wolf ships, but no pilot could fly such a ship and even the best computer guidance systems were inadequate. He needed his own genetically engineered pilots. And he needed this captured Starwolf to show him how to make his own.

"Sir?" the messenger prompted him gently.

"Be patient, son," Donalt Trace said. "It will take you

a few days to overtake that carrier, so we can spare a few minutes to find the best answer."

"Well, at least they showed more sense than I thought they would," the Councilor said as he shut the lid on the message file. "Not such a bad plan, actually. A very good plan, in fact, if you make the mistake of underestimating the abilities of the Starwolves."

"But not good enough, since we're not going to make that mistake," Donalt answered, and struck the edge of the desk in frustration. "Damn! While they were trying to use their brains, why didn't they just stick him in this courier. He could have been right here now, in the one place in the entire sector where the Starwolves cannot get at him. Was that idea even mentioned?"

"Yes, sir," the messenger admitted reluctantly, fearful of the Sector Commander's displeasure.

"And there was, I suppose, some reason why that was not done?"

"Yes, sir. It was felt that the five guards my courier can carry would not be enough to keep the prisoner under control. There was no military escort to protect my ship, and no cargo facilities for the wreckage of the fighter."

"The fighter? That fighter is of no value to me. But no one has ever kept a live Starwolf." He paused and glanced shrewdly at his uncle. "If they are following at a discreet distance, is it most likely that they are using a silent beacon?"

"Yes, that is a possibility," Lake agreed.

"And such a beacon would be located on the ship rather than in the suit of the pilot?"

"They do carry a distress beacon in both the ship and the suit, but those we know about. A secret tracking beacon, however . . . certainly in the ship. They could not hide a long-range beacon in the suit."

"Then this is your message," Trace said as he turned back to the messenger. "Make your best time back to Bineck. The prisoner is to be transferred into your ship, along with two sentries and as many live guards as will fit. Then have the fighter put aboard a destroyer that is to make best speed for . . . shall we say the big sector shipyards at Karran? Do you have that? Do you need written orders?"

The messenger shook his head. "Verbal will be enough, under the circumstances."

"Good. Remember to say nothing of your orders over radio, since there may be ears you know nothing about."

"Military escort, sir?"

"Hell, no! You might as well broadcast your plans aloud! Your only hope is in secrecy and speed. Besides, the sector fleet couldn't save you if they want you bad enough. Hurry, now."

The messenger saluted quickly and disappeared out the door of the Sector Commander's office. Donalt shook his head slowly at the stupidity of the human race in general and underlings in particular. Councilor Lake stood by the window, his hands in his pockets as he stared out across the underground city of Vannkarn. But his thoughts on the matter were plain enough. He was smiling as if at some private joke, amused with his own thoughts.

"It's too late, you know," he remarked after a long moment.

"Yes, I know that. These long delays in travel time are working against me. I've only just now found out what's going on, and for all I know it might already be over." Trace glanced over at him, irritated. "You don't have to look so damned pleased by it all."

"I'm not exactly pleased," Lake answered. "I'm as frustrated as you to realize that we can never deal with Starwolves on their own terms. And yet, where Starwolves are concerned, I have learned to never be too hopeful or depend too much on luck."

"They make their own luck," Trace said. "That is what I want for us."

"You want your own Starwolves?" Lake asked, turning to look at him. "What if our people cannot duplicate their genetic design?"

"Then we clone the one we have," Trace insisted.

"We can surely tamper with his genetic material enough to make use of the information it contains to create our own viable race."

Lake nodded thoughtfully. "Good idea. But what then? Will your new Starwolves serve you willingly?"

"It's not a question of will. As long as we bring them up from the start without a thought in their head except for what we put there, they will be machines to serve us. But I can see that you don't like the idea of using real Starwolves."

"I prefer that we learn how to make our own," the Councilor admitted. "Then we can order their obedience to our will. What if real Starwolves have some instinctive urge to fight us? You could find that your own weapon has turned against you."

7

The late morning sun hung just over the horizon far to the south. Summer was nearing its end and the long day would end with it, for the sun would soon fall below the edge of the world and not rise again for half a year.

The northern polar region of the planet Bineck was in most ways like that of any other world where human life could dwell. Both poles were open ocean, bordered only in part by continents that lay mostly in warmer climates. Bineck was a cool world; even the equator was only temperate and the poles were bitterly cold even in the height of summer, with massive floes of thick ice. Nothing lived on those icy plains, not when the little life that did exist on that world struggled for survival in warmer regions. A few fish did swim below the ice but they were, in truth, only colonists, no more native to that world than the people who had planted them there.

Three small ships shot down through the clear, cold sky through the very center of the magnetic pole, only a few hundred kilometers from the planetary axis. They fell with tremendous speed, nose down with their engines idling to hide them from scanner detection. The transport and two fighters descended wrapped only in the protection of their atmospheric shields, allowing them to move at tremendous speeds with little bother from atmospheric friction. They had begun their approach well outside detection range, building to speed and then drifting along a carefully plotted course that permitted them to complete their run without having to develop the engine power that would give their presence away, braking gradually with minimum reverse thrust.

They entered the upper atmosphere as fast as even wolf ships would dare, nearly seventeen thousand kilometers per hour, dropping down from the very fringe of space to ground level in less than a minute. Leveling out at the very last moment, the three ships engaged their engines just enough to maintain their speed. They flew as low as they could, until their atmospheric shields began to press against the ice only five meters below. At fifteen times the speed of sound, the shock wave created by their shields pulverized the thick ice, throwing it up in a towering plume of snow and splintered crystals.

Flying wing to wing, the ships casually dodged pressure ridges and icebound glaciers that appeared out of the hazy whiteness of the horizon with blinding speed. After a couple of minutes the ice floe began to break up, ending abruptly only seconds later. The ships shot out over open water, a vast curtain of white vapor rising like a storm cloud behind them. Still hundreds of kilometers short of their goal, they began to apply braking thrust to drop speed quickly as they prepared to land.

Hardly a minute later the three ships finally dropped to subsonic speed just as a fortress wall of towering cliffs rose before them. The lead fighter moved to the front as Dveyella took them by a concealed path. The weather had been less kind to the hills since they had been alive; a canyon had cut deep into the unprotected land, providing a hidden passage for the ships until they reached the cover of the high ridge. Dveyella led them at almost a crawl along the back of the ridge, finally slipping through a tight pass that put them almost on top of the wide ledge where they would land.

The transport settled gently to the very center of the ledge, and the two fighters nestled in close to either side. Velmeran left his fighter as Dveyella had instructed, with the generator idling just enough to keep itself cycling, the energy cells charged and the major systems powered up. They might not be able to spare the time for a prestart on the way out. He unstrapped and lowered the boarding ladder; jumping was the easiest way down, but the hinged canopy prevented pilots from jumping back into the narrow opening of the cockpit, and it was a long jump. Fighters had a very long-legged stance to accommodate their turned-down wings and the big main drives they protected.

Dveyella walked around the front of the transport just as he leaped down. She was still fastening on the thick belt that held her guns and a row of heat charges. She turned as the door of the transport slid open. Baress stuck his head out, frowning fiercely. "Do you know how hard it is on a good pilot to have to make the ride down as a passenger?"

"No, but I will surely ask the first good pilot I find," Dveyella replied.

Baress's frown deepened as he stepped down to join them. "Spare me. I came to tell you that a storm is due. A late season warm front is pushing up a line of about the worst weather this place ever sees, and it should be on us about the time you return."

"I can see that for myself," Dveyella said, glancing up at the wall of dark clouds that was beginning to climb above the ridge behind them. Lightning rippled up and down its length, and distant thunder rumbled faintly.

Baress only shrugged. "I am only trying to be useful. Are you sure that you will not need any help?"

"No, we will likely need all the help we can get. But I am sure that you will not leave this ledge."

"I will sit on him if he as much as looks over the side," Marlena offered from the transport door. "By keeping Baress here, the rescuers will at least outnumber the people needing rescue."

"Whatever it takes. Velmeran, we have to hurry,"

Dveyella said as she fastened down her helmet. Velmeran fastened down his own and hurried to join her at the edge of the shelf, looking out over the ancient city. It was an impressive sight, seen from above, filling the valley from rim to rim and extending far to the north. The sprawling structure was composed of a series of massive, featureless stone blocks joined by connecting halls and corridors, unbroken by doors, windows or visible vents. But the greatest part of the city lay below, carved deep into the heart of the mountains.

"Keep your helmet on and your systems to normal," Dveyella warned. "Life has been gone from this world for so long that the oxygen level is still a bit low. Too low to sustain us for what we have to do. Ready?"

"Of course."

"Stay close, then," she said, peering over the ledge to the ground below. "And remember that this is real gravity, not the stuff you practiced in. You will fall faster."

Dveyella casually hopped off the ledge, jumping out just far enough to keep well clear of the cliff face, although she took most of the twenty-meter fall straight down. She landed easily and quickly stepped out of the way, and Velmeran followed. As she had warned, he fell faster than he would have expected. But he was prepared and maintained his balance effortlessly. Dveyella waited until he indicated for her to go ahead.

They kept up a fairly good pace the rest of the way down the slope, running where they could and clearing the more difficult sections in short leaps. Since most of this ridge was composed of tumbled slabs and boulders of solid rock, a good deal of their descent was spent jumping from one massive stone to another. Velmeran was hard pressed to keep up the pace that Dveyella set with ease. But he did not complain, since he thought that he would improve quickly with practice.

The major worry that occupied his thoughts was of Keth and how they might get him back up this slope, especially that final cliff. The dark brown soil and large brown-gray stones were loose and bare of supportive vegetation, as if the entire ridge had just been thrown up by the excavations of some immense machine. Large sections of the crumbled talus were entirely too loose to climb (not in heavy armor) and could only be cleared by jumping. Rain would quickly turn the entire slope into a slick, flowing mass, so they had to be back before the storm moved in.

They reached the bottom of the slope in only a few short minutes, moving stealthfully the last few hundred meters. Fortunately there were enough large stones—apparently the eroded rejects from the building of the city—to keep them well hidden to within the last ten meters of the door. Then Dveyella went ahead to check out the entrance for surveillance equipment and automatic weapons, although she was confident that there were none. This was, after all, only a supply base, an immense warehouse, on a planet where no one but the military was allowed.

It did not take long for her to decide. She paced up and down before the four broad steps that led up to the deeply reset portal, glancing up at the massive blocks of stone framing it and peering into the deep shadows that hid the door. At last she shrugged and signaled for him to join her.

"Nothing?" Velmeran asked as he hurried up.

"Nothing fancy," Dveyella replied. "There might be a simple detector on the door itself, but there is nothing we can do about that. You get down behind these steps and shoot anything that moves when I open the door. Fortunately these sections swing out, not in."

Velmeran drew his guns, one for each set of hands, and crouched down on the large flagstones at the base of the steps, directly in front of the right of the two massive portals. Dveyella took firm hold of the thick handle and jerked it back briskly, using its bulk to shield herself. Nothing stirred within, and Velmeran held his fire. His eyes, large for excellent light sensitivity, could detect no movement. Dveyella watched his response, then drew her own guns and peered cautiously within, first checking the inside walls where he could not see.

"Clear," she said. Velmeran followed her inside, standing guard as she closed the door. "Straight ahead now, until we come to the first major stairwell. Remember to shoot anything that moves; in this place, it will not be your friend. Remember also that the sentries have heavier guns and thicker armor than you do."

They hurried on, moving cautiously from room to room. The main corridor leading in was bisected often by buildings of various shapes, most fairly large and yet only simple, featureless structures. It occurred to Velmeran that these were auxiliary warehouses, perhaps only temporary storage areas for goods arriving or departing overland from other cities, later to be carried down the stairs and ramps to the lower levels. The main warehouses were probably on the lower levels, along with the inhabited areas, where the temperature was even more constant year-round.

Velmeran quickly chased such stray thoughts from his mind. They had just entered a small, rectangular room where the main hall was intersected by two parallel corridors. Dveyella came to a sudden halt at the first of the two smaller passages.

"Sentry!"

Velmeran did not need to ask where, for he could see the machine ambling down the corridor to their left, a tall, heavily armored shell on four long legs. It was perhaps twenty-five meters away, and had already passed the doorways to two adjacent rooms. "Can it see us?"

"I have always suspected that the things are blind to the rear," Dveyella answered, making no effort to hide as she watched the machine. "Nothing back there. They do have stereoscopic cameras in front, like most advanced automatons, as well as echo-location and infrared sensors. It would hear us talking, if not for our helmets."

The sentry turned off to one side, into another chamber to its right. Velmeran had only a brief glimpse of the machine as it turned; it was considerably taller than himself, at least two meters, and the rounded, armored shell of its body was nearly as long. Dveyella watched until it disappeared, its long whip tail dragging under the top of the door.

"I have to see where the thing is going," she said suddenly. "It is headed in the same direction we have to go. Watch these passages for a moment."

Hardly giving him time to protest, she hurried off after the sentry. She crept cautiously down the side corridor and slowly leaned forward to peer around the corner, her guns ready. Then, to Velmeran's consternation, she slipped around the edge of the doorway and disappeared. Suddenly finding himself quite alone, he recalled her instructions and quickly checked each of the remaining corridors, fearful of seeing another of the hulking white sentries ambling toward him.

His unease was based in part on the shadowy presence of the sentry he sensed almost subconsciously behind the wall to his back, or perhaps the presence of its small generator. Nor was it aware of him as it made its ceaseless rounds through the ancient corridors. As it passed the doorway it caught a glimpse of something in the adjacent room, and paused in midstride for a quick double take. For a long moment it stood, as if checking its memory in an attempt to recognize this intruder. Then it began to move again, bringing itself around to face its enemy. It lowered its head to bring its guns to bear and charged at the best speed it could manage.

Velmeran was, unfortunately, facing in the other direction at that moment. He turned to make a second check of the other corridors, only to find the sentry already charging at him. The two adversaries opened fire on each other at almost the same instant. The sentry was a poor shot, shuffling forward at a ponderous pace. Velmeran had better aim, but his own guns could not pierce the sentry's armor. A single bolt struck him in the chestplate early on, knocking him slightly off balance. He recovered quickly and returned fire, this time aiming at the machine's vulnerable points. An instant of concentrated fire destroyed the heavier turret over the sentry's shoulders, then the two lighter guns mounted to either side of its head.

Weaponless, the sentry charged on, intent upon crushing its prey against the wall. Velmeran fired a few more shots, then holstered his guns in time to catch the automaton by its ruined head. The sentry was the heavier of the two, well over a ton, but Velmeran was the stronger. Holding tightly to its head, he swung the machine around as hard as he could. His hope was to throw it on its side and render it helpless. Pulling as hard as he could, he swung it around in three-fourths of a circle. Then its retractable neck snapped, and he was left holding its head.

As surprised as he was, Velmeran thought that was the end of it. But the sentry caught its balance and charged again, and he hardly had time to drop the lifeless head and catch it by the flarings that protected its neck. Slowly it pushed Velmeran back, forcibly sliding him across the stone blocks of the floor until he was braced against the wall. Velmeran began to consider a desperate plan, and leaped aside in the hope that the sentry would run head-on into the wall. He knew that he had to do something immediately, for his strength was fading quickly.

At that moment Dveyella slapped a heat charge against the back of the sentry's shell. A second later the small disk began to glow white-hot; the sentry's shock-resistant plastic coating bubbled and peeled back from that intense source of heat like a curtain, and the metal beneath began to glow faintly red. The charge lasted only a few seconds but the damage was done, for smoke was pouring from every opening in the automaton's hull.

Velmeran noticed the smoke rolling out of the broken neck sleeve before he realized that the sentry was no longer pushing against him but was standing rigidly motionless, its legs firmly locked. He released his hold cautiously and, when he was sure that the thing was dead, began to fight against his helmet, releasing the clips and jerking it off as quickly as he could. He was panting for breath as he leaned heavily against the inert hulk of the sentry.

"Are you all right?" Dveyella asked, her voice sounding thinly through the backup phone in the collar of her suit.

He nodded, still gasping. "I took a hit right on the cover plate of my controls. My air shut down."

"Are all your systems out?" she asked, concerned. If he had lost his cooling as well, he would have to get out of his armor before he cooked in his own trapped body heat.

Velmeran understood what she meant and shook his head. "I have cooling. Only my air is out."

"This is my fault," she said fiercely, to herself. She paused for only a moment before deciding. "Marlena, can you hear me? Trouble. We are coming back out."

"No, wait!" Velmeran said quickly, bending his head to the microphone in his collar. "If we have to try again, it will only be that much harder. They know that we are here now?"

"Of course. That sentry would have warned all the others the moment it saw you. And the master computer would have warned the security officer on duty. Fighters are probably rolling out right now."

"Then secrecy is lost," he concluded. "And now we have to act fast. We must go on. Threl can bring the transport down on the pavement outside the door, so that they can pick up Keth and go on for the fighter as soon as we come out. Marlena and Baress can shuttle our fighters down too, so that we can cover them until they are away. This air is no great problem for me; you keep your helmet on to do the heavy work."

Dveyella crossed her arms as she listened to him, and he thought that she was watching him closely. After a moment she drew her guns. "Valthyrra Methryn, are you listening through that drone?"

"Of course," Valthyrra answered calmly.

"Send your packs in now. Keep them out of the atmosphere, but have them shoot anything in space that moves.

We need the interference they can create as soon as possible. Marlena? Threl?"

"Here!" Marlena answered.

"If you caught that, then carry out those plans. Move the fighters down but do not, I repeat, do not give battle without my approval. Make certain that the cabin air in Velmeran's fighter is working."

"I can fly for him," Marlena offered.

"Professional courtesy dictates that a pilot flies his own ship, if he is able," Dveyella answered, and used one of her guns to indicate the doorway of the main corridor. "We go on, then."

"I hear a sentry coming."

"The one I was following, no doubt. It came running the moment the first sentry gave warning." She pulled a heat charge from his belt and handed it to him. "You can hear it, so you know how close it is. Hide behind the door and put the charge on its back as it comes through. Ignore the head; as you may have noticed, that is not where they have their brains."

Velmeran made a gesture to indicate that he was no longer free to speak aloud, and Dveyella hid in the adjoining chamber. Then he hurried to the doorway opening onto the main corridor and waited, taking up the heat charge and twisting the top as far as it would go. The sentry charged through the doorway. Velmeran slammed the disk against its shell and ducked out the door behind it, just as the sentry began to draw itself to an abrupt halt. The machine lifted a foreleg as it began to turn toward its attacker, and slowly lowered it as the heat charge, activated as its magnetic base attached itself to the thick metal hull, began to fry its electronics.

Velmeran glanced back inside the doorway to find the motionless machine standing in a cloud of smoke that continued to pour from its joints and vents. Dveyella returned from the side passage, pausing only a moment to regard the stricken automaton before she indicated for him to continue on.

"Better," she said approvingly as they hurried down the wide hall. "Our problem is going to be getting back out, since every sentry in the complex is going to be converging on this area. They might try to pin us on the stairs."

Moments later they came upon the stairs they were looking for. The well was square, between five and six meters along each side, with long flights of steps descending down each side. The center of the well was filled by something clearly not of native manufacture; a lift platform, guided by metal rails fitted into each corner of the well. The stone rail had been removed on the nearest side, and a metal shelf extended the floor out to the edge of the lift platform. The Starwolves could see that, while the original inhabitants might have had no choice, the military was not about to lug supplies up and down those steps on the unreliable backs of enlistees. Necessity is the mother of invention, it is said. Then laziness is surely the father.

"I hope this thing is not too slow," Dveyella said as she stepped aboard and triggered it to descend. "Ah, not too bad."

"I do not much like descending blind," Velmeran remarked as he watched steps appear along the side of the platform, starting along one side and proceeding down the next.

"I do not like it either," Dveyella agreed. "A sentry could be waiting for us on any landing, ready to shoot as the platform clears."

"Stop at the next level," Velmeran said suddenly, holstering his guns.

Dveyella stopped the platform level with the next landing stage, and he stepped out. He quickly descended the steps until he passed below the lift. As he had guessed, there was a heavy metal framework that supported the platform and held the field projector that raised and lowered the lift. He climbed out onto the stone railing and leaped out to catch a bar of the framework, then swung up and arranged himself as best he could, facing down, with three of his four hands free. Two held guns, while a heat charge was in the fourth.

"Start down!" he ordered into his collar mike.

The platform started again. Velmeran watched the steps closely, waiting for a white rectangular head to appear over the rail near the corner landings. He did not know if the sentries could elevate their guns very high, although he did remember that the cameras were inset and not able to rotate very far up. He hoped that he could drop a heat charge on the machine before it saw him; he did not care to get into another shooting contest with a sentry.

"Hello, and welcome to beautiful Bineck," Valthyrra's voice, radiating the commercial enthusiasm of a tour guide, announced over their coms. "The weather at your location is threatening, turning to openly hostile at any given moment. I must also inform you that two wings of seven fighters each are taking off from the main base. Your twenty minutes have just begun."

"This will be cutting it close," Dveyella remarked.

"My packs will not be in time to intercept those fighters," Valthyrra continued. "They will have to be your problem. We will get anything else."

Velmeran thought that he could see the bottom now, a square of pale gray stone far below. Five levels were past and the sixth opened beside him, so he was now halfway down. Then he saw an indistinct shape lean out over the railing far below, more than halfway down from where he was.

"Something on the stairs," he warned. "Just passing the second level, I would guess."

"A sentry?" Dveyella asked.

"It really did not look like a sentry's head," he replied. "I believe that it was too small for a sentry, and there were no guns. Whatever it was, I am going to put a bolt through it if I see it again."

"If it is something hidden with a gun, you should know that the two larger, rounded things on your belt are explosives," she offered.

"They are?" Velmeran sounded surprised. "Then I will use one of those if it tries to ambush us as we get nearer. It is dark under here, and it might not see me until too late."

"Reverse ambush," Dveyella agreed. "But do not use the explosive if you get too close, since you have no helmet. Try throwing it from a fourth of a level up."

"I will thank you not to," a third voice said suddenly. "If you two have come to collect me, I would prefer that it be alive."

Velmeran nearly fell out of his perch. "Keth? Is that you?"

"Of course it is."

"Stay at the third landing," Velmeran instructed. "We will collect you there. Do you have a gun?"

"No, nothing. I have been listening to you since you landed. When that first sentry attacked you, the one guarding my door took off at a run. Since he was really the only thing keeping me in that room, I kicked open the door and headed straight for the stairs."

"Why did you not tell us you were coming?"

"I have no helmet," Keth replied. "And the echoes carry far in these old halls. I was afraid that one of the beasts might hear me."

"You would hear it," Dveyella pointed out.

"Not if it was standing still."

"What does this do to our schedule?" Velmeran asked.

"Barring further incident, we might actually be out of here in another ten minutes," Dveyella answered. "In realistic terms, we might just be ready when those two wings of fighters descend upon us."

After another half a minute, Velmeran had Dveyella stop the platform a short distance above the third level so that he could climb out. Keth looked up and saw his pack leader hanging facedown from the framework beneath the platform, his legs and free arm braced wide against parts of the structure, rather like an ironclad spider in a tubular steel web. Keth was at first inclined to laugh, but the expression his pack leader wore warned him against it. Velmeran threw Keth a gun, then quickly lowered himself from the frame and swung out to the landing stage. Dveyella quickly brought the lift down low enough for them to step on, and immediately started back up. When Keth tried to return the gun, Velmeran indicated for him to keep it and pointed up.

"Since you and I have no helmets, we are going to have to be on guard," he said. "If any of those monsters pokes its head over the railing, shoot it."

"Remember that the design of this type of sentry is such that it can rotate its cameras straight down," Dveyella added. "And since its smaller guns are mounted on the sides of the cameras, it can shoot what it sees."

"Is that one?" Keth asked, pointing at the rectangular shape that appeared over the edge of the railing a level up.

Velmeran nodded. "I believe so."

"Oh," Keth said, and began shooting. His aim was surprisingly good, considering that he had seldom practiced with such a weapon. His second and third shots caught the sentry under the chin before it had a chance to draw back its head. "Did I hurt it?"

"I do not believe so," Velmeran said. "No parts fell off. Do we stop?"

"No, we have to get closer," Dveyella answered. "Swat that thing back every time it shows itself."

That did not work so well. The sentry had the advantage, and that advantage increased as the lift platform rose toward it. A moment later it returned and opened fire, and this time the three Starwolves were forced to leap off the platform into the stairs for cover. Velmeran tried to return fire, but it could see him clearly now and shot first.

"Now what?" he asked.

"We do not have the time to spare," Dveyella said as she pulled off her helmet. "Levels are about forty to forty-five meters apart, or three full revolutions of the stairs. If I can climb near enough, I can jump diagonally up from below the sentry to its level."

"I believe I know what you have in mind," Velmeran said. "Will it work?"

Dveyella shrugged. "If you cover me."

A moment later they were climbing the stairs as fast as they could, leaving Keth behind to watch the lift. The climb became more dangerous as they drew nearer to the sentry, since it was soon able to shoot beneath the over-hanging ledge that had protected them farther below. Still, they were able to climb to the run directly below it. Then Velmeran climbed two more flights, keeping behind the cover of the solid stone rail, until he was only two flights below and directly across from the automaton.

The sentry knew that they were up to something. It bent its head down as far as it could, trying to scan the shaft with infrared. Just then Velmeran fired on it, shot after shot slamming into its head, blowing out one camera and the gun beside it. The sentry retracted its head and staggered back. Dveyella leaped as hard as she could against the stubborn pull of real gravity, seeming almost to fly up the narrow shaft. Seven meters up she caught the railing where Velmeran stood and flipped herself atop it. Velmeran shot again, driving the sentry back a second time and blowing out its other camera in the process. Dveyella launched herself directly at the blinded automaton, taking advantage of its confusion.

Velmeran hurried to join her, leaping across the shaft as well, only to find the sentry standing by itself as thick smoke poured from its vents. Dveyella stood beside the doorway in the middle of the landing, cautiously peering down the dimly lit corridor.

"Another coming fast," she said, panting in the poor air. "Keth?"

"Already on my way up," the older pilot responded over com.

"The machinery beneath the lift is unprotected, and we are still only halfway up," Velmeran said. "You are winded, so this one is mine. Take the lift up four flights and wait for me."

"Do you have something in mind?" she asked.

"Nothing fancy. The sentry will think that we are on the way up, so this should be easy."

"I could watch," she offered.

Velmeran quickly placed a hand over his collar mike. "I would prefer that you watch Keth. I do not trust him alone with a gun. He might try something that he would do well to leave alone."

Dveyella reluctantly agreed and joined Keth on the lift as it went by. Velmeran positioned himself by the doorway, carefully out of sight. He did not have long to wait. The sentry had been near enough to fire a quick volley of bolts at the lift as it went by. It charged out onto the landing, slowing as it came out of the passage and finally stopping beside its motionless companion. The lift was ascending, still only two flights up, so it leaned out over the rail and tilted its head back to shoot.

Velmeran had been behind the sentry since it had stepped out onto the landing, unseen in its haste. Dveyella was correct in her guess that they were blind to the rear; they apparently did not even see to the sides very well. Careful to stay immediately behind it, Velmeran watched the sentry's movements carefully. As it leaned out to look up the shaft, he simply crawled between its long legs, lifted it up and heaved it over the rail. The machine fell heavily straight down the center of the shaft, never once bouncing off the sides. He watched until the automaton disappeared into the gloom, and a long moment later a sound like a small explosion echoed back up the shaft. Pleased with his efficiency, he hurried to join the others.

8

Dveyella peered cautiously around the edge of the doorway, and swiftly drew back in alarm and surprise. "I find it hard to believe! There it is, waiting for us, right in front of the door. They must be getting smarter."

"They are getting smarter," Velmeran agreed. "They have learned too many lessons the hard way."

"We have to get that thing out of the way," she said. "Valthyrra Methryn, how much time do we have?"

"Those two wings of fighters are just now beginning to descend," Valthyrra reported. "You have perhaps three minutes."

"Wonderful!" Dveyella muttered, pausing only a moment to think. "Marlena, are you out there?"

"Ready and waiting."

"That machine is backed up to the outer door with its tail in the crack, facing inward."

"Ah, I follow you. Half a moment."

A few moments passed and then one of the heavy doors began to open, slowly and silently, and a single arm reached through to attach a heat charge to the rear hull of the sentry that stood before it. The machine jumped away from the door and spun around. But the heat charge was already glowing and the automaton's legs locked up even

120

as it turned, causing it to fall heavily on its side. The three Starwolves were running for the door immediately.

"Not so smart after all," Velmeran commented as they slipped past the smoking hulk.

He had expected to see violent clouds towering over the city, but the leading edge of the storm had already passed. A seething mass of dark clouds hid the sun, bringing dusk at midday and adding to his feeling that he had been underground for a long time, not less than half an hour. Low clouds and fog already concealed the ledge where they had landed. There was only a light wind here in the valley, although the roiling clouds overhead suggested violent winds within the storm itself.

Marlena and Baress waited just outside the door. Dveyella pushed Keth into their care. "One last task. Pack in those boxes as fast as you can and get out of here."

"Captain?" Keth asked, reluctant to be dragged away to the waiting transport. Baress and Marlena seemed likely to carry him if he delayed any longer.

"Go with them, Keth," Velmeran directed, trying to assume a calm, authoritative voice. "They have your ride out."

Keth allowed himself to be led to the larger ship, although still somewhat reluctantly, and Velmeran and Dveyella hurried to their fighters. Velmeran had hoped that this incident would have cured Keth, that the older pilot would have done enough soul-searching during the last few days to face the truth. Instead it seemed that he had been waiting for rescue so that he could return to the packs; he had apparently assumed that they would have brought a fighter for him. Of course, his real problem had never been age but conceit.

Velmeran climbed into the cockpit of his fighter and sealed the canopy against windblown dust and mist before he began to strap in. The transport lifted immediately. It rose just high enough to pass over the fighters and drifted toward the east, following the perimeter of the city to the landing platform where the boxes containing the remains of the fighter were kept.

"Have you ever fought inside a storm before?" Dveyella asked over ship's com; Velmeran's worthless helmet had gone with Keth.

"I have never fought inside an atmosphere before," he reminded her.

"You will find it remarkably the same," she said. "The greatly reduced speeds are offset by the greatly compressed distances. Union fighters are more of a match for us here; you will find them about as quick and tricky as stingships. But we still outclass this lot."

The two ships rose together into the threatening sky, heading southwest to meet the approaching wings of Union fighters. They went slowly, waiting for their attackers to come to them. Staying within the storm was to their advantage; Starwolves fought by feel under any circumstances, so the lack of visibility made no real difference to them. Blinded by the clouds, however, the Union pilots had to depend entirely on their scanners.

But Velmeran did not forget his own disadvantages. He was used to sudden speed changes of tens or even hundreds of thousands of kilometers per hour, and velocities that were more easily discussed as percentages of light. He was concerned that he might accidentally give his throttle the long throws that he would use in open space. Trying to evade and chase within the confines of this storm, with mountains only a few hundred meters below, would be like trying to fight inside an airdock. There was not much room to run.

The first wing of Union fighters descended into the storm, driving directly at the pair of Starwolf fighters rising to meet them. The wing widened and the fighters launched missiles, four from under the short wings of each ship. And that was a serious tactical error. Union missiles were not very smart—they saw no point in investing much money in something that was going to explode—and therefore they were too easily jammed, evaded or destroyed. The missiles looked about and found nothing. The wolf ships, fully cloaked, were invisible to their rudimentary scanners and heat sensors. As a group the missiles continued on, searching the storm for their prey. Soon they saw the ground approaching and arched back up. Now they saw fighters, but these were their own, bearing warn-off devices. Deprived of legitimate prey, the missiles took themselves straight up to safely self-destruct.

Now the fighters themselves dispersed and closed to attack. Two oriented on each of the Starwolves, while the remaining three continued on toward the city. Ignoring the fighters moving in on their tails, Dveyella and Velmeran dove after the three strays, intent upon stopping them before they found the transport. Velmeran nudged his ship on ahead, centering a heavy barrage on the three fighters and destroying two before the third evaded and ran. He quickly dived after it, while Dveyella obligingly shot a fighter off his own tail before turning her attention to the pair following her.

Velmeran's remaining pursuer moved in close, trying to penetrate his shields with its ineffective cannons. He ignored it for the moment, concentrating on the fleeing fighter ahead. Its pilot, reckless with either determination or fear, dove straight toward the rocky heights above the city. Velmeran clipped its rear engines just short of that dubious safety, sending the little ship spinning out of control. Velmeran skimmed the barren edge of a ridge, pulling up abruptly as a towering peak rose suddenly out of the darkness. The fighter behind tried to mimic that move, only to find that it could not match the precise control. It deflected off a wall of rock to fall end over end into the valley below.

Dveyella had taken one of her attackers with her ship's rear cannon, turning on the other so savagely that it could not even evade. Aware that Velmeran was somewhere far below, she rose alone to meet the second wing of fighters. She strafed them freely, catching two before the others dispersed. She chose her prey quickly, a pair of fighters trying to circle around to the north, leaving the others for Velmeran to catch when they reached him.

She moved in from the side. But at the very last instant they turned as one and drove straight at her, almost as if they meant to ram. Too late to open fire, Dveyella tried to turn away. Her atmospheric shield pierced one fighter, ripping it apart. Its four underwing missiles exploded barely fifty meters ahead of her ship, and she had no choice but to follow straight through the core of that white-hot cloud.

Bits of metal, caught up in her shield, rang against the hull of her ship. An instant later it was through the debris, scorched but whole. Dveyella had not fared so well. Even through the mirrorized windows of her fighter, that flash had been brilliant.

"Was that you?" Velmeran asked over com.

"Did you see that?" she asked.

"It was a funny color for lightning."

"I will be flying blind for another minute. Can you watch for me?"

"There is one on your tail right now."

"I know it," she said. She could sense the Union fighters; her concern was for running into the ground. The fighter on her tail was closing cautiously, its pilot aware that something was wrong. She teased it in and deftly winged it with her rear cannon.

"We are finished here," Threl reported. "How is your vision?"

"Clearing fast," she reported.

"Then we are on our way out. Try not to shoot us as we pass."

"After that remark, you should worry!" Dveyella retorted. "Valthyrra, how is the traffic up there? I sense confusion overhead."

"Fighters and stingships are scattered far and wide," the ship replied. "But we have them on the run. Nothing big cleared the docks. Mind the stingships, though."

"Right. Velmeran, take the lead," she instructed.

"Punch a hole in anything you meet, unless it is dressed in black. I will bring up the rear."

Velmeran fell in ahead of the transport, widening his lead to several kilometers as they accelerated straight up toward open space, while Dveyella moved in as close as she could behind the larger ship. The single remaining fighter gave chase but was quickly left behind. In a last, desperate move it fired all four of its missiles. The pilot, learning from past mistakes, kept them under the superior control of his fighter's on-board guidance system.

The path out was not as open as they would have liked. Three stingships in close formation were closing quickly, and help was still too far away to prevent it. The three wolf ships were still forcing their way clear of the upper atmosphere, and were fairly easy targets. Already the Union ships were bringing their long noses around to align their cannons.

"They are about to open fire," Velmeran warned.

"This old hulk has a few guns that should surprise them," Threl said. "Spread out so that we can all open up. Dveyella, we need your cannons up front just now."

"Make it quick," she replied. "There are missiles just ten seconds behind me."

The three ships moved slightly out of line, each one orienting on a different target. Both groups opened fire at almost the same instant, but the Starwolves had the advantage of deadlier aim and better shields. They opened the hole they needed and went through.

"So much for what lies ahead. What about those missiles?" Velmeran asked. The Kelvessan could not sense such missiles or any type of combustion engines, only the high-energy emissions of crystal drives and conversion generators.

"They fell away," Dveyella replied. "They do not have much range. If those things had real engines, they might almost be deadly."

"We are clear, then," Velmeran said. "Home?"

"Lead the way," she answered.

* * *

Valthyrra Methryn directed the returning group into the upper left landing bay, one of the two abandoned upper bays that were only just being restored to service. The three ships shot into the bay like animals into a den. The transport went in first, coming in quickly to settle in the middle of the flight deck, and the smaller ships set down to either side of it only a moment later. Valthyrra brought in racks for the fighters immediately as spare bay personnel moved in swiftly to lock them down. Two pairs of overhead arms, normally used in transporting racks, were brought forward to pin the transport to the deck. The Methryn was at battle alert, and she could not have unsecured ships on her decks.

The small group waiting to one side approached as soon as the ships began to unseal. Any thoughts that Keth might have had of a triumphant return and warm welcome were quickly dashed. Mayelna and Valthyrra, in one of her usual remotes, went immediately around the front of the transport to Velmeran's fighters, followed by a small group of technicians and Dyenlerra, the chief medic. The younger members of his pack, dressed for battle, silently brought up the rear.

Velmeran had just finished unstrapping when he looked up to see this group descending upon him, not unlike wolf ships descending upon any unwary freighter. His first impulse was to seal the cockpit. Only Consherra was missing from this group of worried mothers; the first officer had been left in command of the bridge. He used the overhead bars to pull himself out of the cockpit and descended the steps of the boarding ladder to meet them.

"Hold up a moment," Mayelna ordered, and waved a technician ahead of her.

"He took a shot dead center of the control panel," the tech said as he inspected the damage. He carefully pried open the panel and pulled down the cracked mirror, only to have it come out in his hand. He slipped it into a pocket before he bent to inspect the controls. "Just a good, hard knock . . . must have kicked something loose. If the cooling is still in operation—which is obvious—then the shot could have done him no harm."

"I could have told you that," Velmeran said.

"Hypermetabolism," Dyenlerra offered by way of explanation. "It is not uncommon for our kind to go quite some time unaware of injuries we have received. Pilots fly entire battles, unaware that their suits are immobilizing broken bones."

Velmeran looked surprised. "Bones? Can our ships fly after impacts that could break our bones?"

The medic only shrugged. "I did not say that it happens often. Just take off that armor somewhere and tell me what you find underneath."

"A leading statement if I ever heard one," Valthyrra remarked.

"Just a moment," Mayelna said, holding him back as the others hurried to check upon the rest of the returning members. "Well, you seem to have come through that one all right."

"So I did," Velmeran agreed guardedly. "I am pleased with the results. Did Valthyrra accomplish what she set out to prove?"

Mayelna caught her breath so sharply that she choked. "What would you know of that? What do you believe Valthyrra's motive was in contriving this?"

Velmeran shrugged. "How should I know? I have only been given to wonder if she means to get rid of me."

"Do you mean . . . she thought . . . you might stay in special tactics?" she asked, visibly shaken by the thought. "But . . . why?"

"For being too popular," he replied. "A child prodigy among pack leaders, and a cause of dissension among the veterans. Political exile, you might say. Does that surprise you? I just might go, if Dveyella still wants me."

"Well, you are certainly free to go, if that is what you want," the Commander said sharply. "But I honestly doubt that Valthyrra has any such plans. And you certainly will not leave this ship without my having something to say about it!"

"I suppose that we will have to wait and see," Velmeran answered, although he was no longer certain what to think.

"I am going to take Keth aside as soon as I can," Mayelna continued as they turned to join the others. "Do not say it! I do not want to hear what you consider your duty. I am one of Keth's contemporaries, nearly his own age. Meran, this means putting an end to a career that has spanned three centuries. He will not want to hear it from a twenty-five-year-old kid who has his whole career yet ahead of him. It would be too easy for him to think that you could have no understanding or sympathy for him, an old wolf being chased out of the pack by the cubs."

"I can see that, contrived analogies notwithstanding," Velmeran agreed reluctantly. "You do it."

"Besides, I have come up with an alternative," Mayelna added. "Do you think that Keth suffers from any failings that would make him an untrustworthy teacher?"

"No, Keth's problem is in his bones, not in his head," Velmeran replied thoughtfully. "In fact, that conceit of his always made the students think that he is better than he ever was. That could be important, if a retired pilot is to maintain the respect of his students."

As they passed in front of the transport, they found Dveyella standing a few paces from the nose of her fighter, wearing a thoughtful expression as she stared at the little ship. The cause of her concern was obvious; the fighter, once matte black, was now a dusty black-gray. It was badly scorched from the explosion it had passed through, and such damage was enough to retire this ship. Too much of its machinery, particularly wiring and hoses near the surface, would have been damaged by the heat. The quartz glass in the windows and focusing lenses would have been weakened, as well as the seals around the canopy and panels.

Valthyrra hovered nearby, the snakelike neck of her

probe stretched to its limit as she inspected the damage. "How long have you had this ship?"

"Three years now," Dveyella replied. "Our ships have a rather limited life expectancy."

"So it would seem," Valthyrra agreed. "I can refit this one as a trainer. But you will need a new one, for your line of work."

"And a very dangerous line of work it would seem," Mayelna added as she walked up behind them. "It cost you a ship and Velmeran a suit of armor."

"Ah, but this was an easy one!" Dveyella insisted. "We did what we intended and returned safe. A good run indeed."

"Good?" Mayelna asked in disbelief.

"A bad one is when they shoot the fins off your ship, so that you bounce through space like a ball," she said quietly, indicating Baress. "Velmeran surprised me, if I may say so without embarrassing him greatly. He thinks quicker than I do, and he will be better than I am in a very short time. With a couple of years experience behind him, he will lead this pack. To be frank, I want him."

Valthyrra's neck snapped around so fast that the hinges popped. "You want him? Are you asking that I transfer him to you? Right now?"

"Not right now," Dveyella said, hiding a smile with effort. "I have only just indicated that I would take him, and I would allow him time to decide."

"It is his decision," Mayelna agreed.

"He is also my best pilot," Valthyrra said, glancing at the Commander in a manner that indicated a fierce glare. "I have plans for him, and I would not willingly part with him. I have no replacement for him."

"It is, of course, his decision," Mayelna said again.

Velmeran, who had remained silent so far, watched in fascination and amusement. Valthyrra Methryn was so agitated that he almost expected to see smoke escaping from the cowling around her retractable neck.

"Yes, and he does not have to decide soon," Dveyella

added. "Several weeks may pass before we are requested somewhere else, and it is customary that we remain where we are until then."

"That is true," Valthyrra agreed quickly, her camera pod lifting hopefully. She turned to look at the larger group standing to one side of the scorched fighter. Dyenlerra had moved in on Keth, and had already attached a portable diagnostic unit to the leads inside the control panel of his suit. "I want to thank you for returning our merchandise safely. Now let us see if it has suffered from its rough handling."

The entire pack was gathered close, silent as they awaited the medic's judgment. Keth himself bore a pained expression of barely restrained impatience, obviously of a mind that all this was unnecessary. Dyenlerra appeared equally exasperated with her patient's unwillingness to co-operate.

"Good enough," she decided as she jerked out the leads. "At least until I can get you out of that armor and properly checked."

"I am all right?" Keth asked with both impatience and concern.

"You are not ill," Dyenlerra said as she bent over the device and pointed toward the lift, indicating for it to put itself away. It turned and rolled off at a quick pace. "Like so many of us, you are getting old."

Keth's reply was a moment of thoughtful silence. Obviously the matter of his age did bother him, whether he chose to believe it or not.

"They did not mistreat you?" Mayelna asked.

"No, certainly not," Keth answered quickly. "They were scared to death of me, although I did nearly starve on their rations. They eat like birds."

"We eat like wolves," Dyenlerra corrected him. "At least they did keep him cool."

"They let you keep your suit?" Velmeran asked.

"Not at first, but I convinced them that I had to have it," Keth replied, obviously pleased with his ingenuity. "I thought that I would need it, since I knew that someone would be coming after me. Actually, it was quite comfortable in those caves."

"We will need a complete report later," Mayelna said. "For now, you report to sick bay for a complete checkup. I want to see you in my office as soon as you are finished."

"Immediately, Commander," Keth agreed with only minor reluctance, well aware that he had been given an order. He departed alone. Some of the others watched him leave but no one was inclined to go with him, no doubt to his annoyance. They were waiting for their pack leader.

"Dyenlerra," Mayelna said softly. "Just what is his condition?"

"About the same as when he left, less about two kilos from light rations," the medic replied. "As I said, he is getting old—fast."

"Would you be willing to declare him unfit to fly with the packs?" she asked suddenly.

"I might have to." Dyenlerra did not seem surprised by that question.

"Valthyrra and I already have, although I would like to have your support on that. Is he capable of being an instructor?"

Dyenlerra nodded. "Yes, he should be up to that for another twenty years, certainly ten."

"Then so it shall be," Mayelna said, and glanced over her shoulder at the younger pilots waiting silently as a group. "I trust that the lot of you can be counted upon to be more discreet than your superior officers. Let this business serve as a lesson to you on the virtues of honest introspection, but do not make the mistake of thinking that foolishness will always be forgiven. I have a present need for an instructor, and as such Keth will be useful to this ship. He might be foolish enough to refuse. Now, forget what you have heard."

No one answered, but there was no question that they took the point to heart. They had matured enough in recent days to recognize a threat when they heard one, although most of them still did not realize that they had been meant to overhear what had been said.

"Then I must leave you," the Commander continued. "There is a war and, unlike Valthyrra, I can only be in one place at a time. Just now I am needed on the bridge."

"I am calling the packs in," Valthyrra said. "We will be under way as soon as they are secure."

"Make it quick, then," Mayelna said as she left with Dyenlerra.

"Well, children, the last order of business is port leave," Valthyrra continued. "There are two packs and several other members of this crew, not to mention our hard-working visitors, who are to be rewarded with leave. There are also eight packs and a large portion of this ship's crew whose tardiness and lack of devotion will be punished by being denied leave. What will be your choice?"

"Kanis!" Tregloran exclaimed, answering for them all. Kanis was one of three places that all Starwolves liked best; the climate was good—meaning cold and dry—the port was interesting but tame enough that they did not have to worry, their kind was very well liked by the locals, and there was no Union base. The others were quick to nod in agreement.

"You are all agreed on Kanis?" Valthyrra asked. "Very well, then Vinthra it is!"

Velmeran looked at the machine questioningly. "Vinthra? Why Vinthra?"

"I have business in Vinthra," she answered simply.

"And since Vinthra is also the capital world of this sector, you also have a lot of brass—if you will pardon the pun—poking your big nose there immediately after your last two encounters with the military."

"So it would seem," Valthyrra agreed. "All the more reason, in my estimate, for going to Vinthra."

Her probe turned and drifted off at a sedate pace toward the lift door, no doubt to return itself to its rack; Valthyrra had transferred immediately to the bridge the moment she was finished there.

"Then we are not going to Kanis?" Tregloran asked, as mystified as the rest of the pack.

"Copperbottom asked us where we would like to go," Velmeran explained the ship's odd sense of humor. "She never promised to take us there. Some of her jokes are older than she is."

Tregloran only shrugged. "The underground city of Vannkarn should be just as much fun."

Dveyella frowned. "Actually, I have had quite enough of underground cities for now."

"You wish to speak to me, Commander?" Keth asked hesitantly, standing in the doorway of Mayelna's office behind the upper bridge.

Mayelna quickly put away her computer terminal, swinging the monitor around on its support arm until it locked into place on the arm and flipped the keyboard over so that the wood grain of its bottom matched inconspicuously with the rest of her desk, while using one of her free hands to indicate the two chairs before her. Although she seemed distracted, she watched Keth closely as he crossed the room slowly to take his seat. It seemed that he was at last beginning to understand how matters stood in regard to his future. Understand, perhaps, but not necessarily accept; he still wore his black armor.

"So, how did your visit to the medic go?" she asked casually.

"I thought that you might tell me," Keth replied nervously. "You have the report. There is something wrong?"

"No, there is nothing wrong for someone your age," Mayelna said, with slight emphasis on that final word. "Keth, Valthyrra and I have a small problem that you might be able to solve for us. We have some busy times ahead of us, and we want more packs for those two bays we are reopening. We have a whole class of students, fourteen in all, just waiting to begin flight instruction. They can be fighting in two years, with another class of twelve ready to

begin when they are finished. All they need is an instructor. I thought that you might want to do that."

Keth looked at her in surprise and mild confusion.
"There must be someone else. I do not have that many
years left, and I would prefer to spend them in the pack.
Surely you can understand that."

"That is not your choice," Mayelna said. "I will not
force you to be an instructor, but you will either instruct, or
you will be retired. Valthyrra and I have decided, and your
physical has proven us correct. You can no longer endure
the stress of hard accelerations. I will not have a repetition
of this previous fiasco, nor will I allow you to be a menace
to the other pilots."

"Commander, that was not my fault!" Keth protested.
"I saved myself when that ship turned in front of me. . . ."

"There is nothing wrong with your reaction time, I
will grant you that," Mayelna interrupted him. "But the
fact remains that if you had time to find that corridor to try
to poke through, then you also had time to turn. Any other
pilot would have missed that ship. I have been waiting for
you to retire since I put you in Velmeran's pack two years
ago. If it is too much for you to admit to yourself, then you
force me to decide for you."

"Commander, it is not fair!" Keth declared in anger,
although he did not look up and Mayelna wondered if he
might cry. The most bitter lies can be those a person tells
himself.

"No, it is not fair," Mayelna agreed. "The great
scheme of life seems to have no respect for a three-
hundred-year career. Nature has no respect for seniority.
Do you think that I do not understand what this means to
you? Flying was my life, all that I ever cared about. I have
not seen the inside of a fighter in the eighteen years since I
came up to the bridge. Day after day I sit in that chair and
watch this ship fly herself and nothing hurts me more than
to see the packs go out, knowing that I will never fly again.
I was young and strong the night Valthyrra called me to the
bridge. But I have grown old, sitting in that chair while the

packs fly without me. And I do not much like to think about it, because I feel like I have lost something that has been very important and dear to me forever. Every day that passes is a treasure lost."

She paused, rubbing her nose absently as she sat back. Then, noticing Keth staring at her, she crossed both sets of arms. "Do not get me wrong. I know that tending the bridge is very important, and I am proud to do it. The fact is, I am of more use to this ship on the bridge than in a fighter. And I quite intend to stay there another thirty years. But I will retire, when the time comes, and Velmeran is going to have to follow me up there. And yet, Great Spirit of Space help him, he will still be very, very young when that time comes, and flying is no less his life than it was mine."

Keth laughed softly. "So that is the great secret! Valthyrra would blow her breakers if she knew."

"I imagine that she knows already. I would spare him that fate, and yet I know that it has to be." Mayelna shook her head regretfully. "This is the talk that I should be having with him, if I had the courage. At least I will have an end to the problem you represent."

"I will be your instructor," Keth agreed, still reluctant. "We are, as you point out, slaves to duty. I am of more use to this ship teaching others to fly than I would be in a pack, certainly more use than I would be retired. I should be glad for the few more years that you are willing to give me. Someday I may even feel grateful."

"Just now, I am sure, you only feel that you have lost something rather than gained," she agreed. "Go move your things down to the instruction bay and start setting things in order. And, if you are smart, you will act like this was your idea as much as anyone's."

Keth smiled as he rose to leave. "Thank you, Commander."

He passed Valthyrra on the way out. She paused a moment to watch him, twisting the remote's long neck around backward, before she drifted on into the office.

Mayelna sat back in her chair, watching the machine closely.

"I take it that matters progressed smoothly," Valthyrra said.

"Very well, indeed," Mayelna said. "Your timing seems to be as accurate as always."

"No, my timing seems to be rather off of late," Valthyrra said, refusing to be teased. "Are you so spiteful that you are actually encouraging Velmeran to join this special tactics team?"

"Velmeran thought that you were trying to get rid of him, arranging for him to go with Dveyella."

"Why would I want to get rid of him?"

"Because he is too young to suddenly be so popular, and he is causing dissension among the older pilots. I just wanted to show him that you have no such plan. If you had a mouth, it would have been gaping."

"Then I quite forgive you," Valthyrra said contritely. "You know, he might have been right . . . about the older pilots. But they gave a very bad showing of themselves, and they have only themselves to blame."

"Just in time for Velmeran to move ahead through the gap of their own incompetence?" Mayelna asked. "Either your timing is very good, or you are about the luckiest ship in the heavens."

"Not so lucky, in the long run," Valthyrra said. "Velmeran is probably going to leave us. My schemes have backfired."

Mayelna raised an inquiring brow. "Are you sure of that?"

"No, not absolutely. Dveyella knows why he must stay."

"And she will give him back to you?"

"No, it is not that simple. Dveyella and Velmeran are very much in love, and they are about as well-matched a pair as I have ever seen. She is going to be making him aware of that very soon now."

▼ ▼ ▼ ▼ ▼

9

▲ ▲ ▲ ▲ ▲

The approach of a Starwolf carrier on a Union planet was an event similar in some respects to an all-out attack, since no one was ever certain that it was not. The big ships would suddenly drop out of starflight halfway into system, hurtling vast and silent into an orbit of their own choosing with no regard for shipping lanes or frantic station controllers. As a rule they maintained com silence unless they had instructions of their own to impart, although they revealed themselves fully to scanners—mostly to insure that all traffic would get out of their way—looming like a mountain on screen.

For the Starwolves, this was a venture into enemy territory, and all this bluff was to insure that they would be left well alone. Their reputation was their strongest defensive weapon, and they guarded it carefully. Freighters scattered in their paths, while ships at station all but shook in their moorings. Union warships discreetly withdrew like predators chased away from their kill by something they did not dare fight. The Union had curious loopholes in its laws to excuse the transgressions of Starwolves, who did not legally exist and so could not be held accountable for breaking laws. It was an uneasy truce at best, and one the

Union hated with a passion. But at least they kept their stations.

The fact that Vinthra was sector capital only made the situation all the more dangerous. Sector capitals were the true inner worlds of the Union; they were the Union, in a very real sense, the bare handful of planets that decided policy for their vast economic empire. There was, at any time, a fleet ready in this system large and strong enough to stand against a Starwolf carrier. Not that they could hope to defeat one of the big ships, but they could drive one away. But the inner worlds were also the homes of the Commanders who would decide if they would fight, and they did not want such destruction brought down upon their own worlds and stations.

Nor was such a world a place for port leave. Starwolves were welcome in the fringe worlds; the black fighters chased away the invasion forces and broke the trade monopolies that could drain a planet dry. But the populations of the inner worlds lived well on the profits of their trade monopolies. Understandably, they did not appreciate Starwolf interference with what they considered their just reward. But the Starwolves did not have to fear greatly, as long as they were cautious. Unioners were generally prudent, and they knew that their unwelcome visitors would level a port, not in vengeance but in stern warning, if any of their number came to harm.

All in all, it was a dangerous and fairly ridiculous situation that neither side liked. The Union did not want wolf carriers in its system, but there was no alternative but to endure it. The Starwolves would have preferred to avoid the inner worlds, but they had to come to the sector capitals to sell their "salvage."

It was not a good place for a young crewmember to take his first port leave. And Velmeran had no desire to take a pack of seven young pilots into the glorified cavern of port Vannkarn. Kanis would have been a better choice, since no one could have gotten into trouble in a place like that. He doubted that any of his students had the discretion to avoid trouble, or even the experience to recognize real trouble if they saw it. And with two-thirds of the ship's crew restricted to ship, they could be too deep in the avenues of Vannkarn for help to find them if they needed it.

His one assurance was that they were armored and armed, as dangerous as a Kandian spark dragon and as hard to kill as a Selvan land crab. So he reflected as Dveyella sealed the last opening of his new armor and, much to his relief, opened the front plate to turn on the cooling. He noticed Dveyella staring at the cover plate as she closed it, and he bent his head forward to look.

"Blast scoring," he muttered in disgust. "Am I to be sent out looking dented and disheveled?"

"It gives you the mean and seasoned look of an old warrior," Dveyella told him. "Would you rather wear your old armor?"

"No. But they could have at least put on a new cover plate when they changed out the controls."

Looking at himself in the mirror, he had to admit, when he considered the effect as objectively as possible, that the Starwolf image was mostly the armor; there was certainly nothing threatening about the person inside. Humans were smaller than they had been when they had first come into space, fifty thousand years before. But Kelvessan were smaller still, averaging little more than a meter and a third, yet, in full armor, they assumed dangerous proportions, tall, powerful and menacing. Male or female, young or old, Kelvessan all looked about the same; partly elfin in appearance, partly innocent waif, anything but threatening. Cute, in a word, and eternally adolescent.

"Ready to rally the troops?" Dveyella asked.

"Gather the children for our little outing, you mean," Velmeran said in mild disgust. "Come along, students. Today we learn what it is like to enter enemy territory under the ruse of port leave, putting our necks on the line in the name of having a good time."

Velmeran fell silent as the door of his room snapped open. The younger members of his pack, who had been ready for some time, had gathered in the common room that joined their suite of apartments. They all looked up at him in surprise and some guilt, the only sound that of seven mouths snapping shut. He assumed that they had been discussing ways to evade their guardians or spend their bonuses in ways they should not. It did not occur to him that they had been speculating on why their pack leader had needed Dveyella's help in getting into his armor, or how forward she would have to be before he realized that he was being courted. And, like everyone else, they wondered whether or not he would go away with her.

"Port leave is supposed to be a time of leisure, of setting aside the dangers of flying with the packs and forgetting fear for a few hours," he began immediately. "Unfortunately, if you go into a place like Vannkarn with such an attitude, you are going to be surprised. Remember that you are above the law so long as you act defensively. Remember also that there are also a number of people in a port this size who might attack you for no apparent reason, who can suddenly turn violent at the sight of Starwolves. Religious fanatics, of a wide variety, who consider us abominations. Some think they have to prove themselves superior to us, bullies who have had some type of martial training and are under the mistaken impression that they are stronger and faster than you are. Others lack the courage to face you and will simply try to shoot you in the back when you are not looking."

"Once in a port like this, a young man thought he knew exactly the right blow to break my neck above the collar of my suit," Dveyella added. "He lived just long enough to realize his mistake."

The students swallowed, wide-eyed with apprehension, as they wondered what she had done to the unfortunate attacker. Especially when they saw that Baress, standing by the outer door, looked sobered by the memory.

"You have checked your guns?" Velmeran asked, and the younger pilots nodded. They had received their belt guns only hours before, and had practiced on scrap metal targets in the holding bay that morning. It had been very little practice, but their native proficiency was adequate to the task.

"Cargo Officer Veyndayk will be waiting for us," Velmeran continued. "Now come the general rules of port leave. Do not buy or sell anything before you have compared prices. Do not order anything off a menu unless you know what it is, since you probably will not like it. Stay away from even the mildest of alcoholic drinks, since they will send you into hypermetabolism. You are free to flirt with humans but be careful with them, since you can hurt them—even kill—without meaning to.

"Ignore those who want favors of you, or seem too fascinated with you. Do not buy from anyone who talks too fast and do not give to beggars or charity; you are too easily taken advantage of. Do not brag, or tell anyone a thing about this ship or our business. Neither a borrower nor a lender be, for loan oft loses both itself and friend. This above all: to thine own self be true."

Dveyella looked at him in surprise. "Shakespeare?"

Velmeran shrugged. "He was always full of advice. Oh, yes. Treg, I know your passion for furry things. Look all you want in port, but by no means are you to bring an animal back to this ship."

Tregloran appeared to wilt inside his armor. "Why?"

"Two reasons. First, Valthyrra would pitch a fit. Secondly, there are very few animals that could survive the accelerations, and many would not be able to take the cold."

The trip down was the easiest part. The pack members were expected to fly themselves down, so that the black fighters would be very much in evidence. Baressa's pack, the only other one that had been granted port leave, was already down when they arrived. Autumn had come to Vinthra. The sun was bright although there was still a bit of a chill to the late morning air, which was to say that it was pleasant by Kelvessan standards. That would not be the case in the enclosed environment of the city, and they would be dependent upon their suits for comfort as well as protection. They quickly converted their armor into the proper costume, belting on their guns and wearing short black capes attached to metal collars that fastened to clips on their shoulders that ordinarily held the restraining straps of their seats.

The actual city of Vannkarn lay underground. At some time in Vinthra's distant past, an immense pocket of magma had formed beneath the surface only to drain away, leaving a single chamber of immense size, a vast oval twenty kilometers long by twelve wide. Such things ordinarily did not last long, but were soon closed by slips and breaks in the surrounding rock. But this one had endured millions of years, as time and erosion stripped away the rock overhead. Finally, after the planet had long been colonized, an oval section in the roof where it was thinnest had broken and collapsed, revealing the vast underground chamber.

In those days the Union and the Starwolves had been in open war, and the black fighters had continually penetrated planetary defenses to strike at stations, factories and military bases. The sector command had been removed to the bottom of the cavern. The opening in the roof had been enclosed by a grid supporting translucent panels that served as a base for the powerful force screen projected into it, making it nearly impervious even to the powerful cannons of the Starwolf carriers. Its only entrances were the trams and freight lifts connecting it to the port.

Later, when the threat of war eased, the underground base had been slowly converted into the seat of government for the Rane Sector. Then the Trade Company had moved in as well, and a city grew to fill the floor of the rocky chamber. And yet Vannkarn was not some dark cavern, but a jeweled city built by the wealth of many worlds. Here it was eternal spring, and while it never rained, brooks tumbled over falls and splashed along sculptured beds.

Vannkarn was a monument that the Union had built in

honor of itself, a tribute to its schemes and grand designs and a celebration of its systematic rape of the fringe worlds under its control. It was the last place in all the Union where Starwolves were welcome, where their very presence was regarded with almost a sense of blasphemy. And, naturally, it was the inner world which the Starwolves frequented most. Sporting in the very lair of their enemy, their presence was a gesture of defiance and a most unsubtle reminder, in the celebration of its own glory and power, that the Union did not always have its own way.

The Starwolves made their way across the landing field to the port terminal where they meant to find a tram to take them down into the city. They entered through the commercial registry, where ship's crewmembers could pass through customs and inspection apart from the confusion of the passenger area. A Class D freighter, just small enough to land, had recently come down, and a handful of her crew was waiting patiently while a rather young and frail-looking duty officer ran their idents through computer check.

The Starwolves had no intention of joining the others in line. They pushed past to let themselves through the turngate, and the duty officer rather pointedly ignored them. But that lack of attention was by no means mutual, for the younger Kelvessan stared in cautious amazement, even fear. This was their first port leave, and none of them had been to the vast carrier facilities at Home Base. And so this was their first glimpse of an actual, living human. They each reacted in his or her own way. To some, men were the legendary creatures of whom Starwolves were only advanced counterfeits. Others saw only the ancient enemy of their race. Such was obviously the case with Tregloran, who stopped short and reached for his gun. Velmeran gave him an impatient shove to send him on through the gate.

They continued quickly down the hall to the wide boarding platform for the trams. This was the main entrance to the city far below, twenty tracks in all. All passengers arriving through the port, either off-world or by air from other cities, entered here, so that there were more people in this one large room than even lived in the Methryn's maze of corridors. The students slowed almost to a stop until the older pilots urged them into the nearest tram. A Starwolf carrier was a curiously sheltered environment, with little direct contact with life outside.

"Were those human?" Tregloran asked uncertainly as they were taking their seats.

"You guessed it," Dveyella said.

"They are not very impressive," the younger pilot remarked.

"I noticed how unimpressed you were," Velmeran observed, still amused that Tregloran had nearly pulled his gun.

"They are very tall," Steena offered. Modern humans were ten to fifteen centimeters taller than most Kelvessan but the fact remained that, from her unfortunatetly low point of view, everyone was tall.

Just then the doors of the tram snapped shut and the tram started off with an uncertain lurch that proceeded quickly to a descent that was just short of free-fall.

"Can we speak with them?" Tregloran asked eagerly.

"If you can speak Terran," Velmeran said, switching to that language. "I hope that you have been practicing it lately. It has been a few years since you had it in school."

"I remember it well enough," Tregloran answered in the same language, with a very allowable accent. Velmeran had a tremendous command of the language, since one of his hobbies was ancient literature. But Dveyella still held the advantage of practical application, since she also spoke five planetary dialects and two alien languages.

The trip down was short and swift, and after only a few seconds the tram began to brake to a sudden stop. Since there was no need for the protection of a roof overhead, the tram ramps opened directly onto an open platform overlooking a wide square formed by the two wings of the port hotel. Looking outward from the platform,

Vannkarn appeared much the same as any other port city. Tall buildings of various shapes and colors rose across the uneven landscape. Wide avenues formed ordered paths between the towering structures, complete with forested parks and fountains, but above a gently curving ceiling of rock replaced the open expanse of sky, the Starwolves standing at the northern edge.

But above all there were humans to be seen by the thousands wherever they turned, nearly half as many in this one city of two million as there were Kelvessan in existence. To Velmeran, humans were descended from the Great Ones of long ago, Olympian gods of antiquity such as Shakespeare, Beethoven, Tolkien and Brahms, who had written the stories and the music he loved, and that influenced his own image of the race. When he fought it was against machines, with only a dim awareness that there were men at the controls. By contrast, Tregloran appeared to see only the ancient enemy of his people.

Most Kelvessan had a quiet fascination with the human race. Some, like Velmeran, believed that humans had greater control over their own destinies, and were free to be whatever they desired. Others thought that humans lived a fairly idyllic and purposeful existence, free of struggle, fear and devotion to duty beyond their own wants and desires. Those, of course, were the dreams. A few port leaves quickly impressed upon a young Starwolf that humans were, by their standards, physically, mentally, socially and morally inferior, greedy, quarrelsome, selfish, bigoted and slow of wit beyond anything they would accept in themselves. Velmeran simply was not "worldly" enough to know that; his image of the human race was still hidden beneath the veneer of what he wanted to believe it should be.

There was an unseen barrier between men and Kelvessan, such as did not exist with other races. Each possessed the virtues that the other lacked. Kelvessan were intelligent, strong, long-lived and lacking the baser emotions and drives that formed the dark side of human nature.

But humans also possessed a naive belief in themselves that lent originality to all things of their creation. It was that self-belief that the Kelvessan had yet to learn, and what Velmeran wanted most to discover in his kind. It had not yet occurred to him that he needed to look inside himself for that belief and confidence.

But the younger pilots were not given time to look around, for there was one remaining task to be completed before they would be free for port leave. Dveyella, the senior officer, took the lead. They boarded a smaller overhead tram that took them from the port entrance to the far side of the cavern. Here, protected by the thickest roof of solid rock, was the sector capital building, the residence of both the Sector Council and the High Councilor, as well as Sector Command of the Union Fleet. It would seem about the last place in all Vannkarn where Starwolves would care to go. And yet they had been coming here for many thousands of years like pilgrims to an ancient shrine.

Near the top of the immense terraced structure was a single vast chamber. Tiles of dark stone covered the walls and floor, and large windows, behind and to the side, were enclosed with panes of gold-tinted glass. Indeed it did seem like a shrine for some sacred or revered object, and yet, positioned on a low stone slab atop a three-step dais, was but a single block of dull gray metal. It was large, two meters high by three wide and eight in length. The metal casing appeared to be quite thick, not unlike armor, and rounded at the edges and corners. Bands of some protective metal also enwrapped it, and yet there was no other feature to it except the twin tracks that ran down each of its long sides and a number of rectangular receptacles on each end, as though it was meant to be interconnected with a battery of computers.

There were few visitors in the chamber and those left quickly when the Starwolves arrived. Dveyella continued to lead the way, walking quickly across the room to stand at the base of the steps, where a rope of gold braid was hung from gilded posts to hold back visitors. She turned to face the students, who gathered about her.

"Do you know what this is?" she asked quickly, but did not wait for them to reply. "You see before you the one great trophy the Union has been able to take in the course of this long war. This is, as well, one of our two greatest shames. It is not likely that you have heard this before. Now that you can see it for yourselves, it is time for you to learn of the two times that the Starwolves have failed."

"Failed who?" Tregloran alone dared to ask.

"Failed themselves," she answered. "Do you know what this is?"

"It looks like part of a large computer," he speculated cautiously.

"This is a memory cell from a Starwolf carrier," she said. "The traits and personal memories of a ship are held in there. There are eight scattered throughout a ship, with enough duplication in the information they store and the computers they drive that even extensive damage does not affect the operation of a ship. That, for all practical purposes, holds the life of a ship. The Theralda Vardon, to be exact.

"The Vardon came out of the early days of the war. That was back when the Union still had the technology and industry to be able to fight us . . . and occasionally win. The Vardon was besieged and destroyed about sixteen thousand years ago, the last of the fifty-seven carriers to be lost, in the years when the Kelvessan were in some danger of dying out.

"Most likely she was ripped apart by a small thermonuclear explosion from a shield-penetrating missile, such as the Union has not been able to build in ten thousand years. According to the Union's own story, a piece of the wreckage was found much later, and the unit was discovered inside. They salvaged it, recognized it as something important and brought it here for safekeeping. Since they assume that we cannot get to it here, they soon grew bold enough to place it on public display."

"Can we get it back?" Merkollyn asked.

"Yes, if we want to try hard enough," she answered. "Since the unit is of no use to the Union, we have let matters stand until we are ready for it."

"Ready for it?" Tregloran, always the quickest, caught a hidden meaning in that.

Dveyella nodded slowly. "That is the second of our failings. You recall, do you not, that we left Terra during the early days? The Union could not get at Terra directly, but they did something that forced us to retreat from the planet for many thousands of year. Just what is not exactly known.

"Now comes the strange part of the story. We lost much in that hasty retreat from Terra. Since we could no longer return there, within time even its very location was recorded only in the memories of the great ships. And the Vardon was the last ship built before the loss of Terra, the last ship that knew where to find it. Since the Union knows even less of Terra than we do, there is no one today who knows where Terra is.

"But Terra was not destroyed. Whatever happened, it was understood from the start that we could return there someday. And our kind has long held a belief, almost a prophecy, although based, I fear, on wishful thinking. The Starwolves have long believed that when the time comes that we may at last win this war, when the Union is waning in strength and we are waxing, then Terra will be found. And the only place where we might discover how to find it is in the Vardon's memory cell."

Tregloran stared in disbelief. "You mean this unit is still operational?"

"Of course," Dveyella replied. "A sudden ripping out of the leads can cause the memory to scramble, but a failure of the system causes an internal protector to preserve the memory indefinitely. The Union has never been able to get at that memory, and they gave up trying long ago. But we can access that memory easily. In fact, we can restore the Vardon to life by installing that unit in a new ship. We have allowed it to remain here until we find a way that we are certain to get it out in a single try, and until we need it enough to make the attempt."

"What is to stop us from trying?" Tregloran asked, as if he thought that attempt might be an interesting way to spend their port leave. At least, Velmeran thought, he had daring.

Dveyella shrugged. "Access is the main problem. The only apparent way of getting our ships inside the cavern is through the dome, which is protected by reenforcing shields comparable to a carrier's forward battle shield. And it would take the concentrated power of a carrier's main cannons to pierce that shield, cooking the city beneath in the process. All this, mind you, while the planetary defenses and a quarter of the sector fleet is hammering away at us."

"I do comprehend the situation," Tregloran replied soberly. The results of such an attempt were obvious, since the Union knew the only way into the city and had planned their defenses around it. The Starwolves could do it, if they were prepared to pay the price.

Dveyella allowed them several minutes to walk about the chamber and view the unit from every side. Soon their thoughts would return to the more immediate problem of port leave, but in times to come they would think often of the memory cell and devise complex and devious schemes to recover it with little or no risk. Such thoughts had occupied the minds of Starwolves for four thousand years, and yet the unit remained where it was.

After a time Dveyella led them down to a lower level of the building, where they waited in a terraced foyer near the main entrance to the sector defense offices. Minutes later a Starwolf in white armor got off an elevator leading down from those offices, somewhat to their surprise. Soon they saw that it was Veyndayk, the cargo supervisor.

"Business done," he said, stepping up to join Velmeran and Dveyella at the rail where they had been watching traffic pass on the level below.

"Did you sell Keth back to the Sector Commander?" Velmeran asked.

Veyndayk laughed. "No, although that might be a good use for old Starwolves. Farstell Freight and Trade bought back a shipment of clothing, conveniently packed in their own shipping containers. And fleet ordnance has just now payed us a finder's fee for an intact cutter."

"A cutter?" Velmeran asked. Cutters were the smallest of the military ships, hardly bigger than a transport, and generally used only for police work.

"My little joke," Veyndayk explained. "We took two intact cutters as riders on salvaged battleships, and one we have had sitting in a forward bay for the last year. We took them apart down to the smallest bolt and rebuilt the ships by taking parts at random. Now I am going to collect finder's fees on those ships in three different ports. That should give the boys in fleet ordnance fits, when they cross-check serial numbers of those parts."

That appealed to Dveyella, who liked frustrating Union officials best of all. "You know, they will not be able to use those ships until they take them apart and rebuild them as they originally were."

"You laugh, but that is probably the truth," the cargo officer said. "Are your pilots ready?"

Veyndayk, as the conductor of the ship's business, always took those on their first port leave about the city to introduce them to the workings of commerce. Buying and selling were new experiences; on board ship, anything they needed was easily gotten from ship's stores. Young Starwolves were also very gullible and in need of careful guidance. Their only protection lay in the fact that not many people would dare to try to take advantage of them.

"Ready?" Velmeran asked. "They have been ready for days."

"Seven at once," Veyndayk muttered to himself, glancing at the group of young pilots. "Well, we already have plans to divide them into three groups. Baress and

Baressa will have Tregloran and his sister, Marlena and Threl will have two more, while Dyenlerra and I will have the remaining three."

"And what about me?" Velmeran asked.

"Dveyella will take care of you," the cargo officer said. "My word, Pack Leader, you have watched over this herd day in, day out for months now. This is your port leave, and I expect that you have it coming. Fair?"

Velmeran agreed reluctantly. Veyndayk called the pack together, gave them his primary instructions and took them away in less than a minute. They would take the tram back to the port entrance, where they would find the rest of their appointed guardians.

"Well, that is safely done. Now we have a night and a day to ourselves," Dveyella said. She stepped over to stand before a thick column covered by panels of Beldiian quartz, rare and expensive and as highly polished as a mirror. Using its reflection, she carefully pulled her long, thick hair out of the collar of her suit, arranging most of its length to cascade over her black cape.

"Baress and Baressa are keeping company?" Velmeran asked. "What do they have in common—besides the same name?"

"Is that not sufficient for a beginning?" Dveyella asked.

"Ordinarily, no. Not for Baressa. She is very careful of the company she keeps. Pack leaders as a rule, although she has briefly entertained officers from other ships."

"Oh? Has she been after you?" Dveyella asked mischievously.

"Hardly! I am too young for her."

"I would never think so."

"Perhaps you do not have very high standards," Velmeran teased in return, realizing too late how that reflected back on him.

"Starwolves!"

Velmeran and Dveyella both froze as their ears picked

up that single voice some distance behind them. Ordinarily they would not have noticed, but there was something about the way that single word had been said. In amazement, certainly. But it was also an accusation, and an acknowledgment of defeat.

"Coincidence?" another, older voice asked. "Neither of us believe that, obviously. You have lost your captive, it seems. A courier should be in soon."

Velmeran saw that Dveyella was staring into the mirrored surface of the column, and unobtrusively shifted his stance so that he could see the image reflected there. The stone was dark, and the images were indistinct. The older man was richly dressed, slightly bent with age but still taller than himself. Beside him, glaring at the two Starwolves, stood a giant of a man to match the deep, forceful voice. Tall and gaunt, he was clearly a warrior. And, judging by the uniform, this was no less than the Sector Commander.

"They have their nerve to come hopping in here!" the tall man declared.

"So? And what can we do about it?" the older one asked. "Come along. Why don't we ask them to dinner?"

Velmeran did not know what to make of that final statement, but the two were indeed approaching. After this, he began to believe that his kind had been given enhanced hearing for the sole purpose of eavesdropping.

"Your pardon," the older man said, and the two Starwolves turned as if noticing for the first time. He nodded to them politely. "I am sorry to disturb you. You are just in port, are you not?"

"We have been in less than two hours," Velmeran replied, trying to hide his amazement at their height. Even the older man had to glance down at him, while the one in uniform was indeed a towering giant of about two meters, a head and a half taller over Velmeran.

"Are you, perhaps, recently out of the planet Bineck?" the older man asked, surprisingly straightforward.

"Yes, we have just come from there," he replied, equally direct.

"Oh? I should like to hear more about it. Could you possibly come to dinner tonight?"

"Of course," Velmeran replied quickly, not pausing to consider whether or not he should. Dveyella looked surprised, although she did not seem inclined to protest.

"Would the seventh hour, local time, be too early for you?" the older man asked. "My residence is on the twelfth floor of the adjacent building, the rather conspicuously pink one. Ask for Jon Lake. I will leave word that you are expected."

"Councilor Lake?" Velmeran asked.

"The same," he answered, and glanced at his companion. "This brooding spartan is my nephew, Sector Commander Donalt Trace. You must excuse his ill temper, but he was born with it. And it has recently been aggravated by distressing news."

"An occupational hazard, surely. I am Pack Leader Velmeran of the Methryn. This is Pack Leader Dveyella, of special tactics."

"Special tactics?" Lake asked. Even his nephew looked at her with interest. "I do look forward to hearing any tales you might see fit to share. Tonight, then?"

"But of course," Velmeran replied. "Dinner with Councilor Lake at seven. Attire is black armor. We would not miss it for this or any world."

"How did you manage that?" Dveyella asked when the two worthies had continued on their way.

"I did not manage it," he insisted. "He asked, and I leaped at the opportunity with due and proper grace."

"High Councilors and Sector Commanders are not in the habit of inviting Starwolves to dinner," Dveyella continued persistently. "Why did he?"

Velmeran shrugged. "He offered for the same reason that I accepted. We are both insatiably curious and are fascinated by the chance to probe each other's secrets."

"No doubt," she agreed. "And at least you seem well able to fence words with that old man."

"He is quick and bright, and no doubt quite dangerous in his own way. But I am willing to take him on. The only thing that worries me is if they will be serving something for dinner I like."

10

As small as they were, Kelvessan had to eat prodigiously to maintain their fierce metabolisms. While on port leave, they would often eat at two or three different places in the course of one meal to hide how much they had to consume to satisfy their enormous hunger. In fact, a large part of what they spent on leave went to feed their deceptively small stomachs. Naturally, they would not willingly pass up a chance for a free meal.

This was one invitation that Velmeran would not pass up, with no regard for what was placed on the table before him. Dveyella was less certain about the matter; she had every intention of going, but she did not share her companion's enthusiasm. By Starwolf reckoning, the Sector Commanders and members of the High Council were the enemy, the ones who made the decisions and determined the policies of the Union. They ran the trade monopolies, ordered the invasions of the fringe worlds and set the traps by which Starwolves died. She could not deny that she feared these two more than she feared anyone in all space, and she marveled that Velmeran seemed ready and willing to meet them in their own element. Still, she would do her best to support him in what she expected to be a fierce battle of minds and wills.

The Lake family had ruled this sector since the days of Unification. The seat of the High Council was the hereditary right of the head of the family, and all other appointments were his to make. Lesser members of the clan controlled the sector trade monopoly, Farstell Freight and Trade, as well as the network of industry that served it. The name of the ruling family had changed often in that time. But the line had remained unbroken, so that Jon Lake, the current patriarch, could trace his ancestry back even before the Union, to the earliest days of colonization.

Word had indeed been left that the two Starwolves were expected. They were greeted politely by the guards at the main entrance and one guard accompanied them up, for he had one of the few keys that unlocked the controls that allowed the elevator to ascend to this upper floor.

Dveyella rang the bell, and a long moment passed before the door opened. It was neither the older Lake nor his nephew who faced them, but a servant in black formal clothing. He occupied the years between young and old, was just slightly tall for the human norm, and he had a nose like a bird of prey and a hairline in the process of a hasty retreat. His look of surprise quickly turned to one of disgust, as if he had found beggars at the door.

"We have come for dinner," Velmeran said.

"Dinner?" the hawk-nosed servant asked incredulously. "As if piracy was not enough, now they present themselves at the door asking to be fed!"

"It's all right, Javarns," Councilor Lake called from somewhere within. "They are expected."

"Starwolves?" Javarns was plainly skeptical, but he grudgingly stepped aside. "Somehow it does not surprise me as much as it should."

"It should not surprise you at all, since we have been cooking for them all afternoon," Jon Lake said as he crossed the room to greet his guests. "I am so glad that you could come. I was afraid that you would not take my invitation seriously."

"We would not think of missing this," Velmeran said as he quickly glanced about the room.

"Well, you are just in time," Lake continued excitedly, as if he were entertaining old and beloved friends. "Do excuse me a moment. Javarns will show you where you can wash your hands."

"A major undertaking, I am sure," Javarns mumbled peevishly. "Is there anything you require? Will you unshell, or are you in the habit of wearing space suits at the table?"

"We are fine, thank you."

"As you wish, sir. Shall I take your gloves, capes or guns?"

Dveyella smiled pleasantly. "We have two rules about our guns. First, we never leave the ship unless we are armed."

"I can appreciate that," Javarns agreed. "And the second rule?"

"We shoot anyone who asks twice."

"Oh." Javarns straightened and pulled his jacket into place. "This way, please."

It seemed that they were indeed just in time for dinner. The Sector Commander was already at the table, drink in hand. He seemed to be in a better temper, now that he had adjusted to the loss of his prisoner, and neither of the two visitors knew just how great a loss that had been to his plans. He even assisted them with their chairs; the furniture of the apartment was all slightly oversized for the convenience of its inhabitants. A pair of firm cushions solved that problem.

Velmeran quickly realized that he needed to revise his opinion about this Sector Commander. He had thought of Donalt Trace as thoroughly military in the worst sense of the word, the perfect, obedient soldier. Obviously there was much of his uncle in him, the intelligence, wisdom and depth of insight that made him a giver of orders. Certainly he was less philosophical than his uncle, blunter and more passionate in both his devotions and his prejudices.

He was also the less dangerous of the two, since there was no danger that the Starwolf could forget that they were enemies.

"You really are a small people," he observed. He meant nothing unkind by that; it was purely an honest observation.

"We were made that way," Velmeran replied.

"I have never met Starwolves before," Trace continued, frowning as he considered the problem. "You know, speaking with you finally makes me realize that you are people. I never thought of you as people before. Starwolves have always been just the enemy, something that will get you if you don't watch out. As . . ."

"As machines?" Velmeran asked when he hesitated.

Trace glanced at him in surprise. "Yes, I suppose so. I am at a disadvantage. You know more about us than we know of you."

"Perhaps not," the Starwolf answered. "The Union has always been just machines to me. Machines are all I ever see, freighters and warships, and it is easy to forget that there are lives in those machines."

"Perhaps it's easier on the conscience not to think of your enemies as people," Trace said, then laughed at himself. "Listen to me! I'm not usually one to carry on this way. And with you, of all people!"

Councilor Lake returned from the kitchen at that moment, still struggling into a leisure jacket of some odd design. He quickly took his seat at the head of the table, the two Starwolves to his right and his nephew to his left. The battle lines were drawn.

"I have an excellent dinner prepared for you," he explained as he took a decanter from the center of the table to pour wine for himself and Trace. He knew better than to offer alcohol to Starwolves. "Vinthran follycrab, cooked in the shell, with a butter sauce that is my own invention."

"Follycrab?" Velmeran asked.

Lake shrugged. "The things crawl up on the beach in early morning, and then seem to forget the way back to the sea. Since they live well out of water, they often march inland for days. It is to their credit, I might add, that if they do find moving water, they will follow it to the sea.

"Now, let me see." The Councilor, glass in hand, turned to the two Starwolves. "I remember that you are Velmeran. But you I cannot recall. . . ."

"Dveyella," she answered.

"De-vay-ella." Lake did his best with the name, and shook his head. "That's not an easy one for a native speaker of Terran."

Just then Javarns appeared from the kitchen, pushing a small cart that bore their plates. He served the two Starwolves with obvious reluctance, almost as if he expected a bitten hand for his reward. He clearly disapproved of their gloves lined up around their plates like the towers of a fortress wall, reaching skyward as they stood upright on their metal cuffs.

They, in turn, eyed their dinner with much the same hesitation, and for better reason. Follycrab, cooked in the shell, nearly filled an entire plate. Their blunt, thick bodies were carried on two sets of legs, and they were armed with two pairs of powerful pincers. Shell plates as intricately articulated as Starwolf armor covered a large swimming tail, half the creature's total length.

"Will there be anything else?" Javarns asked.

"No, not for the moment," the Councilor replied.

"Very well, sir," the servant said as he departed. "I will be in the kitchen, hiding the good silver."

"Good man, that Javarns. Been with me for years. I should have replaced him with a robot long ago," Lake muttered. Then he noticed that the two Starwolves were staring at the creatures on their plates. "Well, what do you think?"

"Icky-poo!" Dveyella declared, simple and to the point.

"Oh, trust me to be a better host than that!" Councilor Lake declared, laughing. "You must realize that in all the time you people have been coming here on leave, we have watched you very closely. It is the only part of your lives that we ever see. I looked up those records and found that Starwolves do eat follycrab, and they appear to like it. I am also aware of how much you eat, so do not fear. There are two more crabs for each of you."

The poor Starwolves did not know whether to count their blessings or curse their ill fortune. Dveyella had lived long enough and been on enough port leaves to have developed a healthy caution. Her rule was to be wary of anything hidden in a stew, under gravy or sauce, had eyes to stare back from the plate or came recommended by humans. Follycrab ran afoul of the final two of those rules, and she feared that the folly would be her own. Velmeran was still young enough to like taking a chance. After a moment of observing the tactics of the Sector Commander, he set about uncrating his own.

"Ah, yes! One of my finest efforts," Lake declared. "Do you not agree?"

"It is all right," Dveyella reluctantly agreed.

"What did I say?" Lake insisted jovially. The two Starwolves were becoming entranced, for the Councilor had a rubbery face that could change instantly to a wide variety of exaggerated expressions. "Though far be it for me to neglect my duties as a proper host, I was wondering if you would mind answering a few silly and possibly personal questions?"

"Not at all," Velmeran replied. "Ask whatever you wish, although we may not answer."

Lake considered that and shrugged. "Fair enough. First, let me see if I have this right. You are Velmeran, and you are De-vayella. Male and female?"

"As far as I know," he answered. "Is it so hard to tell?"

"Well, yes," he admitted. "Starwolves may look very different to other Starwolves, but you all look very much alike to me. I will grant that your armor hides the more telling features. Your height, your appearance, even the length of your hair is the same."

Velmeran glanced at his companion, surprised. "The differences are very obvious to me. If I had to guess, you are misled by looking for the wrong things. Do we both look female to you?"

"Strictly speaking, neither of you look either male or female," Lake said, looking hard at first one and then the other. "There are certain childlike qualities to your features. . . ."

"Velmeran is hardly more than a child," Dveyella said. "But I am nearly as old as you are."

"Is that so? I have seen seventy-three planet years. About seventy-eight or so standard years."

"I am sixty-seven myself," she replied.

"If I may," Commander Trace interrupted. "From what you have said—or how you have said it—I take it that you do not consider yourself human."

"Of course not," Velmeran said. "Why should we?"

"But if you are not human, what are you?"

"We are Kelvessan," he insisted. "Our race is of artificial origin. But we have been around for fifty thousand years, which means that our history is nearly as old as your own. Surely we have earned the right to consider ourselves our own people."

"You will do as you wish, I am sure," Donalt said, still distracted by his own thoughts. "It just never occurred to me that you might think of yourselves as a wholly independent race with a history and culture of your own."

"You were always the first to point out that they are not human," Councilor Lake reminded him. "The only thing that surprises you is finding that they agree with you."

Trace nodded absently, although he kept his true thoughts to himself.

"Perhaps you still hold the mistaken idea that we were bred out of human stock," Dveyella said. "But that is not so. We were generated out of an entirely artificial reserve of genetic stock. Culturally we share a part of the same heritage. Physiologically we are so unrelated that we can barely share the same environment or eat the same food."

"Yes, I can see that," Trace agreed. "As you may know, legend has it that Starwolves were created by interbreeding humans with wolfish traits."

"No, our name refers only to our manner of attack," she explained. "We began by calling our fighter groups "wolf packs"; you were the ones who gave us the name Starwolves. Besides, we are in general agreement that the wolf was a legendary creature that never actually existed."

Councilor Lake stared at her in surprise. "Is that so?"

"It is only a theory, but a sound one," she said. "Wolves were described throughout ancient legend and literature as possessing a wide variety of magical traits. They were given the power of speech in every old legend that I can recall. Shakespeare placed them firmly among all other magical creatures. Tolkien went so far as to suggest that they were only spirits of darkness who could not bear the light of day."

"You certainly seem knowledgeable of scholarly matters," Lake observed, seemingly amused. "Hardly what I would expect of a warrior."

"We all have selective total recall," she explained. "When you have been around for a few years, you tend to accumulate an amazing volume of facts and information. Nor have we ever been under the impression that ignorance is necessarily a soldierly attribute."

The old Councilor nearly choked on his wine, especially when it became apparent that the Sector Commander was unaware that he had been insulted.

Dinner and dessert were soon past and Councilor Lake retired with his guests to the game room. The Councilor was able, with Dveyella's help, to convince Velmeran to meet his challenge in a game of chess. The Starwolf was not at all certain that he wanted to cross wits with the Councilor in so direct a manner, especially since he was under the disadvantage of having no familiarity with the game. He was no more pleased when Donalt Trace took his uncle's place at the game table. Councilor Lake quickly recited the rules, plainly dubious that even a Starwolf's absolute recall was up to such a challenge.

"Are you ready?" Trace asked, equally dubious.

"Yes, of course," Velmeran assured him.

"Oh? Then proceed."

"After you," Velmeran offered in return. The Sector Commander sat in silence for a long moment as he contemplated his strategy, carefully selecting a pawn and moving it forward in bold attack. Velmeran casually sent out a pawn of his own, and the battle continued briskly for several moves to come. After that the Sector Commander began to slow down, although Velmeran continued to move pieces as if he selected them at random.

"If I may be so bold," Councilor Lake said hesitantly to Dveyella, who sat beside him on the sofa beside the game table. He spoke slowly, obviously embarrassed. "Since you ladies only come to port in armor, there is no way to tell. But I have always wondered—since you have two sets of arms—whether you also have two sets of breasts."

Dveyella sat for a moment in bemused silence, the only sound that of her suit cycling on. Before she could reply, Trace roared aloud with laughter. "Ah, you lecherous old fool! There are no wolfettes among the pictures in those magazines you have taken to looking at . . . to refresh your memory in your old age."

Councilor Lake swatted indignantly at the accusing finger that was waving in his direction. "There is nothing wrong with my memory. I look at those pictures to remind myself that I am not so old after all."

"Can a horse do this?" Velmeran asked suddenly.

"Yes, a *knight* can do that," Trace snapped.

"We have only the one set," Dveyella answered softly.

Councilor Lake only shook his head slowly. "It still amazes me, the knowledge our ancestors must have had to build those big ships and then fill them with Starwolves. We could not hope to duplicate either."

"We have never tried," Trace remarked without looking up. The two Starwolves tried not to look surprised, but to them that was a dire threat. The only thing they could not fight was themselves.

"Actually, our genetic design and engineering was accomplished by the Aldessan of Valtrys," Dveyella said quickly, changing the subject.

Commander Trace stared at her in open amazement. "Valtrytians? Now you speak of myths and legends."

"Not so," Velmeran insisted. "The language that we speak among ourselves is Tresdyland, the language of the Aldessan. And our names are of Valtrytian origin."

"Then you have seen a Valtrytian?" the Councilor asked, greatly awed.

"No, but I have seen their ships," Velmeran replied. "There is considerable trade between us, and they are always there to help."

That, Dveyella realized, was a slight but obvious exaggeration. But she also believed that, whatever he was leading to, he had just made his point and these two worthies had swallowed the bait. And the Sector Commander must have swallowed his whole; he sat back in his chair, his arms crossed, and snorted with derision at the young Starwolf's apparent inability to protect trade secrets.

"So that is it. I always did wonder what you pirates did with all the loot you do not sell back, and who maintains your technology," he said. "But what do the Valtrytians have against us?"

Velmeran shrugged innocently. "They do not like the way you do business."

"And what business is that of theirs?"

"The Aldessan are a very old and wise race," he explained. "They have a strong belief in the concepts of freedom, self-determination and the rights of the individual. Naturally they find you objectionable."

"That still does not make it any of their concern."

"Your great and glorious Union is of no concern to them. If you had ever become a big enough nuisance to be a problem to them, then you would have learned the meaning of real trouble. As it is, they have only provided technical assistance to the Terran Republic in the matter of ships and pilots."

"But there is no Terran Republic." Trace pointed out what seemed obvious.

"We are the Terran Republic," Velmeran said.

"You? Just look at you! A band of thieves, dependent upon your petty piracy to keep food in your bellies and your ships in space."

"We may not be Robin Hood," Velmeran replied evenly. "But you are hardly democracy and free enterprise, whatever you pretend. We have kept you to your own space for fifty thousand years. Enough said?"

Trace looked at him in surprise, recalling only too well how the Union had declined, and knowing that the Starwolf spoke the truth. Then he sat back and laughed. "Yes, we do understand each other. We know, beneath all the rhetoric, how matters really stand."

Velmeran smiled. "At least you are an honest man."

"And you are a pert Starwolf," Trace answered. He moved a piece, then watched closely as Velmeran moved another. He glanced up reprovingly at his opponent. "You cannot play chess defensively, or you have lost from the start. You have to make sacrifices."

"I know what I am doing," Velmeran replied. "I refuse to make sacrifices. It is a wasteful, careless way to make war."

"It is only a game!" Trace replied with enough irritation to prove that beating this Starwolf was a matter of life and death.

"You know, Don, there is some logic in that," Lake said.

"What?" Trace stared at him in disbelief. "He has yet to come up with anything I recognize as a strategy. This game will be over in a minute."

"No doubt," Velmeran agreed quietly.

They proceeded in silence through two more rounds of moves before Trace sent his queen in for the kill with a decisive gesture. "Check."

Velmeran shook his head. "I think not."

He sent his king to temporary safety. Trace made the first of two moves that would put his opponent's piece back into check. Velmeran ignored it, moving a piece on the other side of the board. "Check."

Momentarily startled, Trace moved his king to safety. Ignoring the rook pursuing his own king, Velmeran sent a bishop in from the other side for the kill. "Checkmate."

"What?" Trace demanded incredulously, his consternation growing when he realized that he had no options. "How did you do that?"

"It was just luck, I am sure," the Starwolf replied, his innocent tone all the more mocking. "I certainly am not smart enough to have figured that out for myself."

"You were smoke-screened," Councilor Lake said, laughing.

Commander Trace could see that he had been tricked, but he still refused to believe that a Starwolf could defeat him outright. The second time Velmeran led him through an elaborate pretense in a game that lasted nearly half an hour, letting him build up his confidence before moving in for a sudden and unexpected kill. And for their third game Velmeran defeated him in only five moves, just to prove that he could. By then Trace decided that Velmeran was a practiced master at the game and refused to play again.

Donalt surrendered his seat to his uncle after the third game. Privately he believed that if anyone—human—could defeat this Starwolf, it would be Councilor Lake. But at that moment, even before the game began, Javarns entered with a message.

"Excuse me, Commander," the servant said from a safe distance, hardly daring to enter the room. "Your secretary is calling. It seems that a courier has arrived from

Bineck. The Station Commander has come himself and wishes to speak with you."

"I am sure he does!" Commander Trace remarked sarcastically. "Lie to me, more likely. Starwolf, you must have hit that place hard for him to come himself. You were there. Special tactics, I believe you called it. Can you give me an honest report?"

"We got what we were after and got away," Dveyella replied. "My ship was scorched in an explosion, but that was the extent of our damage. We did not leave much of the station, I fear. That was the diversion that got us back out."

"So I thought," Trace said as he rose, and bowed to the Starwolves. "Will you excuse me? This has been a ... memorable evening."

"Well, my young Starwolf, you have just met the Commander of the Rane Sector Fleet," Lake said after his nephew was gone. "You have made a reluctant friend, but also a bitter rival."

"A rival?" Velmeran asked, sitting comfortably back in his own chair.

"Certainly. You have proven yourself superior to him at the chessboard, and that was surely a terrible blow to his pride. I suspect that he will not be satisfied until he has challenged you in real battle."

"But how could I be of any consequence to him?" Velmeran asked. "He is a Sector Commander. I am just a Starwolf, a junior pack leader."

Councilor Lake brushed that aside impatiently. "I may know little of your kind, but it seems obvious to me that you are something special. If all Starwolves are like you, then heaven help us. I only have one Don."

"You seem to place a great deal of faith in him," Velmeran observed.

"Don is my weapon, carefully and completely trained for the sole purpose of defeating Starwolves," Lake said with deliberate pomposity, underscoring his own lack of enthusiasm. "Don's entire life is designed around a single function. One day if all goes according to plan, he will fight Starwolves and win. Or he will himself be destroyed in the attempt."

"You do not seem to be particularly concerned, whichever way it might turn out."

The Councilor sat back in his chair, frowning in serious reflection. "I think that I am going to tell you something that could get me shot for treason if certain of my colleagues found out. Although you people do not realize it you have won the war. The Union is on the decline, in terms of population, economics, industry and technology at a rate so alarming that not one member of the High Council can deny that our doom is at hand. The Union is so overgrown that it will take awhile for the beast to die. And after five hundred centuries, another ten or so is not all that long.

"Now I do not want you people taking credit, as patient as you have been. You have been bleeding us steadily for quite some time, but you have not been a direct threat to our survival since the days of the big battles. Now, however, we suffer from so many ills that your actions can mean life or death to us. And this is the time that will decide our future. If Don can turn the war against you in his own lifetime, then there is a chance that our civilization will get up off its deathbed and start growing again. If he fails, we will not have a second chance."

"But if we are not destroying the Union, what is?" Velmeran asked.

"We see the results, but we can only argue the cause," Lake explained. "Personally, I believe it is because we were not meant for civilized life. Nature gave us hands and a brain so that we could tie a rock to a stick to make a better club. All the rest has been our own idea. Then we began the process of removing ourselves from our environment, the circumstances and conditions that shaped us. Our evolution has stalled out; our civilization promises equal chances for both the weak and strong, and nature intended harsher rules. Cut off from any shaping influence, our species has begun to decline right down to the genetic level.

"The genetic code that defines a human is becoming too foggy and ragged to read properly. Over a third of our population is genetically sterile. Random mutation has driven infant mortality to levels that we have not known since the dark ages. Mental deficiency and mental imbalance claim a quarter of the population. Do you wonder if we are not in trouble? Our race is dying out, for want of proper maintenance."

"But, is this so throughout the Union?" Velmeran asked.

"No, not everywhere," Councilor Lake said, shaking his head. "Three highly mutated races are thriving—or would if we left them alone. And the independent merchants are themselves a race apart. Those four groups might survive, but I doubt that any one of them will replace us. Only you people can do that."

"Us?" Velmeran asked, surprised.

"Yes, of course you." The Councilor drained his glass in a quick swallow and reached for the decanter. "You people are best suited for life as a space-faring race, and for all the reasons that we are not. Machines are your native environment; they can neither dominate nor intimidate you. Have you ever considered the civilization you would build, the lives you would lead, once freed of the task you were made for?"

"Why do you think I fight you?" Velmeran asked in return. "It was intended that we reestablish the Terran Republic, and then remain to defend it. I doubt that it was intended that we should replace you."

"That is fairly much what is likely to happen," Councilor Lake said. "Soon the day will come that we can no longer fight you. The Union will be dissolved and your Republic will return, and the Starwolves will be left to nurse humanity through its old age."

The Councilor sat back and drained his second glass, then crossed his arms and sighed heavily. "That might seem a very dismal prospect, at least for us. But I am satisfied. So many ages have come and gone, and they left nothing behind but ruins. At least we are fortunate enough to have you. The Starwolves are our replacement, made to order, man's own idea of what the superman should be. You are the offspring of the human race, whoever made you. And, I will be the first to admit, you are our betters."

"Then why do you fight us?" Velmeran asked innocently.

Councilor Lake afforded him a startled glance. "Because I am human, for good or ill, and I will not go down without a fight. And I am Jon Lake, High Councilor and ultimate ruler of this entire sector. We have each inherited a duty and I will do what I can to buy time for the Union, even knowing that it must be defeated in the end."

Velmeran only shook his head. "I still do not understand."

"Really?" Lake asked. "I had thought you might. We each have a duty, being who and what we are. The only difference is that my duty is at odds with my conscience. To ease my conscience, the least—and yet the most—that I can do is to warn you of what is coming."

He paused a moment, glancing quickly about the room as if to see if they were indeed alone, then leaned closer to the two Starwolves. "The best minds, human and mechanical, at our service have long been contemplating the problem of fighting and destroying Starwolves. Now we are ready to test our ideas. The first you have seen, and dealt with effectively. The second trap for your fighters is something that you have not seen in a long time, and I fear that it will take Starwolf lives before you remember how to deal with it. The third is something altogether new—Don's own idea, I might add—and that, my friends, is a truly awesome weapon that could well be a threat even to your big ships. Now, that is all the warning that I can allow myself to give. Make of it what you can."

* * *

"I am sorry that Don could not make it back," Councilor Lake said as he escorted his guests to the door. "He was on remarkably good behavior tonight. I think he learned a thing or two."

"So have we all," Velmeran answered as Javarns assisted him with his cape.

"Yes, so have we all," Lake agreed. "But I am satisfied . . . Ah, that will be all, Javarns."

"Very good, sir," Javarns said, turning away. "I will get the valuables back out of hiding."

"Don't let him fool you," Lake said quietly. "I think he was delighted to have a chance to take a good close look at Starwolves."

"Perhaps, but he will never trust us," Dveyella said.

"At least he learned that you are not murderers and thieves."

"Shall we do it again sometime?" Velmeran asked.

"Of course. Your place, next time?" the Councilor asked, smiling mischievously.

"You will probably be welcome, but call ahead for reservations." Velmeran paused a moment, and reached into his belt pocket to pull out a wallet. "Give this to Javarns with my compliments. He will probably want it back."

Dveyella frowned and drew a watch from her own belt pocket. "He will probably want this back as well."

11

"This has been a strange night, and no doubt about it," Dveyella remarked. "Still, I would not have missed it."

Their tram glided silently atop its elevated rail across the width of the city. It was near the middle of the night; the walks and avenues were nearly deserted, and the city lighting had been reduced to a gentle, velvety twilight. By this time there was hardly anyone about but Starwolves, and they had the city mostly to themselves.

When Velmeran did not comment in turn, Dveyella glanced over at him. He sat alone and, for the moment, seemingly unaware of her presence, so lost he was in his own thoughts. She walked over and sat down close beside him. "Meran, do you know what to make of it all?"

Velmeran frowned and shook his head helplessly. "I feel like we are living out that chess game. Councilor Lake has explained the rules, and now he has turned over his seat to the Sector Commander for us to play out the game. I only hope we do as well in life as we did in practice."

"We?" Dveyella asked, and shook her head. "You, Meran. This game is yours. Do you accept what he told you?"

He shrugged. "I do not yet know what to think. The

172

good Councilor Lake might have been in his cups for all I know, considering how well he likes his wine. There is some investigating I mean to do, and I intend to check his theories with a higher authority."

"Who?"

"Valthyrra Methryn, of course. But, beyond that, it is not my concern. I am only a pack leader, and I can do nothing but pass on the warning. Still, it does explain one thing."

"What?"

"Lately I have seen Union officers and Commanders try things that were incomprehensible except for the excuse of rank stupidity, and I have always found that hard to believe. Perhaps that is exactly the case after all."

"Well, I want you to explain one thing to me," Dveyella said firmly. "What was all that business about Valtrytians? I know that the Aldessan are not one of our grand secrets, but we generally do not talk about them either."

"I know," Velmeran agreed. "But it did have its desired effect."

"What effect?" she demanded.

"Councilors and Sector Commanders through the years have dreamed of defeating the Starwolves," he explained. "I just thought that it should be understood that, should the Union ever manage to get rid of the Starwolves, it would still have the Valtrytians to face."

"Oh, I see," Dveyella replied thoughtfully, and smiled. "Meran, you are diabolical."

Velmeran nodded. "It runs in the family."

"So what are we going to do about it?"

"About what?" Velmeran asked, but she quickly signaled him to silence. The tram glided up to its boarding platform, and the door snapped open. Dveyella took him by each of his left arms and all but pulled him out of the car. He did not even have a chance to protest until she had him outside and halfway down the boarding ramp.

"Surveillance," she explained. "Starwolves are under

constant surveillance—so is just about everyone else, for that matter. And what I am going to tell you is the last thing that I would have overheard. They cannot listen in if we are in the open."

"How is that?" Velmeran asked. "They would have sonic scanners."

"But I have a drone," she said, indicating the small device at her belt. "It broadcasts both a high-frequency tone and a jamming wave at matching frequencies, producing a pulsing vibration that blocks both conventional microphones and the crystal receivers of sonic scanners. All they can pick up is a droning sound."

"How did you come by such a thing?"

"Special tactics. We like to make a personal reconnaissance, when we can. And we do not want our plans overheard. And be careful to speak only Tresdyland. As far as we can tell, it is an unknown language to the Union."

They came to the edge of the underground lake and Dveyella paused to look over the edge of the thick cement rail into the dark water far below. The lake was not a natural feature of the cavern; rectangular in shape, two hundred meters wide by three hundred long and smoothly cemented all around, it looked more like an immense swimming pool. The back end ran up against the cavern wall, while the inner end, where they now stood, cut well into the city. The south side was dominated by the port hotel, while the north side, steeply terraced and overgrown with carefully tended gardens, harbored the very best of the city's shops and outdoor restaurants.

"It happened when I was here about thirty-five years ago," she explained. "I was just a new pilot in the pack then, so it was that I was poking about the city alone. I was standing at this very place when I saw a large, dark shape moving toward me underwater. The thing was nearly twenty meters in length and it passed beneath the street directly below me, and as it did I could see clearly that it was a machine.

"After that I did a little investigating. First, I discovered that the lake is seawater. Then I found that it has a tide; the entire level rises five centimeters for noon tide. The lake is down in this hole so that its level is that of the sea. And there is a tunnel directly across from here, in the outer wall; the sea is seven kilometers in that direction. This, my friend, is a secret way into the city, a bolt hole for high officials should Vannkarn ever come under attack."

Velmeran leaned well out over the rail to peer down into the water, although the only thing he could see was his own wavering reflection. He glanced back at Dveyella. "This is how you propose to get into the city?"

"Of course."

"Do you also propose to swim?"

"No, we fly in," she replied, obviously pleased with herself. "Seawater is hardly more dense than some of the mediums we can fly in, such as deep into the outer layers of the gas giants."

"Water has no compressibility," Velmeran pointed out, although hesitantly. Already he could see a way around that.

"Atmospheric shields can be adapted to handle that," Dveyella provided the answer for him. "Compressibility is no problem when you are flying inside a column of water moving at graduated speeds. I have worked out the modifications that permit it, and the computer promises that it will work. And what works for a fighter will work for our modified transport—which we will need to carry the memory cell out of here."

Velmeran glanced at her sharply. "This is not Bineck; you know that. Surveillance is too tight."

She only shook her head. "We can always get down undetected through the magnetic corridor, and Vinthra's magnetism is proportionally strong enough to offset its more advanced scanners. And we will fly underwater from the core of the magnetic corridor to the sea entrance. It will take a couple of hours' travel time due to reduced speed, but it will work."

Velmeran paused a moment to consider that. If they

could just get fighters into the cavern undetected, then they could get what they wanted and be away with little trouble through the dome—by shutting down the protective shields from the inside.

"The first thing is to prove that a fighter actually can fly underwater," he said. "We are going to need a lot of help, and a little proof can break through quite a lot of resistance."

"Of course," Dveyella said. "What do you think I want you for?"

"Me? You want me to test the theory?"

"It is no theory. The computer says that you can take a fighter up to nearly four thousand kilometers per hour underwater."

"Then I will do it," Velmeran reluctantly agreed. "But I want to see your computations."

"Of course!" she laughed. "Come along. In spite of Councilor Lake's generosity, I am still hungry. Besides, I do not want us to be seen standing here too long."

"You suspect that we might be under observation?"

"Lake had quite a lot to say to us tonight, and I do not doubt that he is going to be wondering how we will react to it—whether or not we appear to believe it. And if we do, then he is smart enough to know that we will be after the memory cell sometime very soon. That is our disadvantage. He has to know what our next move will be. And if he guesses our strategy, he will know how to block it."

"Bait?"

"Perhaps," Dveyella agreed thoughtfully. "He might be tempting us to take a chance so that he can trap us."

"He also said that the Sector Commander will soon make his second move against us," Velmeran added. "I can believe that they have quite a few tricks up their sleeves that they are now ready to play. We will not have our own raid ready tomorrow or even next week. I think that we should wait, force them to make the next move, and see what they are up to."

"Of course," she agreed.

Velmeran glanced up, suddenly realizing where they were going. "Are you taking us up to the Terraces? Those places are expensive."

Dveyella shrugged. "So what? Piracy pays well."

They followed the northern edge of the lake halfway to the wall of the cavern, to where the rocky ceiling overhead was now beginning to slope down quickly. There they found an artificial stream that leaped and splashed along a stair-step course down a steep hillside. Walkways weaved around and along patches of forested gardens, so that here, late at night, they might well have been outside and not deep underground. There were but a very few people along those paths, as late as it was. The two Starwolves took a table in a small open-air cafe, nestled on a small platform of rock that leaned slightly out over the brook.

"In all the worlds I have known, I think that this place is one of my most favorite, very late at night when no one is about," Dveyella said as they waited for their meal.

"Do you often come here?" Velmeran asked.

"I have come to Vannkarn five times now," she replied absently. "The first time was nearly fifty years ago. Only thirty years past I sat on this very terrace with a boy I loved but who would not love me. He knew that I would be going away as soon as another ship needed me, and he knew that I would not leave my pack to stay with him. I had not expected that I would ever try that trick again."

"I have been here twice before," Velmeran offered. "Since this is the Methryn's territory, we see it more than anyone."

The waiter approached and set down their plates as quickly and discreetly as he could before retreating. Starwolves were not good for business; their presence could frighten patrons away and prevent new ones from coming. No one, of course, was going to tell them that, so they were generally served quickly and quietly in the hope that they would go away.

"I have been thinking," Dveyella began hesitantly. "I

have asked if you will fly in my pack. That is no longer possible."

Velmeran looked up, startled. "Do you not want me?"

"Certainly I want you," she insisted, although she would not look up at him. "But Valthyrra Methryn wants you as well, and she needs you more."

"And what about what I want? Do I not have any choice in the matter?"

Dveyella shook her head slowly. "Mostly people do enjoy such freedom, but those of greater ability have the greater responsibility. My own responsibilities have forced me to this decision, responsibilities to myself, to you, and to all Starwolves. I hope that you can recognize your own responsibilities and face them bravely."

Velmeran only stared at her in disbelief. "What are you talking about? I am only a pilot . . . a good one, perhaps, but still just a pilot."

"Yes, you do keep saying that. I do not know if you are afraid of the responsibilities in themselves or because they are at odds with your own desires." She paused, frowning. "Meran, I have been on half the ships in the fleet. I have met most of the Commanders and pack leaders, and I have heard enough about the rest to judge correctly. Someday soon you will command the Methryn. And if Councilor Lake spoke the truth, that this ancient war will be decided within our own lifetimes, then you and possibly you alone will win it for us.

"Meran, do you honestly believe that I am the first person, in all these years, to find a way into this city? That is actually only the best of three effective plans that I have. Others have surely discovered some of those plans for themselves. The difference is that no one has ever decided that the time has come to try, or knew how to actually go about doing it. You know what must be done, how it should be done and, I believe, how to make certain that it is done."

"And you will decide that for me, whether I like it or not?" Velmeran complained bitterly.

"Yes, by that much the choice is mine," she agreed. "I tell you that there is much that you must and will do in your lifetime, but I also promise that you will not face that future alone. If you cannot come with me, then I will stay with you."

"But . . . what of your own pack?"

She shrugged, unconcerned. "What pack? Two fighters and a transport? I have told you that Threl and Marlena want to retire soon. And Baress is no longer as delighted with the business as he used to be; he is my younger brother and wished only to stay with me. And I want to stay with you."

"Why?" Velmeran asked in the bewilderment of innocence.

"For love, if nothing else," she replied. "I have never loved and known that it was real. And I do not believe that you would even know what love is, or you would have known this long ago."

"But I . . ." Velmeran began to protest, but hesitated.

"Do you not?"

"Perhaps I do; I do not know. Perhaps, as you say, I do not even know what it is. I guess that I have always thought of love as a human indulgence. I have never sought love; perhaps I could have known it before, but I refused to recognize it. It frightens me, and I do not know why."

"Why?" Dveyella asked. "We are Kelvessan, what they call Starwolves. We were made for a purpose, yes. But our lives are our own. Are you afraid to claim the rights and privileges of being a real person, afraid that you will fail? Decide now whether you are a person or a machine. But I must leave you if you decide that you are a machine, for a machine can never return my love."

Velmeran sat for a moment in silence, and Dveyella thought that she saw the beginnings of tears in his eyes. And that moved her to pity, for she had not suspected that he was indeed so lonely and afraid.

"I still do not know if I love you," he said at last, not

looking up. "But I think that I could, for it seems that my heart would break if you were to go away."

Dveyella smiled. "Is that not love?"

She paused and glanced up, for a Feldenneh, a balladeer, was approaching timidly while the other musicians in her group waited near the entrance of the little cafe. Canine in form and clothed only in her own thick coat of fur, she looked to be no more than a large wolf walking with unusual grace on its hind legs. She held in her arms a gelvah, half harp and half guitar, the instrument of the Feldennye street balladeer. She stopped beside their table and dipped her slender snout over the upper neck of her instrument.

"Fair night, noble Starwolves," she said in a rich, velvety purr. "If it would please you, I have a song that I would give you."

"It would please us greatly," Velmeran replied, reaching for a coin in his belt pouch. But the Feldenneh quickly laid a slender hand on his arm.

"Please, it is my gift to you," she said. "The Feldennye do not forget that we come and go as we please because of you. A small gift, compared to what you give us. The people of the wolves are gracious."

"Who is a wolf?" Velmeran teased.

The balladeer smiled. "I have for you a very, very old song, as old as my own world. I fear that my poor translation does not do it justice."

She nodded to her fellows and struck the opening chords, then lifted her delicate muzzle to the night and sang.

Fair night, and darkness surrounds us softly,
Hidden where none in the world may see.
Here we are alone.
This night is our own.
Fair nights that we share joyously.

Come love, for love is the force that binds us.
Short is the time that we call our own.
Though night soon must fly,

Love will never die.
It lives in the cherished memory of this fair night.

The balladeer reset the tone lever of her gelvah and shifted smoothly into another song, now playing solo to the accompaniment of her fellow musicians. She turned and walked slowly away into the night as she continued to play, and the music carried clear and bright through the dark and deserted streets.

Dveyella rose and held out a hand to her companion. "Come. I know where we can get a room for the night, one cool enough to be comfortable to us."

"Why do we need a room?" Velmeran asked innocently.

Dveyella smiled tenderly. "Meran, promise me that you will never completely grow up."

They left together, silent and unnoticed, descending the curving path back toward the hotel at the port entrance. Near the top of that same passage, on a bridge overlooking a short waterfall, the balladeer paused to sing again. Her words carried through the clear, still air, echoing among the rocks of the underground stream, but still did not reach the sharp ears of the two Starwolves. For they were already gone.

Fair night, fair night delay!
Night is the realm of love.
Cherish the moment that love's fortune has spared you.
This night shall pass, and the light of dawn shall find you,
Disturbing your dream of love.
Beware! Beware!
Or night shall pass,
And dawn will find you alone.

Vannkarn was at its best in the later hours of the morning, from the time when the shops first opened until the midday meal. Then everyone seemed to be out and about the city; then the avenues were cheerfully noisy and all the stores from the simple stalls of the port market to the elegant and expensive shops of the Terraces, were filled with eager and alert buyers. At this time even Starwolves could mingle freely with travelers, tourists and native cave dwellers and no one seemed to take much notice.

But that morning it was too easy for Velmeran to dream of other things, after all that Dveyella had taught him the night before. It was not accurate to say that he had lost his innocence; that was a tall order for anyone, but she had put a sizable dent in it. At the very least he had learned that there was considerably more to this matter than he had thought; he had taken a mate, and now had to consider the consequences. True, his old loneliness had vanished and he felt more at peace with himself than he had in a long time. On the other hand, his cherished privacy was thoroughly and irrevocably invaded. He was frightened by the prospect that Dveyella might turn up pregnant, as unlikely as that was, and yet he was only too eager to try again.

Unfortunately, he did not seem to have any choice in the matter. Dveyella had decided that this was what should be, and he could not say no. Which was his own shy way of admitting that he wanted it just as much. Some things simply had to be, regardless of the risk. Let others think what they will. He was happy. Worried, but happy.

They were making their way through the crowded avenues leading to the more expensive shops of the upper Terraces when it came. Velmeran stopped suddenly and turned with abrupt swiftness. Dveyella saw the beginning of that move and interpreted it as one of alarm and in the same instant turned also, a gun in each set of hands. Two score humans nearly died of fright in the following moment, but that was all Dveyella could see.

"What is it?" she asked softly, putting away her guns.

"It seemed to me that I heard someone calling me," Velmeran replied uncertainly. "Someone is looking for me."

"Who?"

"Commander Trace, actually," he said, and shrugged at his own unwillingness to believe what he had just said.

Before Dveyella had any opportunity to comment, Donalt Trace himself appeared as if summoned by the mention of his name, approaching from a side street not fifteen meters away. He wore dress uniform, as he had the night before; towering a head above anyone else in the crowd, he could have no more disguised his identity than the two Starwolves might have. Having seen them as they passed, he now hurried after them as they waited.

"Val treron de altrys caldayson!" Dveyella exclaimed softly in Tresdyland before switching back to Terran. "Speak of the devil and he shall appear! But how did you do that? Telepathy of that order is a purely Aldessan trick. You are worth more than I thought."

Velmeran had no time to reply to that, even if he had an answer. He turned to the approaching Sector Commander and bowed his head as well as his armor would allow. *"Val edesson, Commander Trace."*

"Good morning to you, young Starwolf," Trace answered pleasantly. "I certainly hope that I have the pleasure of addressing Pack Leader Velmeran. I have been most of the morning looking for you."

"Oh? Surely there are not that many Starwolves in Vannkarn."

"As a matter of fact, there were five hundred and seventy-nine at last count," the Commander said, indicating for them to proceed to a small open-air cafe just ahead. "And, if I may say with no malice intended, they all look alike to me. But there are very few in black armor, and I believe that I have learned to recognize the two of you."

They took a corner table at the cafe, as far from the open as possible. Although feared and often hated, Starwolves in armor generated intense interest in themselves. But for a pair in black armor to be seated at the same table of a fashionable cafe with the towering figure of the Sector Commander was a sight never before seen in the long history of Vannkarn. Commander Trace was apparently unconcerned about the amount of attention they drew. He ordered cold drinks, nonalcoholic, for them all. And yet, for all his urgency, he seemed at a loss to know how to begin.

"You wanted to speak to us about something?" Velmeran prompted.

"Actually, I wanted to finish our conversation from last night," Trace began, still hesitant. "There are some things that I would ask. The martial creed does not allow you to sit down with your enemies and talk like friends. Can you understand that?"

"I believe so," Velmeran said.

"I admit that I have always thought of Starwolves as just machines cut from the same mold, identical and lifeless. Interchangeable components, you might say, for sticking behind the controls of your fighters. You have challenged me to think of you as people, and now I want to know more."

Velmeran understood only too well the Sector Commander's purpose in coming. It seemed that Donalt Trace was a wiser, more open-minded man than Velmeran had first given him credit for being. He had thought that he knew his enemy well enough, having sifted through every legend, myth and prejudice to come up with his own idea of what Starwolves should be. Confronted with reality, he accepted his error and sought to correct it. Velmeran, however, had no intention of being the source of the Sector Commander's better understanding of his enemy, especially since that knowledge would be put to defeating his own kind.

In truth, Velmeran hardly knew what to think. The Union had always underestimated the Starwolves, much to their own detriment. Why change things now? The Union could easily battle itself to an early death. On the other hand, if Union High Command had a better understanding of its enemy, it might be a little more interested in an early surrender. Velmeran quickly decided that he had already said enough the night before.

"Do you allow nonhumans in the military?" Velmeran asked suddenly after they had been talking casually for well over an hour.

"What?" Trace glanced up, startled. "Nonhumans? You know the Terms of Unification. Each race is a society in itself. Members of one race have no business in the affairs of another."

"With exceptions," Dveyella pointed out.

"With a very few exceptions," Trace corrected her.

"And yet several races are under Union rule," Velmeran observed.

"That is different. We control on the governmental level, but we do not interfere on the cultural level. Damn it, Starwolf, face facts. We cannot allow hostile alien elements within our own space. The Kalfethki would drive us mad with their ritual murder and terrorism if we allowed them free travel."

"The Feldennye are hardly a threat."

"And we make sure of that," the Commander said firmly. "How can you tell who will be a threat and who won't? Knowing you two, if I were to come upon a civilization of your kind, alone and untroubled, I would suspect that you would be the most peaceful, harmless souls—if you have souls—in all space. But I also know better."

"An interesting point. Although, for the likes of Feldennye and ourselves, it takes an enemy to make us fight," Velmeran said. "But returning to my original question, which you did not answer. In this sector you have the Kalfethki and two Feldennye worlds. I do not see you as one not to take advantage of a resource, and each does have something to offer."

"True enough, and I do admit it. We have been using Feldennye in clerical and highly skilled technical areas for some time now. We have no choice. Our own people can no longer do what they can. The Kalfethki are useful in some tasks, but they are also a tremendous security problem. I think that our new Shepherd sentries are much better."

"I did not find them all that dangerous," Dveyella commented.

"You did not?" Trace asked, eyeing her skeptically. "Do you think that we would do better with Kalfethki guards?"

"No, your sentries are superior to Kalfethki warriors —which, I am afraid, is not saying much. Your machines are loyal and more difficult to kill."

Trace laughed in private amusement. "I would suspect you of smoke-screening me, if I didn't know what you did to my sentries at Bineck. One, they say, was picked up and tossed down a stairwell."

Now Dveyella laughed, pointing to her contrite mate. "Ask him about that!"

Trace stared at him in amazement. "You picked that thing up yourself? My dear Starwolf, those mechanical beasts weigh over two tons!"

Velmeran shrugged. "It was not all that heavy. I thought that you had a better idea of just how strong we are."

"So I've heard." He paused for a moment, frowning at his own thoughts. "Does it never bother you, knowing that your race was made for a purpose?"

Velmeran frowned as he considered that. "Yes, we do think about it often enough. We know that we were made for a specific purpose, and that we would not exist at all except for that purpose. But I prefer to think that we were designed not for the specific purpose of flying starfighters, but for the more general function of space travel. Consider the independent traders, who have lived aboard their ships for tens of thousands of years now. They have become as much like us as nature can manage: small, strong and quick."

"And yet it seems to me that you are still as tied to your assigned task as if you had been a living machine,"

Trace observed. "Having been born a Starwolf aboard a Starwolf ship, you had little choice in the matter."

"Actually, very few of us are pilots."

"True, but you are a warrior and a leader. I can see that clearly enough just talking with you."

"Then, in a sense, our destinies are largely guided by our abilities and opportunities," Velmeran said. "My choices were no greater or less than your own. You are of the Lake clan, and you are the warrior of your generation. And so you were destined to be what you have become, or were shaped to be. Where then is your freedom?"

"I could have refused," Trace insisted.

"Could you? Have you ever thought about what your other choices might have been?"

"I cannot be anything but what I am," Commander Trace said, perhaps to avoid a more direct answer.

"That is also the truth for me," Velmeran said, and rose from his chair. "I am afraid that we must go now, since we both have packs waiting that must be back to the ship by noon port time."

Trace rose as well to stand towering above the two Kelvessan. "Then this must be our final farewell as friends, for if we ever meet again it will be as enemies. You are at least my equal. Time will tell which of us is the better."

"And who will that be?" Velmeran asked.

"The one who makes the fewest mistakes, of course."

"Well, what do you make of it all now?" Dveyella asked as they made their way quickly to the tram port.

"I think that Councilor Lake was telling us the truth after all," Velmeran replied absently. "Donalt Trace has something very much on his mind, something far beyond the petty mischief that Sector Commanders have always made for us. He is making plans for that last big battle. Götterdämmerung."

"What?" Dveyella asked.

"Ragnarok," he added, to her complete mystification.

He seemed to have resorted to a language that was neither human nor alien.

Dveyella would have asked for further explanation, but they were within sight of the tram platform and their packs were waiting. They had been in port less than a day, but to Velmeran it seemed like several. He wanted to collect his students and retreat to the ship before anything else could happen.

The first thing he saw was that Tregloran had ignored the warning about bringing home small, furry animals. Then he saw that this particular animal was neither alive nor real.

"Treg, what is that . . . that beast?" he demanded.

"Ah, Captain!" Tregloran replied jovially. "This is my wolf."

"Your what?"

"My wolf," the younger pilot replied. "An authentic replica of a real Terran red wolf, about one-tenth life-size and handmade by the nicest lady you could ever hope to meet . . . for a human."

"That is a fox, authentic in detail and about life-size," Dveyella said.

Tregloran returned an exaggerated look of indignation. "I have her word!"

"Let me tell you a story," Dveyella said, indicating for them to proceed up the ramp to the tram. "I read this many years ago, although I do not recall who wrote it. I am inclined to say Aesop, although I know that it was one of the Roman poets.

"It seemed that there was once a nursemaid who was having trouble with an unruly child. Finally she threatened to feed him to the wolves. A credulous wolf, passing by at that moment, overheard and sat by the door all night, waiting for a free meal that never came."

Tregloran glanced back. "Meaning?"

"Meaning that if you are a gullible wolf, do not believe everything a human tells you. Especially if it sounds like a bargain."

The Starwolves filed into a tram waiting at the bottom of the inclined shaft, the other passengers allowing them a car to themselves. The students' first port leave was drawing to an end.

"What does this do to the Councilor's theory of the decline of human intelligence?" Dveyella asked as the tram began its rapid ascent.

"Humans have always had a gift for deviousness and an ability to lie shamelessly," Velmeran replied. "And we have always been uncomplicated souls, our gullibility at odds with our own intelligence. It seems that human duplicity is still as great as Kelvessan simplicity."

Tregloran, in the seat ahead, glanced back over his shoulder. "If it gives you two any peace of mind, I should tell you that I was not fooled for an instant. I know a fox when I see one."

"Then why did you buy it?" Velmeran asked.

Tregloran shrugged. "Because I like it."

12

Mayelna glanced up as a pair of freight tenders emerged from the bottom of the monitor screen. Valthyrra Methryn had more than her share of audacity, setting herself in orbit just ahead of the station and then flying backward to face it, the cannons of her main batteries open and extended. Valthyrra seemed to court trouble, and yet her record was surprisingly clear of such undesirable incidents. She knew exactly how to play the game, and Mayelna knew better than to interfere.

"That is the last of it," Valthyrra reported as she swung her boom around to the recessed area of the upper bridge. "I am securing the holding bays."

Mayelna nodded, not looking up from the readout on her main console monitor.

"The last of the packs are in," Valthyrra continued. "We have fourteen crewmembers planetside due to come up on the last two transports within the quarter hour."

Mayelna nodded again.

"Velmeran and Dveyella are on their way up to the bridge."

Now that was news! Mayelna hit the hold button on her monitor and indicated for Valthyrra to bring her camera pod in a little closer. "Do they seem to have reached an understanding?"

Valthyrra chuckled mischievously. "That is an interesting way of putting it! Dveyella has moved her belongings into the cabin that Keth vacated a few days ago—the one adjacent to his own."

Mayelna only stared with open amazement. "Do you mean . . . ?

"Their understanding appears to be a personal one," the ship explained. "As, I believe, I did warn you it would be. Sheesh! If I had had my wits about me, I would have planted a bug on that boy. Then we would have heard some very interesting conversations indeed."

The result of that came as a surprise to them both.

"Son of a bitch!" Consherra, seated at her station on the middle bridge, declared. She gave her console a four-fisted thump that threatened to demolish it. "Son of a bitch!"

Then, to the speechless astonishment of the entire bridge crew, she leaped from her seat and left the bridge in a cold rage.

"I must say that I do not care much for her choice of terms," Mayelna remarked in the stunned silence that followed. "Makes it sound like I had something to do with it, and I do not like this any better than she does."

Valthyrra's pod turned to face her so sharply that the boom rattled. "What are you complaining about? You are only losing a son. I am losing the best would-be Commander this ship has ever had. When I think of how hard I worked to get that . . . girl on board. And if you had named him Commander-designate when I asked. . . ."

"I wish I had! Great Spirit of Space, I wish I had!" Mayelna returned, then shook her head and sighed. "Where did I go wrong?"

"Twenty-six years ago, when you thought you were too old to get pregnant," Valthyrra offered. "Quiet, now. Here they come."

"Act natural," Mayelna warned as she bent over her

monitor. Valthyrra aimed her pod upward as if she were giving the ceiling a cursory inspection, and a whistling sound came from her speakers. Mayelna silenced her with a sharp rap on the underside of her camera pod.

"I want you to meet my mother," they heard Velmeran say teasingly from the corridor outside the right wing of the bridge, speaking louder than he was aware.

"I have met your mother," Dveyella teased in return. "She is a real bitch."

Valthyrra turned her camera pod to the frowning Commander. "That would seem to make it unanimous."

Velmeran and Dveyella marched into the bridge, well-pleased with themselves and each other and totally oblivious to everything that had occurred prior to their arrival. Mayelna and Valthyrra both returned to their roles of complete innocence, the ship's cameras glancing about the bridge at everything except the approaching couple. But Valthyrra's impatience quickly got the better of her; she focused on the two Starwolves as if they had materialized out of the very air.

"Ah, Meran!" she exclaimed. "Pack Leader Dveyella. Did you have a good time?"

"Excellent!" Dveyella agreed happily. Mayelna made a rude noise.

"There is something that I would like to know," Velmeran said quickly. "Have you kept any statistics on the genetic deterioration of the human race?"

"Genetic deterioration?" Valthyrra's lenses seemed almost to blink in confusion. "Actually, it is hard for me to make any valid observations, but that does not change the fact of its reality. Our own human worlds are in slow decline, and there is every indication that the Union worlds are proceeding at a much greater pace. Especially the inner worlds—it is getting so bad that if all the machines were to suddenly stop, it is doubtful that they could ever get anything running again."

"Why?" Velmeran asked.

"Because Mother Nature is a stern mistress," she explained, the information analysis, storage and retrieval systems in her warming to the task. "The one rule of all life is change, and the driving force is survival. But that is a game that modern, civilized man has not been forced to play in nearly sixty thousand years. Nature intended that only the best should thrive and multiply, but for so long now nearly everyone survives—and reproduces indiscriminately. Change continued, but in a random, ineffectual manner, and once begun the process accelerates itself.

"Which, mind you, is all theory to explain what we have been observing since before I came out of the construction bay. What the future holds is even more speculation. But if the race is protected so that these conditions go undisturbed, then the present deterioration will continue."

"Which may very well happen," Velmeran said. "Since we are likely to take over the management of the human race in the very near future."

"The Kelvessan cannot provide for the entire species," Valthyrra answered. "I have often thought, when considering the problem, that the best thing we could do for humanity is to systematically destroy its entire civilization. I have even wondered if our very purpose is self-defeating. The Union has existed for most of recorded history, and we have been a catalyst, a unifying force, acting to keep it alive. I do believe that, had it not been preoccupied fighting us, the Union would have split into its various sectors and reduced itself to smoking rubble within the first few hundred years of its existence."

Velmeran brightened, seeing the logic in that. "Of course they would have. They would even yet. And a collapse of their civilization, a return to the most primitive of conditions, would also mean a return to the old laws of survival and natural selection, and the species would rejuvenate itself."

"Then you do understand," Valthyrra said approvingly. "That is our dilemma; wreck a civilization, and possibly save a species. But I already know that it is not our place to make that decision."

"The Union itself seems to be of the opinion that there is little hope," Velmeran offered. "They believe that they are already doomed to extinction, except for a few mutant races that are no longer strictly human."

"In a sense, there is very little of the race left that is strictly human," Valthyrra said as she glanced at the main monitor. Then, realizing what he had said, she snapped her pod around to face him. "And how is it, pray tell, that you are privy to what the Union thinks on the subject?"

Velmeran shrugged indifferently. "Councilor Lake explained it to us last night over dinner."

"Councilor Lake. The Councilor Lake, who runs this sector like he owns it—which he does?" Mayelna demanded. "And how did it come to be that you had dinner with Councilor Lake?"

"He invited us," Velmeran replied. "Just the four of us, Dveyella and myself, the Councilor and his nephew Donalt, the Sector Commander. We dined on Vinthran follycrab."

"But . . . why?" Mayelna demanded in exasperation.

"Apparently for the sole purpose of warning us. The Union knows that it is doomed, but it seems that the High Council intends to die fighting. Councilor Lake warned us to expect war the way we used to fight it, for as long as the Union's resources hold out. He said that we can expect two new, deadly weapons that will soon be used against us."

"But why would he warn you about what must be the Union's most secret plans?" Valthyrra asked.

"Because he knows that the Union cannot win. And I believe that, for a number of reasons, he wants us to win. Most of all, he believes that we will prosper once the war is over, and we will gradually take over complete dominance of their own civilization. That way we will keep the machines running and, if the human race does face extinction, it will be a gentle, painless death."

"Their civilization is more fragile than they might believe," Valthyrra said. "The heavily populated industrial planets are wholly dependent on off-world food supplies.

An interruption of that supply would starve those worlds in a matter of only a few short weeks. Eight- or nine-tenths of the Union's entire population would be destroyed before we could do a thing to stop it."

"Lake trusts us not to strike at civilian targets," Mayelna pointed out. "According to his plan, I am sure, the Union will fight for as long as it has warships in space and then it will surrender."

Velmeran nodded. "That just might be his plan. But that is not our immediate problem. That warning of things to come is."

Mayelna glanced up at him. "Do you have any idea of what that is about?"

"No, we will just have to wait and see." He shrugged helplessly. "Forewarned is four-armed."

Mayelna put her head in her hands and muttered a most dire obscenity. Then she lifted one hand to wave them away.

"Go away, children. All this business is simply beyond me, and I want no part of it." She glanced up at Valthyrra's camera pod accusingly. "Why did you never tell me about any of this?"

"You never asked," the ship replied simply. "We have waited a very long time for the Union to realize that it is doomed, knowing that it will begin the last phase of this war. We have known that we will have to be very careful if we are to save anything of what will otherwise be destroyed."

"But what would happen if we drew back and refused to fight?" Dveyella asked.

"The Union will fall apart very quickly once interstellar trade begins to fail," Valthyrra explained. "Then greedy men will seize control to wring what they can of dying worlds. Faced with starvation, entire populations could erupt into uncontrollable violence . . . or entire populations could be put to death so that the chosen few might live. As I said, the deaths of worlds will not be measured in years or generations, but weeks or even days. Or perhaps even seconds, if they turned their own planetary defenses upon themselves."

Velmeran shook his head slowly. "You envision a very dark future indeed, but I fear that you are right."

"You should be pleased," she told him. "Your stupid little dinner party was the turning point of this entire war."

"Then, by your leave, I will contemplate the future from the safety of my own room," Velmeran said as he and Dveyella turned to leave. Then he stopped short and turned back. "I am forgetting the real reason why I came. Dveyella wants to stay with us, and we would like to know if she can fly with my pack for now."

Valthyrra's camera pod bobbed as she momentarily lost control of her voluntary functions. She glanced at the Commander, but Mayelna only stared back in speechless confusion. She turned back to the younger pilot, pausing a moment to check her breakers and relays as an excuse to gather her wits.

"I see no reason why that would not be perfectly acceptable," she said in a surprisingly even voice. "Although I think that it would be something of a waste of her own abilities as a pack leader."

"We had thought that it would only be temporary," Velmeran explained. "Once Keth's students are ready to fly, I thought that we might disassemble my pack to form two new ones, the other under Dveyella's leadership."

"That sounds good to me," Valthyrra agreed, suppressing an uncharacteristic urge to giggle with hysterical relief. She glanced at the Commander.

Mayelna shrugged. "Suits me."

"So be it," Valthyrra declared with an air of finality. "You will be going out to hunt within the next few days."

"We were the last to hunt," Velmeran cautiously pointed out. "Remember? We ended up the hunted."

"With eight entire packs humbled, no one is going to complain," Valthyrra insisted. "And I want your children to make another run. Their confidence is high now, and I want them to hunt again before they lose that."

"A good idea," Velmeran agreed. "By your leave, Dveyella and I will get down to serious business."

"I would have thought that you had done that last night," Valthyrra remarked as the two young Starwolves left. Whether or not they heard her, Mayelna certainly did. She reached up to give the camera pod another swat.

"I actually got my way," Valthyrra muttered after a long moment. "Just when I thought that I had screwed things up beyond any repair, I actually got my way."

"Through no effort of your own," Mayelna added. She returned the monitor to hold and sat back wearily. "And I remind you that you have not had your way completely. I have not yet named him Commander-designate."

"If you do not, I soon will." That was no threat, but a promise. "Why do you think Dveyella gave up special tactics to remain with him?"

"To indulge her infatuation for my poor baby!" Mayelna replied hotly.

"She could have had him entirely to herself; he meant to go. He wanted to go," Valthyrra insisted. "This was her idea. She knows."

"Whoever had the idea, I do approve of one aspect," Mayelna said. "At least Velmeran will live to see his first hundred years. And not come back crying because his beloved mate ran out of her own portion of luck."

"Then we are actually in agreement?"

"Well, partial agreement," she amended. "I do not approve of this business. Velmeran is simply too young. What is the point of love anyway. It can be among the worst of personal catastrophes, and yet people go looking for it like fools."

"Command has turned you into the machine I never was. I would bet that you have never had a passionate thought in your entire life."

"Oh?" Mayelna asked, glancing up. "Do you suppose that I got Velmeran out of ship's stores? Besides, he was not out looking for his fate. Love jumped him from behind."

"It also seems to have done him a great deal of good, and I like the improvement."

"Yes, I can tell the difference," Mayelna reluctantly admitted. "What do you suppose Consherra is doing?"

"She is in her room crying."

"I had always considered them a likely match," she mused, and turned to her monitor yet again. "It is Consherra's own fault. Actually, I do believe that I could like this Dveyella very well indeed."

"Oh, indeed!" Valthyrra agreed.

Mayelna frowned, realizing that she had quite forgotten what this report was even about, and quickly set it back to its beginning. Thirteen officers at their posts did their best to pretend that they lacked both good hearing and natural curiosity.

"If it be love indeed, tell me how much," Valthyrra quoted softly. "There's beggary in the love that can be reckon'd."

Mayelna glanced up. "What?"

"Shakespeare."

Councilor Lake sat at his desk, bent over the long printout of some report, peering so closely at the print that his nose almost touched the page. Donalt Trace paused at the door, having seen that his uncle was not yet aware of him. He was suddenly impressed by just how old Jon Lake appeared after his return from the Union High Council. He was shrunken and frail, half-blind and more than half-deaf. Uncle Jon had not been a young man for as long as he could remember, and he was no longer all that young himself.

Councilor Lake suddenly became aware of his presence and hastily put down the report, somewhat guilty for having been caught peering at it so closely. His vision had been artificially corrected as much as possible, and yet he stubbornly refused to wear his glasses.

"Hello, Don! Do come in," he said jovially, indicating

the chair in front of his desk "I was just thinking about you. What brought you in?"

"Oh, just sneaking around to see if you were asleep at your desk again," Trace teased.

"Not this time," Lake said. "Have you been busy today?"

"No, not really. You know how business is, waxing and waning like the three moons of Maldeken. In terms of that analogy, there are no moons tonight."

"Maybe they just haven't risen yet," the Councilor said, pushing a report, still in its metal folder, across the table to him. "This should keep you busy. Your test ship arrived and is ready for fitting with bays for those new Tracer automatic fighters. They're sending her straight into airdock. Now what do you plan to do?"

"What else can I do?" Trace asked. "We load these machines and send that freighter back out to run the lanes until someone takes the bait."

Councilor Lake frowned. "I hate to think that our two young friends will be out there with those things."

"So do I, but it can't be helped. The Rane Sector has been the Methryn's private hunting ground for a long time now. I want those missiles tested here, in this sector, where the two of us have absolute control over their use." He paused a moment, reading the report. "At least they have the launchers up to one hundred percent. Those things are too expensive to lose because they explode when launched in starflight."

"When a twenty-two-ton missile converts its entire mass to energy, the term explosion is something of an understatement," Lake remarked dryly, then frowned as he glanced down at the papers that littered his desk. "I heard that you visited with our two young friends again this morning."

Trace glanced up at him in surprise. He knew, better than anyone, that Jon Lake employed many spies, electronic and living, to watch the movements of his associates and underlings, but he had never suspected that he was a subject of such scrutiny.

"What of it?" he asked casually.

The elder Lake shrugged, as if it was an unimportant matter. "I can guess why you wanted to talk to them again, and I approve. Did I not invite them to dinner? But it did cause a bit of talk—not quite scandal—and Rik heard of both incidents. He thought it beneath our dignity to consort with Starwolves."

"Oh? And what business is it of his?"

"He will be the next High Councilor of this sector, and I will at least give him the courtesy of hearing his opinions before I tell him to shut up," Lake replied. "We're in this mess now because we spent too long pretending that our enemy didn't exist. Whether we win this war or lose, at least you and I have started something good."

Trace glanced up at him, startled, "Lose? How can you even doubt?"

"You may be right, but I still have hope," Councilor Lake teased, then stopped short, suddenly aware that his nephew took this all very seriously. Donalt Trace, so thoroughly trained—perhaps too well trained—in his belief in himself, his own kind and the rightness of his cause, could not even consider the possibility of his own failure.

Or so he thought, although in truth Trace had been gnawing upon those same doubts since his final meeting with the two Starwolves hours before. He could admit to himself that Velmeran might be the better of the two. He even told himself that he could accept his defeats, so long as he could learn from them. There was room in his own mind for doubt, but it shattered his confidence entirely to hear his uncle express such doubts. He had never realized that so much of his own confidence depended upon his uncle's belief in him. Now he felt alone, empty and afraid.

Councilor Lake leaned back in his chair casually, his hands clasped behind his head. "Nothing has changed, really. You are still the only real hope we have of defeating them, or I would not divert half the profits of Farstell Trade to building your weapons. But will it be enough? Don, you have to have the right weapons to defeat them, and the best that we can give you might not be enough. That has been our failing before, as much as bad leadership. You know the weapons you need, but can we make them for you?"

"I can design weapons that you can build."

"But you have no one to use them."

Trace frowned. "I need Starwolves of my own. We can build fighters to match their own for speed and performance. But there is no mechanical brain that I can put inside the thing to make it fly as well as they can. To fight Starwolves, I need Starwolves. Fighting them would be easy enough on their level. But I work under such a handicap that I have to be ten times smarter than them to come out on top."

"Which you cannot be every day. Lord, Don, if you could capture and keep a Starwolf like Velmeran or Dveyella, I would move worlds to see that a viable race is created from their genetic stock." The Councilor paused a moment to reflect, and shook his head sadly. "They just have too many advantages. Velmeran might be smarter than you are and beat you at chess a thousand different ways, but he was designed for that. But I sincerely doubt that anyone can be bred for wisdom and insight. That is where I hope you will prove superior."

"And yet young Velmeran has more than his share of both wisdom and insight," Trace pointed out.

"Yes, what is it about that boy that is so special? He surprised even me—and I thought I knew Starwolves better than to underestimate them. There was really nothing he said or did that impressed me so much as just that tremendous sense of presence he seems to radiate. I fear, Don, that you have met your match."

"That remains to be seen," the Commander said coldly. "But I do know now just who my enemy is."

"You did not fare so well against him last night," Lake reminded him.

"I could have done no better against a computer, and

I'm told that there is a portion of every Starwolf's brain that is very much like a computer in its functions. But real life is very different from a game of chess. For one thing, some of my best pieces are not on the board but hidden under the table where he can't see them. Surprise has always been our best weapon, and I know how to use it."

"Just as long as you remember to play the game on your terms and not on his. Unfortunately, someone like Velmeran is very likely to play the game by your rules and still win."

"We will see," Trace said, rising swiftly to stand beside his chair. "I will take a look at that decoy ship."

"You might wait a couple of hours yet. I told them to stay clear of the area until the Methryn leaves, which should be any time now."

Trace shrugged. "Good enough. I have enough to do up at the station to keep me busy until they get in. I hope Rik sent me a decent ship."

"One of his best. Medium bulk freighter, and only five years old."

"Good! Send him my thanks."

"All right. Stay out of trouble," Councilor Lake called after him.

Trace smiled to himself as he paused for the door to open. Trouble was the very thing he had in mind.

The Methryn was barely an hour out of the Vinthran system when a rumor ran through her many decks like the echo of a meteor strike reverberating within her armored hall. Or, rather, a series of related rumors, and all of it surprising. Velmeran, it seemed, was going to stay. Dveyella had disbanded her own pack to stay with him—an occurrence that had caused Consherra, the normally reserved and capable second in command, to abandon her post while on duty. And, strangest of all, they had dined, by private invitation, with personages of no less import than Councilor Lake and the Sector Commander.

Valthyrra Methryn did not believe that she should be

made to endure confusion or be forced to assemble what she could of the story from bits and pieces. She considered that an accounting of that evening with Councilor Lake was very much her business, and she sent a probe, the most formidable of her remotes, to Velmeran's cabin to demand, entice or beg an explanation. As it turned out, she had no need to worry. While Velmeran and Dveyella were not willing to discuss such matters with the rest of the crew, they were willing to tell her anything she wanted to know about the time they had spent with Councilor Lake and his nephew. And since they had each committed most of those two conversations to selective recall, they were able to report to the very words.

For the most part, Velmeran related the story himself, since most of the two conversations had been directed at him. He sat, together with Dveyella, in the two large chairs in his cabin. Valthyrra's probe was perched precariously atop Velmeran's desk, so that its relatively short neck could place its camera pod on a level with the others. Velmeran was not entirely pleased to have her there, since the desk was of real wood, purchased on port leave months earlier, and the probe weighed over an eighth of a ton.

The probe's camera pod looked thoughtful. "What I wonder is if this was something Lake has been calculating for some time or if it was just spur-of-the-moment, because he was so impressed with the two of you and, as Dveyella so eloquently phrases it, well into his cups."

"Do you suppose that he might regret what he did and warn the Sector Commander?" Dveyella asked, then paused. "No, he cannot do that, can he?"

Valthyrra laughed. "I do not see how he can possibly explain that he told all the Union's best secrets to Starwolves over dinner. For better or worse, he cannot change what he has done."

"But do you think that he did tell us the truth?" Velmeran asked.

"Yes, I believe that he was completely honest with you—as far as he knew," she answered thoughtfully. "As I indicated before, I think that he is mistaken on a few points. But after careful thought, I believe that I now understand his motives a little better."

"How is that?"

"Councilor Lake is interested in saving as much as he can of many things: his race, his civilization and the wealth and power of the sector families. Yes, they will fight only so far and sue for peace, making the best deal they can in the process. Dethroned emperors of worlds, they would at least live on as merchant princes."

"Councilor Lake will not be there to negotiate that surrender," Dveyella pointed out.

"True, but he has trained his replacement well. It is a shame that the younger Lake—Richart, I believe—could not have been there as well." Her camera pod made some ambiguous gesture that might have been anything from a symbolic appeal to fate to a helpless shrug. "You, Velmeran, will live to see an end to this war. Perhaps you will even win it for us."

"What about the prophecy?" Dveyella asked suddenly.

Valthyrra's camera pod regarded her with a decidedly wide-eyed stare. "In my experience, there is no such thing as prophecy. Just educated guesses, wild guesses and things that never come to pass."

"And which do you suppose this to be?"

"This is the case of an educated guess," she explained. "We want the Vardon's memory cell in the hope that it will show us the way to lost Terra. Have you ever wondered how that was supposed to win the war for us?"

"How?"

"Because Terra holds the original Home Base of the Kelvessan Fleet. Terra and her moon have the construction docks and support factories for the assembly of Starwolf carriers—ships so technically advanced that they make me look like an antiquated hulk. Can you not see how the possession of such ships could win this war for us?"

"Yes, if there were crews for them," Velmeran said.

"Our ships operate at only a fraction of their fighter capacity now."

"Because that is all we have been able to use for some time now," Valthyrra said. "Five thousand years ago your race was in danger of dying out. At that time there were only eighteen thousand Kelvessan divided between twenty carriers and one freighter. Now there are sixty thousand divided between twenty-seven ships. And, as you shipborn ones are inclined to forget, there are now five and a half million Kelvessan who do not call themselves Starwolves but live in our stations and on human worlds. We can recruit a few shiploads of pilots and crewmembers from their numbers. And the rest are surely ready for a world of their own."

The idea obviously appealed to Velmeran, who smiled broadly. "Just imagine, the cradle of human civilization becoming the home world of the Kelvessan. But where would we live? There are few portions of the planet that we would find comfortable."

"Yes, there is that," Dveyella agreed. "And I wonder if there is anything left. We have no idea what forced the evacuation of the planet."

"Well, we will have to see," Valthyrra said. "We have to find it first. And for that, someone has to go after the Vardon's memory cell."

Velmeran was so deep in his own thoughts that he did not notice both Valthyrra and Dveyella staring at him expectantly. Although his qualities as a leader were beginning to manifest themselves quickly, he was still very much a child in one respect. Although he could make decisions in a hurry in an emergency, he still waited for his elders to initiate any spontaneous action. Since he did not comment on this idea, there was no way to tell what he thought about it. Valthyrra realized that the time had not yet come.

"I also wonder about these new weapons," Velmeran said after a long moment. "I wish that we did not have to just wait until those weapons are used against us."

"If we had some idea of what those weapons are or

where they are being built and tested, we could strike first," Valthyrra agreed. "Once we know what a weapon is, we are always able to neutralize it or guard against it. That is why all this talk of new, secret weapons does not worry me greatly. Those weapons tend to work well, if at all, only the first time they are used. Also the Union is in a constant cycle of forgetting and reinventing technology, so that they seldom come up with anything we have never seen before. You say that these are designs that Commander Trace himself worked out?"

"That is what Councilor Lake said," Velmeran answered.

"According to my intelligence work, Trace has had years of training in various fields of engineering," Valthyrra mused. "Because he is of undeteriorated human stock, he is much smarter than anyone who works under him and so he does it all himself. Engineering computers must take his finished plans for conversion into working designs."

"And can we take anything that he throws against us?"

"Yes, if we are careful. The effectiveness of a weapon depends most upon the cleverness of the user and the carelessness of the victim. You know yourself that carriers have been destroyed by simple means when they are caught unprepared, while at times the best of plans have gone awry for no apparent reason."

"And if Commander Trace has a fault, I suspect that it is his own impatience to act when he is sure that he is right," Velmeran mused.

"His second fault is that he believes that he is right until proven otherwise," Dveyella added.

"As well as the two of you have him figured out, we have nothing to worry about," Valthyrra said, amused. "It is strange to think that this ancient war is finally coming to an end. It will be nice, never again running this endless patrol."

Velmeran glanced at her, startled. "You are a fighting ship. What will you do when the war is over?"

"I shall probably be decommissioned," she replied dryly.

"What?" he demanded. "You are not exactly a machine to be thrown away."

"No, and there certainly will be enough police work for me to do for some time to come. Humans are capable of incredible mischief. But, once our duties are fulfilled and our fates are our own, I am sure that our old alliance with the Aldessan will be strengthened. They made us both, you and I. At least they drew up the specifications. We are like them in heart and mind. Someday I would like to be an explorer, a long-range research vessel. I would need no special modifications."

13

Leaving Vinthra, the Methryn followed the freight lane directly to the Kalleth system. There she paused outside the system itself and far enough to one side of the freight lane to remain undetected. The Kalleth system was near to Vinthra, still very much in the inner systems even if it was not one of the rich inner worlds. Indeed it lacked a single world that could have been made even remotely inhabitable. It was just a system consisting of four gas giants and a wealth of ore-rich moons and debris, with a total population of nearly a billion divided between several large mining colonies and stations. Bulk freighters brought in all the necessary supplies and equipment, and left shifting all the mass they could manage in raw ores.

Velmeran approached this run with as much apprehension as he had the last time. Instead of demoralized students and an older pilot who should not have been flying, he now had seven eager and possibly overconfident students and a girl he could not quite consider his subordinate. In truth he had little to fear for the younger members. After their last battle, they were out to prove themselves experienced pilots and the only danger was that they might try too hard. But Dveyella was another matter altogether, and one that he did not know how to approach.

"Dveyella, we must be pack leader and pilot now," he reminded her gently, almost questioningly, as they rode the lift down to the bay.

"Meran, for as long as I fly with you, we must always be pack leader and pilot to a certain extent," she answered. "For now, we must forget that we are anything else. I will follow your orders without question or condition. You must not be afraid to give me those orders."

Velmeran smiled uncertainly. "Yes, I know. The problem is more likely to be with me, not you."

"Why? Because there is love between us, or because I have been a pack leader myself."

"Both, perhaps," he admitted.

"If that is the case, then I will leave the pack," she told him. "There are other things that I can do aboard this ship. But there is no one else I love. I will never allow anything to come between us."

The lift deposited them on the lower flight deck and they went directly to their ships. Time was running short, for their target ship would already be on the edge of the system before they could overtake it. Steena and Delvon would have as many chances at the freighter as time allowed before he let Dveyella pull it down—if necessary.

The nine fighters thundered out of the bay, holding formation so tightly that even Velmeran was impressed. He did not know whether they were inspired by their past performance or if they operated under a collective urge to impress their new member, but he was grateful for the change. The last time he had taken this pack out for battle, he had been concerned that Vayelryn might bump wings in her nervousness. Now she snapped her fighter up into its running position above the pack with casual precision.

Shayrn brought her own pack in close behind his own and the two formations moved as one into starflight. They were upon their prey almost immediately. Valthyrra Methryn had been flanking it as closely as she dared, every scanning device she had turned on it, remembering the misfired trap that had awaited them last time. She reported a crew of seven and a half-filled hold, mostly inexpensive bulk items and what appeared to be an uncertain number of very small ships, smaller even than fighters, but nothing that she could identify as dangerous.

Velmeran intended to verify that at even closer range, bringing his own ship to within a thousand meters of the freighter to allow his own scanners to pick it over as best they could. There was something about this that seemed wrong, but he had no idea what. His own readings confirmed Valthyrra's. He lifted slightly above the freighter and dropped back a short distance.

"Have at her!" he announced to the waiting pilots.

Delvon came in first, quick but careful in his approach, and fired. His target was an easy one; he missed, but not by much. He dropped back to await his second pass as Steena took his place. She was just moving in when Velmeran realized what he did not like.

"Scatter!"

His cry sent every fighter of both packs heading as fast as they could directly away from the freighter. Hardly an instant later nine small shapes shot out of openings in the freighter's hull, curious little ships that seemed to consist only of a generator, a large star drive in rear and a slightly smaller one forward for braking, and a single turret that might have belonged on a destroyer. Their targets had been selected before their launch. Each shot unerringly after one of the nine fighters of Velmeran's pack. And their speed was terrifying.

For the Starwolves, this was a new and frightening experience, for they had never met anything in actual battle that could match the speed of their wolf ships and their own reflexes. These machines could not only pace them, but at first threatened to overtake their prey. The fighters dodged and twisted as best they could, but their deadly pursuers reacted with the barest instant of hesitation. These were obviously robots, the best automated missiles the Union could build. Nothing but a Starwolf could have survived aboard them.

The Starwolves engaged their star drives at full thrust in an attempt to flee. Now the drives of the pursuing missiles flared like sustained explosions of raw energy, the roaring of those crystal engines filling the heads of the pilots and confusing them to an extent, their special senses blinded by that violence. The machines were tearing themselves apart, their drives unable to sustain more than perhaps a minute of that terrible abuse. But that minute was all they would need.

Then, as the first few seconds passed, their responses began to deteriorate as their engines overheated both themselves and their on-board systems. Velmeran destroyed his with a shot from his tail cannon after luring it in. Dveyella took out her own, and the free ships then went after the remaining missiles. The one weakness of the machines, they soon discovered, was that once locked on target they appeared to be blind to all else.

Steena was in the worst trouble. She had been in her run at the moment of Velmeran's warning. Three shots had glanced off the hull of her fighter before she was able to evade; the damage was not obvious, but the ship remained slow to respond.

Dveyella went to her aid, moving in on the missile with careful deliberation. Perhaps her attack was too slow. The machine proved to be more alert than she had anticipated, and sensing this new danger, rotated its turret completely around. Dveyella was not even aware of her own danger until it fired directly into her ship's forward hull. The stricken fighter tumbled off to one side, engines flaring but out of control, as the missile circled around for the kill. An instant later it was ripped apart as Velmeran dived to her aid, too late.

"Dveyella?" he called out questioningly as he fell in beside the damaged ship, but he could not wait for a reply. "Report!"

"All clear!" Tregloran answered for the rest. "We have them all."

"Valthyrra?"

"Coming!"

"Make certain of that freighter," he insisted.

"I am already on it," she replied. A pair of powerful bolts lanced out of the darkness of space, locking with deadly accuracy on the bulk freighter that cruised seemingly unconcerned into system. The vast ship was vaporized by the explosion of its own generator.

"Dveyella?" Velmeran asked again as he brought his fighter in close to her own. The damage was not extensive, but it was all concentrated on the right side of the cockpit. A gaping tear in the tough material of the hull ran from where the seat would have been to a point two meters back. The forward window as well as the one on that side were shattered but had not popped out.

Had Dveyella survived that? Was she dead, stunned or simply too busy at the moment to respond? Even as he watched, the fighter righted itself and swung around on a new course, back to the Methryn. The remainder of Velmeran's pack gathered protectively about the two fighters, and Shayrn brought her own pack in close behind.

"I have control of her ship," Valthyrra informed him. "I will bring her straight into the bay. Help will be waiting."

At that moment Valthyrra was putting packs into space with clockwork efficiency. In contrast with that, her bridge was a scene of confusion. She was silently giving special orders throughout the ship, but her conversation with the packs was open and the bridge crew was beginning to understand that something was very wrong. Mayelna stood tensely beside her seat, watching the main screen attentively. Valthyrra condensed her map of long-range scan to project a set of graphs beside it. They represented Dveyella's failing life, the vital readings from her suit.

"Do you have that?" she asked of someone not on the bridge.

"I do now," Dyenlerra, the medic, replied over inter-ship com. "Great Spirit of Space, what hit her? Valthyrra, I want total life support equipment moved to the bay immediately."

Mayelna stirred for the first time, pouncing on the com controls in the arm of her chair. "Dyenlerra, answer me. Can you save her?"

"I can save her, yes," the medic responded, then hesitated. "Commander, you know what tough little machines we are. To put it simply, that girl is dead right now. But I can save her yet, if we can get her in before she realizes that."

"Velmeran?" That weak voice, as though echoing from the dead, brought instant silence.

"I am here beside you," he answered. "Valthyrra is taking you home."

"Where are you?" Dveyella asked weakly, uncertainly. "My windows are glazed."

"I am just off your right side," he was quick to assure her.

"Dveyella, do you hear me?" Valthyrra cut in gently.

"Yes, of course."

"Can you tell me how you are hurt? We need to know what to do for you."

"There is a pipe . . . or a rod . . . that has come through the hull," she answered slowly. "It has penetrated the armor on my right side, just below my lower arms."

"Is it in very deep?" the ship asked.

"I suppose," she said uncertainly. "It . . . it comes back out the other side in about the same place."

Mayelna closed her eyes and sat down wearily. Dveyella's hope was almost gone. Her body had tightened hard against the rod that had transfixed her, even torn veins and arteries, so that her blood loss was minimal. Ordinarily she would have survived an amazingly long time with such damage, but with ship and suit penetrated her wounds were exposed to the harsh emptiness of space. The terrible cold stabbed at her through the breaks in her suit and the rod, at first red hot, was now a spear of burning ice. She was quickly freezing, and she knew it.

"It would seem that I was wrong, Meran, when I said that nothing could come between us," she said, seeming to gain both strength and awareness. "Nothing in our lives can be that certain."

"Please, I wish that you would not say such things," Velmeran pleaded helplessly. "We will be back on board in a moment."

"Oh, I have not given up all hope," she assured him. "I have a fairly good idea of what my chances are. Because they are not good, there are certain things that I would not have unsaid. Soon I may be only a memory to you. I want it to be a happy memory and not a bitter one. We did not have time for many happy memories, but I would prefer that you remember only those."

Velmeran did not know what to say, if indeed there was anything that he could say. On the Methryn's bridge there was silence, a tense, fragile silence as they waited for fate to decide this desperate race. Consherra wept silently but stayed at her post. Valthyrra was running at her best sublight speed and wishing that she dared a short jump into starflight. But she could not bring Dveyella in any faster, not without killing the girl with stresses that she could no longer endure. All of her packs were out now, for all the good they could do, and she was closing quickly.

"Commander Trace is to be complimented on his new weapon," Dveyella said after a long, uneasy moment. "He was so angry at you when he could not beat you at chess. And the balladeer's song was so beautiful. That night was worth a lifetime. I remember that you were so afraid. . . ."

"You were quite enough to frighten anyone," he said when she seemed to falter. "You asked me that night if I loved you, and I was too confused to know. That is something I do not believe I ever told you. I hope that I did not have to."

Mayelna struck her armrest so hard that portions of it shattered. "Damn it, Valthyrra, you have to get that ship on board now!"

"Do you think that I am not doing my best?" Valthyrra

demanded, swinging her camera pod around. Then she paused. Mayelna had to wipe her eyes to glare fiercely at the staring lenses. An instant later the Methryn began braking hard to match speeds.

"Meran, are you there?" Dveyella asked suddenly, urgently. "Meran? I have no control over my ship."

"Valthyrra is bringing you in," he reminded her gently, although there was no mistaking the raw fear in his voice. "She is turning in front of us now."

Valthyrra said nothing, but too many of the life signs that she had been monitoring were beginning to fail.

"Meran, where are we?" Dveyella asked, only partly reassured.

"We are coming up behind the Methryn fast now," he promised her. "She is perhaps fifty kilometers ahead now. If your windshield was clear you would be able to see her lights."

But Dveyella did not hear him. Too many of her vital signs had abruptly ceased and others were failing quickly; whatever reserve of strength or fierce determination that had kept her alive was gone. Mayelna buried her face in her hands for the moment's indulgence in grief that she could spare, wondering at the same time how she could tell Velmeran. Valthyrra watched her for a moment of silent pity before turning away.

At Valthyrra's silent command the nine packs broke their running formation to thunder past the two lead fighters, engines flaring as they broke away to either side, the ancient final salute of the wolf ships. Then Velmeran's own pack broke away in pairs, one to either side, leaving the two lead ships alone in their hurtling approach toward the waiting bay.

Mayelna rose and shifted her suit into place. "Valthyrra, prepare a new heading into system. We will be going to low starflight speeds."

Valthyrra stared at her in disbelief. "Commander..."

"This has all been too fast for Velmeran from start to end. It is best, for his sake, to be done with it now." She stepped to the edge of the upper bridge to address the crew. "All officers to the bow deck. Consherra, do you think that you can come with me?"

The second in command nodded quickly, wiping her eyes, and paused only to collect her gloves and helmet from their rack behind her seat. Valthyrra called a lift to the bridge and held it for them, ready to rush them to the landing bay. If Velmeran was comforted by their presence, and if he drew from them the courage to do what he must, then they must be there. Later, she knew, he would want to be alone.

The two black wolf ships hurtled through the rear portal of the bay, still wing to wing. The front landing gear of the damaged fighter would not respond. Valthyrra brought it in gear-up, blowing the bolts so that the down-swept wings folded up flat.

Velmeran was out of his ship almost the moment it touched the deck, leaping from under a half-open canopy. A single bound took him completely over the second fighter, so that he was the first to arrive. He pulled open a small panel in the hull and keyed the canopy release. The lock mechanism released and the canopy clicked open a fraction, but the damaged struts would not lift it. Impatient with the delay, he took hold of the edges of the canopy and pulled back until it ripped loose, then threw it well to one side. Benthoran and an assistant, hurrying to his aid, hesitated at that unaccustomed display of violent strength.

But Dyenlerra was undaunted. She had her head beneath the canopy even as he was pulling it loose, removing the helmet from Dveyella's suit and opening the chestplate for the leads of her own diagnostic equipment. She waved Velmeran aside, then took the leads offered to her by the silent automaton. But she did not need the judgment of the medical scanner, not after all the battered ships that she had attended in the Methryn's bays. She could save almost any life, but she could not give one back.

Velmeran waited so patiently, she wondered if he really understood that death was irrevocable. Dveyella's

THE STARWOLVES / 217

eyes were shut and her face was pale, but she seemed only to be asleep, leaning back in her seat. The rod had penetrated the suit by only two small holes, and the armor hid the terrible damage that it had done. Dyenlerra turned to the medical scanner for its verdict, only to wonder that Dveyella had stayed alive and alert for as long as she had. She looked up at Velmeran and shook her head slowly. This was not the time for excuses or regrets.

His reaction to that was the same calm acceptance, as if he had already surrendered any hope he might have had to the inevitability of fate. Then the Methryn thrust herself into starflight and he glanced about, confused. Mayelna stood silently behind him, unnoticed until then, Valthyrra hovering at her side in the form of a supple-necked probe. Consherra, standing farther away, would not turn to face him. No one spoke a word, but he understood that a final task remained.

Turning back to Dyenlerra, he nodded gravely. She bent to remove the leads of the medical scanner, and together they unstrapped the suit from its restraints. Velmeran carefully lifted Dveyella's body from the ruined cockpit, holding the lifeless form in his four arms for the medic to extract the deadly rod that had transfixed it. Then he started toward the lift, not looking back to see if the others followed.

That ride up to the Methryn's bow was the longest that he had ever known. The others could only guess what thoughts filled his mind as he held the body of his mate in his arms for the last time. Grief, certainly. Rage, or as much of that emotion as his Kelvessan nature would allow, and frustration at a fate he could not control. He was alone, left with only a handful of memories of the short time that he had shared with Dveyella, and vague, fearful visions of a future without her. But beneath all the hurt was something he could not yet recognize, something that was strong and reassuring. He thrust it from his mind, offended by something good in the depth of his misery. And yet it remained, the force underlying his will, giving him the strength to do what must be done and to face the future that would follow. Later, perhaps, he would try to discover what it was.

The lift slowed to a stop and its doors snapped back, opening upon the forward observation deck. The wall across from the lift was lined with windows, now opaque from the glare of some external radiance. Directly ahead were the wide doors of the airlock, leading out onto the observation platform, the very tip of the Methryn's bow. Velmeran paused, bending slightly so that Mayelna could secure his helmet, while Dyenlerra quickly replaced Dveyella's. Then the others secured their own suits as they approached the airlock.

When the outer doors of the airlock opened, it was upon a blinding glare. The Methryn had shot inward to the heart of the system during her short jump into starflight, so that its sun loomed just off her bow. The observation platform was crowded with scores of silent, motionless suits, the white of officers and the black-trimmed white of other crewmembers, all except for the armored forms in solid black. All about the bow of the Methryn hovered nine packs of fighters and the remains of a tenth, so steady and still that they appeared suspended motionless.

Velmeran glanced down again, toward the slender tongue of the platform that extended out over the black bulk of the shock bumper which housed the Methryn's main battery. He walked slowly to the very end of that platform, down the narrow aisle formed by the ship's most senior officers. Mayelna and Consherra, as Commander and first officer, remained close behind him and to either side. Valthyrra's probe had remained behind, her presence felt in the ship itself.

Velmeran stood for a long moment in silence. Perhaps there should have been words, but he felt that anything of real importance had already been said. Even as he wondered where he would ever find the strength for this final act, he released his hold upon the lifeless form he carried. At the same moment the Methryn began to brake gently, so that it seemed that Dveyella's body was drifting away with increasing speed, welcomed into the fiery radiance of the star ahead and quickly lost in its blinding glare. The fighters broke away to either side, engines flaring, in their own salute. Then the Methryn herself began to turn slowly, the crewmembers on the platform turning in small groups to retreat back inside. Velmeran did not notice. As far as he was aware, he was alone.

As he would always be alone.

A short time later, Velmeran stood at the window of the rear observation platform, watching as the last of the fighters returned to the ship. Dveyella's star was now a point of light far behind, but he meant to stay and watch it recede into the distance until it was gone. Just as her body was long since gone, consumed by its fiery touch.

He had returned to the bay and had waited long enough to see that his pilots were safe. But he did not approach them or allow them to know that he watched. They were frightened and confused, for this was the first time that they had seen death. And he knew as well that they grieved with him, and for him. They would not have known what to say if they had had to face him, and so he spared them that pain.

Something had occurred to him, almost as a shock, as he had stood there in that dim corner of the bay. The crewmembers hurried about their duties. The fighters had come in, and the pilots had departed to their own cabins. Life did go on, just as time had not hesitated for an instant. The life that had been Velmeran and Dveyella was dead and past. But the life that was Velmeran alone remained, with duties and tasks to be done. Even if he had met death with her, or in her place, little else would have changed. That simple, self-evident realization had the ability to surprise, and he had taken it with him to the observation platform to gnaw upon in his thoughts as he waited out the Methryn's departure.

Dveyella had said that he should recall her in happiness and joy, not in bitterness and sorrow. And as much as he was consumed in grief, as much as he would have liked to indulge in the self-pity of the belief that he would grieve forever, he knew that it would not always remain so. He had been surprised that life continued after her death because he had never envisioned a future without her, and he had tried to deny that he could live without her even as that dreaded future became present reality. As long as he continued to live, he would continue to be challenged by the future just as he was stalked by the past.

Below he could hear the closing of those big doors as the bays were sealed, the distant vibration as fighters in their racks were being transported up to their storage bays. He looked back at the distant star a final time, striving to impress that vision forever upon his memory, aware that this glimpse would be his last. A moment later the Methryn leaped into starflight.

In the time that followed, as his grief became numbed by acceptance, Velmeran came to realize that he regretted most the lack of something real and solid that stood for the short time that he and Dveyella had spent together. At least, if he had nothing material to stir his memories, he still had the memories themselves. Cherished memories.

And a dream.

Gradually he became aware of that dim, curious feeling that had underlain his pain and confusion from the start, like the drone note of a song on the balladeer's instrument. Surprisingly, he found it to be courage. Not the thing that he had always assumed to be courage, the bravery required to get inside a wolf ship and face danger and death. This courage was an inner strength, a confidence that was new to him. Dveyella had made him content to be Kelvessan and a Starwolf. Curiously, that contentment remained. Together with courage, he wondered if it gave him the strength to face what he had always feared. To face himself, what he was, what he did not like in himself and what he wanted to be. Indeed, he was certain of that strength, and it delighted him.

Courage of this sort was the seed of resolution. And resolution combined with a dream was the foundation of the future.

At last he slept, exhausted physically, mentally and emotionally. Kelvessan never slept unless they were very tired. Ordinarily he did not much like it, this unfamiliar and disquieting retreat into oblivion, but this time he welcomed it as a temporary escape from his torment.

As few as his hours of escape were, he awoke to a greater sense of peace than he had known, or at least a greater sense of acceptance. He was by no means free of the pain, nor would he ever be completely free of it. But this awakening was in some ways a rebirth, for this was the beginning of a new life. His short life with Dveyella had come to a sudden end. Nor was this a return to the life he had known before she had come, for he was by no means the same person. That Velmeran had been a child, unsure of himself, of what he was or what he wanted, afraid to try because of the greater fear of failure.

The Velmeran he had become was still a child in many ways, he knew that, still afraid of others, perhaps even more afraid of being hurt. But he no longer needed others, certainly not someone braver and surer than himself to lend him strength. He knew for the first time what he was, as a Kelvessan and as a person, and he accepted it even if it did not completely satisfy him. He knew as well what he wanted. No longer would his existence be defined by what was expected of him, only what he expected of himself.

The Methryn remained in starflight. Velmeran had no idea where she could be going, and he did not particularly care. Both Mayelna and Valthyrra stayed well away, and he was glad for that. For a time his only contact with the ship outside his cabin door was a simple remote that brought him food from time to time. As long as it appeared that he was to be left alone, at least he could take some advantage of it. Valthyrra, impatient to know what he thought and felt, was at first mystified and then delighted to discover that he was making extensive use of his access terminal to the ship's computers. She was even more surprised when she figured out what he was planning to do with the data he sought. Problems did have a way of working themselves out, she realized with satisfaction.

The Methryn's destination was Alliolandh, a planet of a small system just on the fringe of the Rane Sector. Alliolandh was a rugged, barren world, cold and wet, empty of all but the most rugged life because nothing else could survive there. It was the type of place the Starwolves could appreciate, one of a few places in Union space they could visit without being concerned that Unioners were watching them.

Velmeran was on the com as soon as he felt the Methryn leave starflight, asking to know where they were. Korleran, the communications officer, hardly knew what to make of that question, and she did hesitate when he asked her to relay his request that his fighter be brought to the deck as soon as possible. Apparently her delay was to consult with a higher authority, for Valthyrra herself came on a moment later to assure him that it would be done. The incident left him to wonder if the crew was beginning to think that he had fallen out of his orbit. Soon, he reflected, their suspicions would either be confirmed or denied.

It was planet dawn over the area where Velmeran wanted to make his run, and so he landed his ship on a narrow stretch of beach backed by rugged peaks and ridges of broken rock to wait an hour or so for daylight. The morning wind was cool and fresh, so he took off his armor to sit naked in the sand and watch the rolling waves. This was a rare privilege, for the Starwolves had no planets of their own, only a very few places where they could put aside both their armor and their shells of remote dignity.

Curiously, the Kelvessan did not consider themselves at odds with nature. As completely engineered as their own race was, they remained living animals. Although their own world was a machine, they welcomed planetside life with fascinated delight. There were, of course, many aspects of nature that frightened them: the unaccustomed openness that they normally associated with empty lifeless space, the great beasts in the wild and the strange sounds in the night. Those were unwarranted fears, born of unfamiliarity, since there were few things in nature that could harm them. Still they welcomed, even longed for it, perhaps because they recognized it as something they thought that they could never have.

As soon as the morning sun was well up, Velmeran put himself back into his armor and returned to his ship. He realized, as he took his fighter above the tumbled heights, that he could not have wanted a better day, at least not on this turbulent world. For a time he flew along the coastal mountains, weaving around rocky peaks and up narrow valleys, just for the joy of flying. He told himself that this was an evasive maneuver, knowing that Valthyrra was surely watching, that her attention would soon turn to other matters if she thought that he was only prowling up and down the coast. The truth was that he was just a little frightened. His computer projections insisted that this could be done, but his doubts remained. Failure would surely mean his life; even if he survived the crash, he doubted that he could get out of his suit before he drowned. But this had to be done.

He turned out over the open sea, still keeping his speed down and his attitude low. At the same time he fed his microdisk into the ship's computer, waiting nervously as it digested the instructions he gave it. But it was agreeable, quickly indicating that it was ready. At his order the on-board computer began to reform the atmospheric shield that protected the ship like an invisible shell. Slowly the shell narrowed and elongated, altering its already tapered form to become a slender shaft a hundred meters long and no wider than the tips of the fighter's down-swept wings.

Velmeran made a final check of his scanners, insuring that he was indeed over open, clear water. Then he brought the nose of the fighter down gently, reducing speed, carefully inserting the tip of that reformed shield into the sea. There was no indication of contact except for a momentary loss of speed until the ship followed its shield under the waves. There was a smooth, rolling shock as the shield around the ship filled with water, and then it was completely under and leveled off perhaps thirty meters below the surface. He realized that he had succeeded, that the fighter was cruising at five hundred kilometers per hour underwater.

Dveyella had been right. Water was just another atmosphere, considerably denser, to a ship that flew tucked within layers of water at graduated speeds. The fighter was not trying to force its way through a heavy medium, but flying within a bubble of water that was moving at a speed equal to its own. There was still considerable drag transmitted to the fighter from the forward cone of the shield, so that it took a larger portion of the wolf ship's considerable power to maintain the same speed. Already he was traveling faster than most unshielded vessels could have gone.

But this speed was nearly as worthless to him as complete failure. Slowly he fed power to the engines, gradually building speed to just below the four-thousand-kilometers-per-hour speed limit the computer had projected. He could tell that the ship was indeed approaching its limit; it continued to hold smooth and steady, but responsiveness had deteriorated to a dangerous level. He tried not to think of the danger of hitting something in the water, since he could not use the debris shield; it would not have acted upon the molecules of water itself, but there was enough suspended silt and microscopic life that the drag from the shield would have been like opening a large parachute. He trusted that the atmospheric shield would throw anything like a fish away from the approaching ship.

Satisfied that his plan could succeed, he reduced

speed by half and brought the fighter back up into the sky, then applied speed again as he drove the ship straight up into the morning sky. The dream was still a very long way from being a reality, but now he knew that it could be done.

14

$\blacktriangledown\blacktriangledown\blacktriangledown\blacktriangledown\blacktriangledown$

$\blacktriangle\blacktriangle\blacktriangle\blacktriangle\blacktriangle$

Velmeran made three practice runs before returning to the ship. The first order of business, he decided, was business, and that meant checking into the condition of his pack. He realized guiltily that he had not given his students a single thought since the attack. That was not exactly the truth, of course; he had thought of them often those last three days. Now was the time for him to be pack leader again.

Finding the members of his scattered pack was no small task, for they had hidden themselves throughout various parts of the ship. Four had retreated to their mothers' cabins, the only place they could find in a hurry. Kelvessan maintained loose ties with their parents and many, like himself, did not even know their father. He was surprised to find that Baressa was the mother of the twins Tregloran and Ferryn; that not only served to explain where they had acquired their quickly developing talents as pilots, but also reassured him that he was not the only Starwolf on this ship with a disagreeable dame. Few pilots were offspring of mothers who were themselves pilots, since the pilots had less time to devote to having children than other female members of the crew.

The other members of his pack had simply hidden

themselves in holes of their own finding, and it took Valthyrra's special talents to locate them all. Velmeran had them in their suits and down to the landing bay before they were hardly aware of what was going on. He had begun to realize that his students were quickly becoming very accomplished pilots, but any pack that was going to fight with him needed to know a few special tricks. Returning to the same coastal region, they spent the rest of the morning, local time, practicing high-speed low-level runs over both land and water and stalking each other in mock combat.

It was later in the morning when he became aware of a ship coming into the system, and moments later he recognized it as a Starwolf carrier. That surprised him, although he realized that, if he had not been so involved with himself, he should have expected it. Leaving his students to play on their own, he returned immediately to the ship. The incoming carrier was approaching fast, dropping out of starflight at the very last moment, so that it was braking into orbit even as he climbed out of the atmosphere.

The strange carrier settled into orbit barely its own three kilometers' length behind the Methryn. Passing close beside her as he made his final approach, Velmeran looked her over as best he could. Since no Starwolf ship, from carrier to fighter, bore markings of any type, he still had no idea who it could be. He was somewhat annoyed with himself for not anticipating this. Even after such a disaster, the Methryn would not retire to such a place as this simply for a break. Warning the other carriers about the new weapon was a matter of priority, but she would have already sent word far and wide. There was only one reason why she would call other carriers to her here. A council of war was about to take place; the Starwolves were going to exact dire payment for Dveyella's death.

Just after he passed the second carrier, a single fighter shot out from beneath it to fall in line directly behind him. He wondered who would be in such a hurry; perhaps it was her Commander, coming to confer in person. Mayelna did

not fly herself, mostly because it was too harsh of a reminder of what she had given up. But Commanders were
always chosen among the pack leaders, and some kept their
own fighters even if they did not fight. He knew that he
would.

Since Valthyrra must have directed the pilot to follow
him in, he landed just to one side of his usual position in
the center of the deck, allowing the second fighter to set
down beside his own. Their racks were brought in together.
Although Velmeran did not lack assistance, he saw Benthoran go to the aid of the visitor. He did not think about it
until he was on his way to the lift, passing in front of the
two fighters. He saw Benthoran speaking with the pilot, a
tall, thin and rather good-looking girl. Benthoran called
him over with a wave of his hand, although Velmeran
joined the pair with some reluctance.

"Captain, can you show our guest to Mayelna's
cabin?" he asked.

"I was not aware of any difference in the design of our
carriers," Velmeran snapped, bad manners born of his
preoccupation. Realizing that, he shrugged and attempted a
smile. "Actually, I was on my way to the bridge anyway."

Leaving her helmet with her fighter, the pilot joined
him quickly. But they did not speak until they entered the
lift. As soon as the doors snapped shut, she placed a hand
on her chestplate and bowed her head in polite greeting.
"Pack Leader Daelyn."

"Pack Leader Velmeran," he replied.

She stared at him, first in surprise, then with a curious
intentness. "Pack Leader Velmeran? Your mother is Commander Mayelna?"

"Yes," he replied uncertainly. Had he already acquired
this kind of reputation? He thought it best to change the
subject. "I had wondered if you were the Commander
coming over to talk business."

She laughed easily, apparently satisfied with him.
"No, although I am Commander-designate of the Karvand.

This is only a social call, although we will certainly have enough business to discuss when the Delvon arrives."

"Have you known Commander Mayelna long?" Velmeran asked. Now that he knew most of what he wanted, he wondered if there was still any point in going up to the bridge.

"Oh, yes. All my life, in fact," Daelyn replied. "I was born on this ship and lived here until thirty years ago."

"You flew with Mayelna?"

"Quite some time!" she laughed, with a look of terror that told him that she had indeed known Mayelna very well.

The lift came to a stop and the two parted company, Velmeran hurrying on to the bridge to find Consherra. If Mayelna was in her cabin, he knew that he could get all the news he wanted from the helm or the ship herself. Daelyn took the side corridor to Mayelna's cabin. Mayelna was stationed, as always, behind a monitor; only Valthyrra knew what occupied so much of her time. This time, however, she had apparently been hard at work on some task of her own, for her desk was strewn with lists she had made and diagrams she had drawn up. Whatever it was, she abandoned it quickly enough when she saw who was calling.

"Daelyn!" she exclaimed, leaping up. "Valthyrra warned that you were wanting to board, but I did not think that she meant so soon."

"After all these years, I was not going to be slow about it. You do look well," Daelyn said, although that was not entirely the truth. Her last memory of Mayelna was that of the Starwolf who had not changed a day in three hundred years, while the Mayelna she saw now was beginning to grow old. That startled her, perhaps, but it did not worry her. What did worry her was the fact that Mayelna looked as tired as if she had personally fought half the sector fleet in a twelve-hour running battle.

"You know, I will never get used to seeing you behind

a desk," Daelyn continued. "I can only remember you in black armor, the meanest wolf on this ship."

"I am still mean," Mayelna said, very matter-of-fact. "Ask anyone. You left this ship a long time before I became Commander."

"You chased me out," Daelyn corrected her.

"I did no such thing!" Mayelna insisted. "I was asked to make a decision as though I were the Commander."

"Gelvessa Karvand thought me capable enough."

"Yes, and she got a bargain. So it would seem that— once—I did make a mistake," Mayelna admitted, with obvious reluctance. "A very bad mistake. And you were gone. Do you regret it?"

"Gelvessa has named me Commander-designate," she said, by way of reply. Then she saw Mayelna's reaction to that. "Really, do you have to look so horrified? I know that you would not approve. . . . "

"No, and time would prove me wrong again," Mayelna interrupted impatiently. "My problem is more acute. I need a replacement now."

"And no one suits you?" Daelyn found that easy enough to guess.

"If you have waited these many years to point out my mistakes and shortcomings, then you are too late. Is this your idea of revenge?"

"No, because I really do have no regrets . . . except, perhaps, one," she frowned. "I met Velmeran on the way up."

Mayelna glanced at her expectantly. "So?"

"He seems like you. Just as mean and ill-mannered. And even more brooding."

"Then you have not met Velmeran," the Commander remarked as she leaned back. "He is quiet and introspective, yes. But not mean. This is a bad time for him, and I hate for you to have to meet your younger brother under these circumstances."

"He has been in trouble?"

"He has been in trouble for a long time now. His first

pack was shot out from under him; he was one of two survivors. Then I let Valthyrra make him a pack leader of seven students and one old fool who should have retired. Now he has lost a pilot the last two times he has led his pack out. That girl we lost was flying under him."

"That is bad," Daelyn observed.

"She was also his chosen mate."

"That is worse."

Mayelna nodded slowly. "Through no fault of his own. Any other pack leader would have lost more. He is the best pilot I have. The best leader as well, I am beginning to think."

"From you, that is high praise." Daelyn did not mean that as a joke.

"Then you know that it has to be the truth. He is better than I ever was. That is why he is going to have to command this ship when I go."

"Is that so bad?"

Mayelna glanced up at her. "You are a pilot. You should know."

"I understand."

"I hate to do this to him, since I know that he would not want it himself," Mayelna continued. "Fate is kind and cruel to him at the same time, but lately it seems that he has been made to suffer more than his share. I would shed a tear or two for him, if I were not so mean."

"It seems to me that you are not nearly that mean," Daelyn said. "I do not know him, but it seems to me that he has the strength to endure this."

Mayelna shook her head slowly. "He never was that strong before. Dveyella gave him something to love and to believe in. But he had to stand by and wait for her to die when no one could do a thing to help her, and I wonder if his strength has died with her. That is one thing I am still waiting to find out."

Daelyn glanced over her shoulder, as if she expected to see her brother standing there, and shrugged. "The Velmeran I met was very strong. Whatever he was up to, he seems quite resolved about it."

"He was out running his pack," Mayelna said. "Some tricks that he had learned flying special tactics. What he has in mind . . ." She shook her head helplessly. Then certain pieces fell suddenly into place, and the shape they revealed frightened her. "Of course. He knows who killed her, and he wants payment from the source. Damn that Valthyrra, she knew this from the start."

"What?" Daelyn was bewildered, but concerned by her mother's obvious distress.

Mayelna caught her in a firm stare. "Daelyn, you have to help me put a stop to this."

The Delvon arrived barely two hours later, and a meeting was called in the Methryn's largest council room as soon as representatives of the three carriers could gather. The main table was filled to its limit. The two visiting ships were represented by the usual probes, perched on the arms of their chairs with their long necks snaking about as they observed the gathering. Each ship was represented by Commander, helm and Commander-designate, seated together in small groups. Valthyrra Methryn held forth from on high, enjoying the greater mobility of her camera pod.

Velmeran was seated near the head of the table with the delegation from his own ship, by all appearances in the role of Commander-designate. Mayelna wondered at that. He would be expected to testify, certainly, since he had been in the middle of all these strange events. But that did not earn him a place at the council; he should have been with the other pack leaders in the crowded gallery, waiting to be summoned. But she was ready to bow to the inevitable, and this might even begin preparing him for that task. She was even just a little proud to see both of her children in that same honored position.

Valthyrra called upon Velmeran to testify from the very start, having him take up the story from it's true beginning with the evening he and Dveyella had spent with

Councilor Lake. He recounted the Councilor's exact words, relying upon his total recall to quote accurately. He was allowed to continue uninterrupted to the end, although at that point the Kelvessan members of the council wanted to know more about the possibility of the extinction of the human race. Only the ships themselves were not surprised. For them, the only real news was the discovery that the Union had finally recognized the threat.

Schyrrana, Commander of the Karvand, shook her head slowly. "This is all quite beyond me. I came here to deal with the worst problem I have faced in my entire life, and now you tell me that the war is nearly over. Mayelna, you have had time to think on this. What do you make of it?"

"I think that these animated hulks that we call home have been keeping secrets from us," she replied. "But if they say that it is true, that they have been keeping watch for some time, then I am ready to believe it."

"Lake is faced with the destruction of all human civilization," Valthyrra explained. "And, being a close approximation of an honest man, he is willing to sacrifice the Union to save the civilization that it has always fed upon. He is going to throw the resources of the Union against us, forcing us to fight and knowing that we must win. He knows that we are the only thing that can save his civilization; by defeating it, we also accept the burden of caring for it."

Schyrrana snorted derisively. "That certainly is having the last laugh!"

"Wait a minute," Korlan of the Delvon interrupted. "We still have this new weapon to deal with. Is there any way that we can detect it in advance, or neutralize it?"

"This weapon is just a variation of the old Wolfhound missile design," Valthyrra explained, putting up a schematic on the main viewscreen. "They used it to limited effect in the early days of the war, and again when I was young. Its main fault is obvious enough. Detection is simple, because you can scan them inside your target ship. I saw the ones that were used against us inside that freighter, but I mistook them for something else."

"But is there a way to fight them?" Korlan insisted. "Ignoring the ships that carry these missiles is no answer, since the Union would quickly put a clutch in every military and commercial ship it has."

"Actually, we have a very simple method of dealing with them," Valthyrra said. "Before, when we knew that we were after a ship that carried wolf-chasers, we would send along an adapted transport that carried a powerful field generator. The first pack would run in and lure the missiles out, and the transport would blind their scanners with a static distort. Then the first pack would destroy the helpless missiles, while the second pack would go in after the ship itself. That is one reason why the packs run double to this day."

"Also, when we went after military targets, we would lay down a blanket distort from the first," Gelvessa Karvand added. "Then they would most often realize that they could not even launch at all."

"Still, they are very dangerous, when you suddenly get nine in your face when you are not expecting it," Thenderra Delvon said. "Velmeran was lucky to come away as well as he did."

"He did not lose any ships in the initial attack," Valthyrra said. "He warned his pack away at the last moment before the wolf-chasers launched, and that was what saved his pilots. Dveyella ran into trouble when she went in to help someone else."

"How did he know?" Thenderra asked.

Valthyrra turned her camera pod to regard the younger pilot. "Meran, I never have figured out what did clue you to the trap. How did you know?"

Velmeran shrugged. "A lucky guess, for the most part. Lake's warning of a new weapon was very much on my mind. I was not about to take a chance, when my fighters were right on top of that ship and it still did nothing to evade. It seemed to me that we were being lured in."

"The stories I have heard about you must be true," Korlan said. "I do not know if any other pack leader would have made that connection."

"The next question, I suppose, is what countermeasure we are going to take," Gelvessa said. "I suppose that we are in agreement that we must answer this attack with some action of our own."

"That is simple enough," Valthyrra said, and brought her camera pod around to face her young pack leader. "Velmeran, will you explain your plan?"

He glanced up at her sharply, understanding only too well exactly what she meant. "You have been watching me."

"Of course," she replied with no shame. "It was not hard to figure out what you were planning. Now I would like for you to explain it to everyone."

Velmeran had only a moment to collect his wits. And, after his initial resentment, he could see that it was very much in his interests to ally himself with Valthyrra. They shared a dream. She needed him to do it, and he needed her to arrange the opportunity.

"I intend to recover the memory cell of the Vardon," he announced simply. "I have discovered a way to get an attack force inside Vannkarn undetected."

He paused then, knowing what the reaction to that would be. The only members of the gathering who did not appear surprised were the mechanical manifestations of the visiting ships. Mayelna looked dismayed, but he had expected that. What he had not expected was the eagerness he began to detect.

"I have been made aware that there is an unknown and unguarded entrance to Vannkarn," he continued. "An artificial tunnel, leading down from the lake near the port trams to the sea several kilometers away. A special attack force can approach the planet through the magnetic corridor and fly underwater to the entrance of that tunnel."

"Fly underwater?" Korlan asked, stilling a second outburst with that important question.

Velmeran nodded firmly. "The atmospheric shields of our ships can be adapted for underwater flight. . . ."

"In theory!" Schyrrana interrupted.

"In fact!" he insisted. "I have done it myself—three times—in the seas of the planet below. I was able to achieve a test speed of nearly four thousand kilometers. That means a two-hour flight from the polar corridor to the tunnel entrance, but it can be done."

"Assuming it is done, what then?" Schyrrana asked.

Velmeran frowned, hastily assembling his plans. "I know of a transport, adapted for Dveyella's special tactics team, that has a large cargo bay and handling arms that can be used to carry out the memory cell. My computer projections show that a transport can fly underwater as well as a fighter, so that is no problem. Aside from that . . ."

"Assuming that you have the complete resources of these three ships at your command," Valthyrra told him gently, encouragingly. "You are giving the orders. Tell us what you need."

Velmeran sat back for a moment, deep in thought. "I would like to lead ten full packs into the city, mostly to serve as a distraction. Tregloran and I will guard the transport during the securing of the memory cell. There is another pilot, Baress, who is very familiar with special tactics. I will send him with a pack or two to destroy the generators that power the dome shields and planetary defenses. With all the major power systems out, we will simply punch a hole in the dome and leave unopposed.

"By that time, the system fleet will be closing in to intercept us. That is when the remaining packs will attack the Union Fleet from behind, coming in two or three large groups. They will crush the fleet between them, and we will shoot a hole for ourselves during the confusion. Valthyrra, I am hoping that the ships will have acquired maps of the Vannkarn complex, especially of the generator stations."

"Of course," Valthyrra replied. "Actually, we have always known about the underwater entrance."

Korlan glanced at her questioningly. "Why have you never gone after the memory cell before?"

"The time had not yet come," she answered simply.

"And this is the time?"

"Has it not been said that the memory cell would not be reclaimed until the end of the war was drawing near, so that it can show us the way to Terra? Who do you think started that rumor? Besides, we have never had someone like Velmeran to go after it."

Mayelna made a small derisive sound that only those nearest to her could hear, her first contribution to the conversation in some time. Valthyrra Methryn was about to get her way in everything she had ever wanted. Mayelna wondered what she could do to stop this, although it already seemed too late for that. She wondered if she should even try.

Velmeran studied the map that Valthyrra had brought up on the main viewscreen for him, quietly comparing notes with her. At last, seemingly satisfied, he leaned back. "It can be done. I will need Baress, Threl and Marlena."

"Here!" the three answered from the gallery.

"Threl, do you want a chance to fly that transport underwater?" Velmeran asked, turning to face that section of the gallery.

"That is the only place that I have not flown it," the pilot answered.

"Baress, you have the greatest special tactics experience of us all. Will you go after those generators?"

"I will, if I have the proper help."

"Do you think Baressa's pack would be a good beginning, if she is willing to go with you?"

Baress considered that, and brightened. "That would be a very good beginning. I would also like Kalgeran's pack, from the Delvon."

Velmeran glanced at Thenderra Delvon. "Is that agreeable?"

"Do you even have to ask?" a pilot called from the gallery, bringing laughter from most of the gathering.

"That makes three packs to follow me in," Velmeran mused as he returned to his seat. "I would like to have ten—certainly no less than six. Not only will we need that distraction inside the city, but we certainly need that firepower to get back through the system fleet. I think that our ships should make two or three suggestions each, and we will decide from among those."

"Easily done," Valthyrra said. "Then we are in agreement that this is what we must do? Karvand?"

Commander Schyrrana quickly consulted with her ship, first officer and Commander-designate, and there was no dissension. Daelyn was grinning with mischievous satisfaction. Schyrrana nodded. "We agree."

"Delvon?"

"No complaints here!" Korlan insisted, not even pausing to consult with his ship or officers. There was no need; they all nodded eagerly.

Valthyrra turned her pod to Mayelna, who sat well back in her chair, deep in thoughts of her own. "Commander?"

Mayelna glanced up sharply, at first surprised. But she also nodded in agreement. Consherra offered no opinion, aside from a very bewildered stare; this whole affair left her speechless.

As soon as the council was over, Velmeran made as inconspicuous a retreat as he could manage. His problem was compounded by the fact that his only way out lay through the middle of the gallery, so that he was caught between the crowd of pack leaders and officers gathered there and Mayelna behind. Noticing the look that Mayelna gave him, he knew that he would do well to flee. And being a first-rate Starwolf, he was unequaled in his talent for dodging and evading. He had made it to the corridor outside before Baress stepped out of the crowd before him.

"Velmeran, I would like that place in your pack, if you will have me," he said. That was not only enough to bring Velmeran up short, but make him forget that he was being pursued.

"That position off my right wing tip does not seem to be a lucky place to be," he remarked. "But if you will have it, then I would be glad to have you. I am sure that Valth-yrra would agree."

"Of course I do," she replied for herself. She had managed to be the first out the door by having a probe lying in wait, ready for her immediate use.

At that moment he was grabbed and spun about, tightly pinned by four arms in a fierce hug, and soundly kissed on the mouth. Startled, he drew back as far as he could, only to find himself in the arms of the Karvand's Commander-designate, Daelyn.

"Velmeran, you are fantastic!" she declared. What was this?

"I know," he replied uncertainly, still too surprised and confused to know what he was saying. "I mean, I have to be . . . I try."

She released her hold on him, and he remembered too late that he was supposed to be running for his life. Mayelna caught both of his right arms and, with Daelyn holding his left arms, he was herded quickly down the length of the corridor, up a flight of steps and into Mayelna's office. Valthyrra followed, none too close, while Daelyn remained on guard by the closed door.

"Do you have any idea what you have gotten us into?" Mayelna demanded as she backed her prey across the room. "Do you even know what you are doing?"

"Of course I know what I am doing!" he replied hotly. Having been brought up short by a corner, he decided that it was time to counterattack. "Three entire ships agree that I indeed know what I am doing. You are the only one who is dissatisfied. Do you want me to call everyone back and tell them that I cannot play this game, that my mother says that it is too rough for me?"

Mayelna blinked in confusion, taken off her guard by his determination. Momentarily at a loss, she turned on

Daelyn, an easier target. "You! I thought that you were on my side."

"You told me that I was on your side," Daelyn replied, undaunted. "I decided otherwise. He is right, you know."

"Of course he is right!" Mayelna exclaimed in frustration, throwing up her hands. "He has a disturbing habit of always being right. He is also the only one capable of getting away with this. But I still do not have to like it."

"What do you not like?" Velmeran demanded. "Is it the Commander who objects to me, a young and inexperienced pack leader taking entirely too much upon myself? Because I want us to be more aggressive when you would have us remain defensive? Or is it the overprotective mother who refuses to accept that I am quite grown up and able to decide these things for myself?"

"Under the circumstances, I am equal shares of both," she answered. "Velmeran, I no longer question your abilities. You are already a far better leader in battle than I ever was or will be. Your ability to never miss a trick amazed me. But I question your motives. What are you trying to prove?"

"You tell me," Velmeran said in return.

"Very well. The last time we talked, you were afraid that you were just a machine, a weapon of war built for one specific purpose. Now I wonder if you are willing yourself to become that machine. Dveyella might be gone, but you still have life. Are you trying to deny that?"

"Is that what you think?"

"You are not the same person you were before," she said. "I did not really understand you before. But I hardly even know you now."

"To the contrary," Valthyrra interrupted. "This is the real Velmeran that I always knew existed."

"You keep out of this, chips-for-brains!" Mayelna snapped impatiently. "You put him up to this. You put the idea in his head."

"Actually, he was the one who gave me the idea," Valthyrra countered.

"This is something that I must do," Velmeran added. "But for my own reasons."

"And what are your reasons?" she demanded. "Do you think that you can avenge yourself and Dveyella upon the ones who killed her? Vengeance is a human passion, and I am not sure that even they found quite the satisfaction in their revenge as they always thought they should. But you are not human, so stop pretending. Revenge will not help her death sit any easier in your conscience; it will not help you to forget, and it certainly will not bring her back. She was beyond your help the moment she died, so you cannot say that this is something you want to do for her."

"No, not for her. For me, Mayelna! This is what I must do for me, and for every Kelvessan alive today and who will live in days to come!" Velmeran declared so fiercely that Mayelna was driven back by his wrath. "I am Kelvessan, and I want that to mean something. I want my kind to be able to go where they want without fear of being shot. I want my people to be whatever they want, to have worlds of their own, to write their own music and their own stories and build their own monuments. I want this war to end now, not for the sake of some alien race but for my own. Someday I think that I might even like to have children, but children who will be free to be whatever they want.

"I know now what I am, what I want to be. Yes, I am a warrior, a Starwolf, but that is now my decision based upon my talents and desires, and not just because it is expected of me. Let me do what I can . . . what I must. Help me, if you dare, because I need all the help I can get. But if you are afraid, then kindly get out of my way. I know what I have to do, and I can do it without you."

The silence that followed came almost as a shock. Valthyrra was so startled and cowed by that violent outburst that she had drawn the probe's camera pod into its protective cowling and was peering out cautiously. Daelyn, on the other hand, was smiling with satisfaction. Mayelna simply stood where she was, staring aimlessly at the floor, deep in thought. After a moment she glanced up at him, searchingly.

"Is this what you have decided, those long days you spend alone in your room?" she asked gently.

Velmeran nodded slowly. "I have faced death as I never have before. Dveyella's life was dearer to me than my own. I could not face life alone without first coming to terms with it."

"Yes, I suppose so," Mayelna agreed. She reached out and took up his hands in hers, urging his attention. "Meran, I always knew of the conflict in your heart and soul, your dissatisfaction with your inability to choose your own lot in life. I hated to have to force a fate upon you. You said it yourself, that you want children who are Kelvessan and free to be what they want. That freedom is one thing that I could never give my own children, and that hurt me. But now I think that I am satisfied after all. Daelyn found her own life, even if she had to leave this ship to do it. Now I trust that you have found yours, and I am sorry that your lesson had to be such a bitter one."

"Daelyn?" Velmeran asked suddenly, and stared at the girl. She grinned and waved at him.

Mayelna smiled. "I believe that you have met your sister. Half sister, at least."

"Sister?" he asked. "Nuts! I was hoping for another kiss."

"You can talk to Consherra about that. Right now you will listen to me," Mayelna said, in the Commander's voice. "Meran, I see something of the future that you must face. I suppose that is what everyone must see in you, that your life is tied up in some great and terrible fate, and that is why it is so easy to believe in you. I believe you, and I will give you all the help I can."

Velmeran stared at her in surprise. "You do?"

"Have I not said so from the first?" she demanded in

exasperation. "I know who led the counterattack against that fleet. And I know as well who took over leadership on that expedition to retrieve Keth when Dveyella thought that it was time to pull out. Did you think that Valthyrra was the only one listening to every word that went over your com? Someday, left to your own devices, it might even occur to you how much I love you. And I hope that you will make the equally amazing discovery that you might just have some love for me in return."

"You love me?" he asked. "I do not recall that you have ever said that to me before."

"I have always told myself that actions speak louder than words," she replied gently. "That is just a coward's excuse, and I have had a hard lesson in how actions can be misinterpreted. Therefore I will say it plainly: I love you, Meran. Not because you are my son, or my best pilot, or because you are the most unique person I have ever met. No excuses or conditions. I love you just because of yourself, for you are special to me."

Velmeran nodded and swallowed nervously. "You are my mother. . . ."

"And sometimes we need the help of someone who loves us," she finished for him. "I understand. Meran, there is no one here who does not love you. I have shed tears for you, because I shared your grief. Many of us did, more than you might imagine. Others would have, if glass eyes could weep. But you never did. Something was lacking, I suppose. Something that still needed to be done."

He smiled uncertainly. "Ghosts of more than one nature will rest more easily now."

"Then let them rest," Mayelna said. She took him in her arms and held him tightly while he cried.

15

Even as the Starwolf carriers were gathering for their council of war, Jon Lake received some very disturbing news. News that frightened him as nothing in his life had frightened him before. With the packet containing the report in one hand, he stormed into the Sector Commander's office. The secretary and two guards in the outer office, under strict orders to admit no visitors, were undecided as to whether or not that applied to the Councilor as well. During the moment of hesitation, he was already past.

"Idiot!" the Councilor spat like an angry cat at the startled Sector Commander as he came through the door. "What are you trying to do?"

"Hello, Jon," Commander Trace said casually as he sat back in his chair, waving the astonished guards out of the doorway so that it would shut. "Yes, I ordered that test moved up three weeks. What of it? We lost the freighter because her captain did not get the hell out while he had the chance. But we did get Starwolves."

"A Starwolf!" Councilor Lake corrected him.

"Oh?" the Commander asked innocently. "My report said three. Ah, well, we will improve. Even one was a good start."

"The wrong one!" Lake declared. "You moved that test up so that you could send your trap after the Methryn, knowing where she was and that she would probably be hunting again. Why, Don? Were you trying to get Velmeran?"

"And why not?" Trace demanded. "He made me nervous. Too damned smart."

The Councilor did not reply to that, but opened the package he held and pulled out a photograph, which he threw down on the table. "Do you know who this is?"

"Starwolf," Commander Trace replied, hardly bothering to glance at it. "I cannot tell one from another."

"You should know, since you dined with her only a week and a half ago. There was a two-man prospector poking around the asteroid debris in the system, surveying for metals. Suddenly they saw a Starwolf carrier coming into system fast, and it seems that they recognized a Starwolf funeral when they saw it. They kept the body on scan until the carrier left, then rushed in and snatched it up at the last moment. And, being a company prospector, they turned the body over to Farstell rather than to the military. Since they sent the report on a military courier, it came to me instead of to you."

"What became of the body?" the Sector Commander demanded, almost greedily. Alive or dead, a Starwolf was a valuable possession.

"You needn't concern yourself, even though I can imagine you hanging her head from a post as a warning to all Starwolves. I have already ordered that body destroyed in our own sun, according to their own honors," Lake said with considerable heat, then grew cold and menacing. "Are you too big a fool to realize the consequences of your actions? Velmeran knows that you were after him. Now he is going to demand payment."

"What can he do, just one Starwolf?" the Commander asked, unconcerned, even contemptuously.

"Have I not taught you to understand them better than that?" the Councilor demanded. "They accept a certain amount of risk, but they always make us pay. They made us pay through the teeth for that last trap, and that was nothing personal. But you have made it something personal. Damn it, that girl was his mate. He is going to make us pay for her death if he has to take apart this entire planet, and the Starwolves are going to give him all the help he needs."

Councilor Lake walked over to stand before the window, staring out over the city. "I am going to take what steps I can to prepare for their attack. The first thing that they are going to have to do is crack the dome to get their fighters in. I am going to arrange to have the dome shield fail after only one or two determined hits from their big cannons. That power will be of more use in the planetary defense system."

Trace stared at him disbelief. "The dome shield has to remain up. It will delay them long enough for our fleet to move in."

"And let them fry this city in the process?" the Councilor asked, and shook his head. "I will not sacrifice this entire city for a block of metal. Also, we have to get our people out. I will warn Richart and everyone else to get to the sub the moment we see a Starwolf carrier coming in. Both of the sea gates will remain open from now on. Fortunately we should have a few weeks before they can put together an attack."

Preparations for the attack were made even before the Starwolves left Alliolandh. The nine packs that were to accompany Velmeran's own into Vannkarn were quickly selected and transferred to the Methryn, where they were serviced and fitted with the big auxiliary cannons they would carry on their raid. The Methryn's packs that would not be a part of the attack force were divided between the Delvon and the Karvand for their own servicing. Everything had to be ready before their arrival at the Vinthran system.

Velmeran wanted to lead his attack force down just

before dawn, local time, so that they would be coming up into the city early enough to catch most of its population still at home and in no real danger. He thought that a courier would have taken three days to arrive with news of the attack, and he wanted to make his raid before any major countermeasures could be arranged.

He was certain that Councilor Lake at least suspected the possibility of a counterattack on Vannkarn. But he still believed that the element of surprise remained on his side, simply because Lake would not be expecting anything so soon. Hopefully he would also be expecting the Starwolves to come in the obvious way, through the dome. Velmeran doubted that he would do anything drastic to block the sea door even if he did suspect the possibility, since that was his own bolt hole. And even if he did, Velmeran would simply take his packs airborne to the port, where they would blast away the roof of the port building and fly down the tram tunnels, using their big cannons to clear the tracks. The plan was as nearly foolproof as he could hope.

The plan was that the Methryn would go in alone, coming in as close to Vinthra as she could to launch her packs. Then came the tricky part, for the assault force had to drift in almost powerless to avoid detection, at a speed slow enough that the most gentle braking would prepare them for planetary entry. They would be six hours in space and two more underwater, eight hours and more before they would return to their ships. Fortunately they would have to rely upon hypermetabolism only during the battle itself, only about twenty minutes before they were clear of the planet. The problem was that, for Kelvessan, that was entirely too long without eating.

Mayelna hurried down to the landing bay for a final word with Velmeran during the short jump into system. Valthyrra, in the form of one of her hovering probes, was there ahead of her. They waited beside his fighter as he made a final check of his pack.

"All ready?" Mayelna asked as Velmeran approached.

"Ready and eager, in fact," he replied. "It is hard for

me to remember now how they were only green students only a short time ago. Now I trust them enough to take them with me into Vannkarn."

Mayelna smiled. "To tell the truth, not that long ago I wondered if you would ever be a good pack leader. Now here you are, leading three entire ships on one of the greatest raids the Starwolves have ever attempted. In fact, I believe that you have assembled history's largest special tactics team."

Velmeran shrugged, as if it were unimportant. "I know better than to ask you not to worry."

"Just as I know better than to ask you to be careful," she said. "When you come back, there is something else that I must talk to you about."

"I understand," he answered, glancing down shyly. "It occurs to me that I should thank you—both of you—for making me what I am today. All your best efforts have paid off, it seems."

"Or in spite of our best efforts?" Valthyrra asked pointedly.

Velmeran laughed. "I am not sure how you did it, but I am what you have always wanted me to be."

"You are what you want to be," Mayelna corrected him. "That is the only thing I ever wanted. I never really doubted you, nor do I expect less of you than you are."

"It is time," Valthyrra interrupted gently.

"No long speeches," Mayelna promised, and turned back to Velmeran. "You have never asked me about your father. . . ."

"I am my mother's son," he said, smiling. "I hope it does not surprise you to learn that I have always been satisfied with that."

"Good luck, Meran," she called as he turned and started toward his fighter. She tried to ignore the fact that Valthyrra was staring at her, not him. At last she had to gesture impatiently for the probe to remain silent.

"What if he had asked?" Valthyrra insisted. "You have no more idea than he does."

"Shut up!" Mayelna hissed under her breath. They retreated across the bay as the line of fighters began to power up for flight. "It was something that I had to know."

Moving as one, the ten packs of the assault team penetrated the outer edge of Vinthra's atmosphere, still braking gently with their forward engines. Looking down, directly above the center of the magnetic pole and not too far from the planetary axis, they might well have been descending toward a world of ice. An endless, featureless expanse of white lay below them, disappearing into the haziness of the horizon in all directions. The ice cap was not really all that large, but their altitude was now less than two hundred kilometers and they were coming down vertically.

They were able to brake harder as they penetrated deeper, now that they were well within the protection of the magnetic corridor. And that was well, for they had a lot of speed to lose before they reached the surface. They were only a hundred meters above the icy plain by the time they were able to cease braking and begin a wide, spiraling circle.

The lead fighter moved out from the rest, descending toward the solid ice floe. Velmeran activated his auxiliary cannon, and the big gun swung down and forward on its struts into attack position. These cannons were so powerful that they were mounted below the cockpit so that their flash would not blind the pilot, and moved a meter out from the hull to avoid searing it. In power they were comparable to the main battery of a Union battleship; a single shot from them could rip a smaller ship in half, and they could fire up to three shots a second.

Velmeran did not dare concentrate too much firepower on the ice, since power of this type could be detected. A two-second round of six shots left a steaming crater a hundred meters across. The brisk wind had carried most of the steam away by the time he circled back, and he could see that the center of the hole was more than clear enough of debris for safe access. He retracted the cannon and triggered the modified atmospheric shield for underwater travel, then dived toward the center of the pit.

Penetrating below the surface was as easy as he had hoped, although he did hear fragments of ice ring harmlessly against the hull as the shield filled with water. For now he kept his speed well down, barely a hundred kilometers, as he waited. His own pack followed as soon as they saw that he was safely installed in underwater flight, moving up in single file directly behind him until they were only ten meters apart, their overlapping shields forming a single long corridor that reduced drag for the entire group.

The other nine packs continued to dive through the steaming passage, assembling by packs beneath the ice in their own shield tunnels. These in turn lined up side by side, so that any accident that might occur in one pack was not likely to involve others. The single transport followed last of all, flying alone behind and slightly below the packs. Once they were all in place, Velmeran began to increase speed gradually, taking them up to the transport's maximum safe speed of thirty-eight hundred kilometers. The gently glowing ceiling of ice overhead began to streak past, and the packs dropped down to avoid the massive icebergs trapped over the years in the floe. To the pilots it almost seemed as if they were flying upside down, passing over an inverted landscape.

After a few minutes they passed out from beneath the cover of the ice floe into open water. Now Velmeran had to be more cautious, watching his scanners constantly for the presence of aircraft overhead. The nature of their atmospheric shields was such that they absorbed in the tail any pressure wave formed by the forward cone. But he knew from their test runs in the seas on Alliolandh that they were leaving wide trails of dense bubbles, white trails when seen from high enough. He doubted that anyone would figure out the meaning of the trails themselves, not soon enough to matter, so long as they did not observe that fast-moving leading edge. It was a necessary risk.

Two hours of flight time brought them to the shallow coastal waters west of Vannkarn. Now Velmeran relied upon the course plotted by his ship's computer, using its guidance to bring him to a point where the underwater tunnel must terminate. Submerged ridges of the coastal range made towering underwater cliffs that stretched for hundreds of miles along this shore. Reducing speed to five hundred kilometers, he began to cast about for that opening. The nine other packs fell back to follow his own in single file.

Velmeran did not need long to find the tunnel entrance, for it bore its own markers. Two red beacons pierced the murky water, below which shone the white radiance of the tunnel's lights, illuminating the striking blue of the tunnel walls. He aimed his ship toward that opening, aligning with the passage early both to insure that his shields would be centered and to have a look up the tunnel. Activating his accessory cannon, he began his run. He was committed now. If he did find the passage blocked, the cannon had better be enough to clear it. Otherwise the others would be alerted to his failure by the explosion of his ship.

His fighter shot up the tunnel like a bullet within the barrel of a rifle. Soon he could see that the passage was clear to its end, although the illumination decreased to almost total blackness near the far end so that no betraying glow would be seen from the inside. He had passed two sets of sea doors, both invitingly open. Were the Lakes so confident that this way would remain unknown that these doors were always open? Or were those doors for use only in severe weather outside, isolating the underground lake from betraying disturbances?

Velmeran's fighter shot out into the lake and he arched up sharply before he ran out of traveling room. The calm lake suddenly erupted into violence, a massive column of water rising toward the cavern ceiling as it was carried aloft in the atmospheric shield, collapsing back like a fountain as it was discharged. Velmeran followed the curve of the cavern roof, dropping his atmospheric shield altogether and bringing up his debris shield and defensive screens. Even as the column of water collapsed it leaped back up again, each time ejecting a black fighter.

At first the fighters flew high over the city as the packs reformed, then dived down in groups to dodge and dart among the buildings and avenues. For the first minute or so they might almost have been at play, slipping in and out among the suspended walkways and elevated tramways, making it plain to anyone about that Starwolves were here and they should take cover, which they did quickly, the small, early morning crowds seeming to evaporate in an instant.

Now the Starwolves went to work, turning their lesser guns on unimportant targets. Most of those packs were there just to create a diversion, darting in and out so fast that the entire city seemed overrun by thousands of wolf ships, keeping the population frightened and in hiding. Skyways and tram tracks collapsed under their assault. Wooded parks and sculptured gardens exploded in flames from the bolts of their larger cannons. The Starwolves had no complaint against the civilian population, and they destroyed nothing that could not be easily repaired.

Only the Unioners knew what they thought of the sudden plague of Starwolves inside their impenetrable city. Only a very few knew of the underwater tunnel and, with the dome still intact, there was no logical explanation for how they might have appeared. And once inside the cavern, there was nothing that could be done about them. All the planetary defenses lay outside. And Union pilots could not get their own fighters and stingships inside, even if the Starwolves had. For once they held an entire city for ransom, for as long as they dared.

The only thing that Councilor Lake could think about that morning was that it was entirely too early to be up and about, especially after spending half the night and a bottle of wine with a trade delegation. But this was the time to act on getting these new missiles installed in a number of freighters for a better test of their effectiveness. Especially since he and Donalt Trace were in complete disagreement on the effectiveness of the last test.

"I consider it a success, since it did kill a Starwolf," Trace argued. He was seated at his desk, reading the review of the incident, while his uncle stood near the window that overlooked the city.

"And I consider it a failure, since we lost the freighter," Lake countered. "Obviously our goals differ."

"Are you telling me that you would just as well abandon this entire project?"

"No, not yet," the Councilor said, turning to look out the window.

The first thing he saw was a familiar black shape streak past. He blinked, but it was already gone and he was not even sure that he had seen it. Had it been only a manifestation of his fears come to haunt him? Of the wine? His senility? But he looked again, this time more closely, and saw that his beautiful city was being overrun with wolf ships. How could an invasion force have gotten this far without his being aware? The dome shield was rigged to fail, but only after a few determined shots that he would have heard. And yet, when he glanced up, he could plainly see that the dome was still intact. Suddenly he understood —only too well. He had left the door open for them.

"Don, do you remember that young Starwolf we had up for dinner?" he asked casually.

"What, Velmeran?" Trace asked without looking up from the report he was reading. "What of it?"

"Well, he seems to be paying us a return visit."

The Sector Commander glanced up, and saw at once what he had meant. It seemed that wolf ships were coming out of nowhere to fill the interior of the cavern. And he knew exactly what it meant. He leaped from his seat and was out the door before his uncle could do a thing to stop him.

"Don! Wait!" Councilor Lake called after him. "You are running into a trap. What do you think you can do about it?"

He paused, aware that it was already too late. Donalt Trace was running to meet his fate at the hands of a Starwolf he owed a life. It did not matter that he knew where to find Velmeran, for that knowledge in itself did not give him the power to stop it. Would he realize that in time to save his life?

It took less than two minutes to get all the packs inside the city. By that time the streets of Vannkarn were completely deserted; if modern man was not as intelligent as his predecessors, he was also less brave. The Starwolves prowled the passages of the city that, by all appearances, was completely empty, a marked contrast to the Vannkarn they knew on port leave. As long as they did not fire directly into the shops and buildings, there was little danger of hurting anyone.

The city was not completely defenseless, although it might as well have been. Scores of automated sentries began to amble out of the many buildings, alerted to the attack by their master controllers. These machines were never intended to fight; they served police duty, walking the halls of empty buildings at night or strolling dimly lit walkways. Even their biggest guns were inadequate against the defensive shields of the black fighters. Once the Starwolves realized what was firing at them, they began to use the automatons for target practice.

As soon as all of their ships were inside the cavern, three of the packs broke off from the rest to gather in loose formation above the city. The transport, the last ship to emerge from the lake, hurried to join them.

"Baress, are you ready?" Velmeran asked over ship's com. In a sense, Baress had the most important task. They could leave without the memory cell if they got into serious trouble. But they could not easily get away until he destroyed the generators that powered the dome shield and planetary defenses.

"Ready and willing," he replied, breaking away from Velmeran's pack to set himself in the lead position for the others.

Baressa and Kalgeran led their own packs as they followed him, shooting across the city. The entrance of the corridor leading to the power complex lay in the north wall of the cavern, down at street level. It was a tight fit for the fighter, but no more than the underwater tunnel. Here, however, they could expect some opposition, sentries and guards with guns, and blast doors that could be secured. Baress would go in first to lead the way, and his fighter had enough firepower to clear any obstacle except solid rock. He found the entrance and dropped down to street level, beginning his run.

The power complex lay a kilometer to the north of the city, an artificial cavern cut well back into the rock of the mountain above it. Self-contained, the complex had only this one entrance. Double sets of massive steel doors served to guard the passage at either end. The doors at this end were still open, and he made sure that they would stay open before he began his run. He brought the big accessory cannon to bear on the walls to either side of those portals, wrecking the locking mechanism and tracks.

The next instant he was inside the passage, ignoring the steady barrage of light-energy bolts that streamed down its length as he focused his telescopic vision on the doors at the far end. After a moment he could see that they were closing, the halves moving slowly inward. He had no intention of racing them, but slowed until they were closed and securely locked. Then a hail of bolts from his accessory cannon ripped those doors apart in an instant.

The generator chamber of the power complex was a rectangular cavern, bisected by a main corridor. A second corridor ran the length of the chamber, lined on either side with a total of fifty massive generators, each adequate to serve the needs of the largest battleship. The two packs fanned out as they entered, drifting slowly through the installation as they centered their lesser cannons on the computer controls of each generator. They had to insure that the generators were safely shut down, since a damaged and malfunctioning computer could force an overload. As safe as total conversion was for general use, a forced explosion of one of these generators would rip out a large section of this range, leaving a gaping crater several kilometers across. A chain reaction of several could destroy this entire world. Once the generators were stilled, their big cannons would insure that the planetary defenses would remain down.

At the same time Velmeran led his own pack west across the city, to where the government building stood massive and gray in the dim lighting of early morning. Their task was in truth an easy one, and Velmeran expected no trouble. The pack spread out to circle the building, while Velmeran searched the top of the building for the proper chamber. There were several such chambers in that same area, all a part of the sector museum, with very similar design and window patterns. At last he was forced to draw back and turn his ship's scanners on that area of the building.

Centering on the indicated chamber, he drifted in slowly, hardly more than a walking pace, and cautiously pushed the nose of the fighter through the window. The glass shattered easily, falling away. He drifted on inside that opening and brought the ship to a motionless hover as he made a quick inspection of the room, then brought the fighter down to floor level. Tregloran came in through the opposite window and settled in as well. Chance had put the younger pilot on the side of the chamber where Velmeran wanted him, the guns of his ship facing down the short corridor toward the double doors that were the only entrance.

Finally the transport approached the side of the building, hovering before a section of the wall indicated by its own scanners, the end of the short alcove branching off the main chamber. While Threl held the transport steady, Marlena made use of a special weapon, a unique combination of energy bolt and projected field. She played it across the outer wall. The wall shook, splintered and crumbled away beneath the blasts as if it were being beaten by an immense hammer. Two large slabs of polished gray marble were reduced to rubble beneath those blows and the inner wall quickly followed, leaving only a twisted steel framework. She sliced that away with an ordinary cutting laser, and the transport drifted through that rough opening.

Threl brought his ship into the main portion of the chamber and edged it over until its cargo bay was even with the memory cell. Marlena had opened the large bay doors and now extended the handling arms out to receive it. The arms took firm hold of the unit and Marlena tried to lift it from its display stand. But the unit did not rise. Instead, the transport shifted slightly, tilting dangerously off center. Marlena quickly released the pressure and Threl fought to regain control of the ship before it slipped sideways off its field drive suspensors.

"Velmeran, that thing is fastened down," Marlena said over com.

"I suspected as much," he replied. "Give me half a moment."

He brought his ship down to the floor, landing gear up so that the cockpit was tilted down. He quickly climbed out and signaled to Marlena, who threw him a light and a hand-held cutting laser. With these in hand, he walked quickly to the end of the unit and flashed the light underneath it. The memory cell had inset tracks running down all four of its long sides by which it was locked into its cradle inside the ship. The Union official who had overseen the installation of the unit had made use of the bottom set of tracks, installing mechanisms that locked it down to the dais. He quickly cut loose the two locking bolts, then crossed quickly to the other end to free those bolts. He had just finished when Tregloran interrupted him.

"Captain, we have company," the younger pilot announced casually, even amused, so that Velmeran knew that he was in no real danger. If there had been any real trouble, he would have fired at first sight.

Velmeran turned slowly. Not five meters away stood a towering figure of a man, his legs braced as he held a gun centered on the Starwolf. He might have almost been a law officer making an arrest, so sure he seemed to be that he had the situation well under control. But that was hardly the case, for Velmeran knew that the little gun could not so much as dent his armor. He stood for a moment, regarding the intruder with an appearance of mild surprise and patient tolerance, even though he was securely helmeted.

"Commander Trace," he acknowledged at last, switching on the com link that gave him contact with the world outside his suit.

"Pack Leader Velmeran," Trace answered coldly. "I knew that I would find you here."

"So?" Velmeran asked, drawing his own gun. "What do you expect to be able to do about it?"

Commander Trace hesitated as that very question occurred to him. Somehow he had thought that if he could just get here in time Velmeran would be defeated and he would win, as if those were the rules of the game. But that was not the case at all. This game went to the player with the greatest advantage, and just now Velmeran possessed every advantage. His confusion gave way to real fear, for he knew that he was facing his own death. And when the Starwolf raised his gun to take aim, he turned and fled in open terror. He knew that his one, remote chance for life depended upon getting himself out of that chamber.

Velmeran hesitated, astonished at this turn of events. Defeated and fearing for his very life, the plight of this man evoked his sympathy. For once Velmeran saw him as he was, not a personification of evil or the enemy of the Kelvessan, but a man. In spite of his prejudices, his blind hatreds and his disregard for the lives and rights of others, he also possessed rare courage and a selfless devotion to duty. For good or ill, he was human. And for the first time Velmeran understood what being human really meant, both the familiar and the alien.

Velmeran realized something about himself—what he was in comparison, and what he believed himself to be. Killing this man would give him no satisfaction, nor would it restore some balance in his own sense of justice. Dveyella's death would not be vindicated in blood, but by the accomplishment of her dream. Vengeance was his for the taking, and he did not desire it. He could not hate this man, not as Commander Trace hated him.

He shot anyway, because it was his duty.

Commander Trace's back exploded in a sheet of flames, and the force of that explosion threw him forward to land with bone-crushing force just short of the open doorway and the safety he sought. He lay there motionless, the material of his uniform burning lazily. Velmeran had no more time for that matter. Turning back to the transport, he saw that Marlena had done nothing to load the memory cell.

"Get that thing on board!" he called impatiently. "We have to get out of here now."

"I did not want to be a distraction," she replied, working the controls of the handling arms. The unit lifted easily from its cradle where it had lain for thousands of years, and the arms retracted it back into the ship, drawing it into the bay. The fit was so tight that it did not appear likely to go, although the measurements Valthyrra had provided insisted that it would slip in with a third of a meter to spare. Velmeran tossed the cutting laser and the light into the bay even as Marlena began to close the door.

"He is gone!" Tregloran warned suddenly.

Velmeran turned quickly to see that Trace's body had indeed vanished. He had either revived enough to drag himself out the door, or someone had quietly collected him, dead or alive. Velmeran suspected the latter. Either way, there was nothing that he could do about it. He wanted Donalt Trace dead for the same reason that he would want to deprive the Union of any valuable weapon. But at that moment he had to get his attack force away.

"We have to be on our way out," he said, and waved the transport out of the chamber. "Swing that ship around and get out of here, Threl. We will guard your back."

16

The transport spun around in a half circle as Threl cautiously pivoted the ship to face back the way it had come in. He then led the transport down the side corridor and out the impromptu entrance of the gaping hole in the outer wall. Once the larger ship was clear of the building, the two fighters rose to the ceiling and passed out through the broken windows. It might have seemed easier for them to have followed the transport out, but they could not. As small as they were in comparison, their wingspan was too wide for that opening; the boxlike hull of the transport had no wings or fins.

What they found outside appeared at first glance to be absolute confusion. The government building had apparently been replete with automated sentries. Scores of them had appeared on terraces and rooftops to shoot at the circling wolf ships. And the Starwolves had been entertaining themselves with picking off those sentries. But the sentries were a self-sacrificing diversion, occupying the Starwolves' attention while the inhabitants of the building fled. Indeed, the Sector Residence and the Farstell Trade building had been evacuated as well; Velmeran applauded Councilor Lake's wisdom in guessing his next move.

The wolf ships now dropped to street level for the

final phase of their attack. They began to streak in low and fast, firing rapid bursts from their auxiliary cannons into the lowest levels of those three buildings, so that in barely half a minute they were all reduced to smoking rubble. This was not wanton destruction but a calculated strategic move. The destruction of those buildings also meant the destruction of the bureaucracy they housed. The management of both the government and the trade company in this sector would be seriously impaired for months or even years to come.

Once that task was complete, the Starwolves withdrew to the upper levels of the cavern, forming into their separate packs. Velmeran found eight present, including his own; the two that comprised Baress's assault force had not yet returned.

"Baress?" Velmeran called.

"We are on our way out," he answered promptly. "The planetary defenses are down. Cut a hole in the roof and start out. We will join you in time to bring up the rear."

Velmeran waited no longer. Flying out over the middle of the city, he dived down to make some running room and arched up toward the dome, aiming a blast from his accessory cannon to its very center. As the smoke cleared he saw blue morning sky beyond and shot through that small opening without hesitation, his pack following him closely. The transport slipped through the hole next, and the remaining packs brought up the rear. The second attack force shot out the tunnel leading to the power complex in time to fall in place behind the others.

Once all the wolf ships were clear, they began to accelerate quickly, at the same time reforming into the tight arrowheads of their running formations. Velmeran's pack took the lead and the rest gathered into a defensive sphere about the transport. Once assembled, they accelerated straight up, leaving the planet by the shortest course. They were aware that a fleet of Union destroyers and battleships such as they had never seen lay directly in their path, waiting to intercept them.

At that moment four more groups of five packs each suddenly appeared at the same instant, descending upon the Union fleet with frightening speed as they closed for the kill. Warships tried to adjust to the new attack, frantically pivoting to face incoming ships. The only result was that the fleet was in a state of complete confusion as their new attackers began to rip them apart with cannons they did not normally expect on fighters. The Starwolf forces closed quickly to crush the Union ships between their concentrated barrage, the packs separating to strike at different portions of the fleet, then separating again as fighters went after individual targets. They shot to kill, their accessory cannons tearing entire ships apart in a single pass.

Velmeran's assault force stayed in tight formation, concentrating their own fire on anything in or near their path, opening a hole for themselves through the enemy fleet. Six of the packs fell behind the transport to guard the rear as they shot through that opening unopposed. Then they were out the other side, and the six following packs circled around to return to battle. Two of the remaining packs dropped back behind the transport as they prepared to cross the Union's second line of defense.

Farther out, in an arch behind the first fleet, awaited the stingships. Their original task had been to go after anything that tried to break from the main battle. They now prepared themselves to intercept this small group fleeing with their prize. Thirty carriers worked quickly to release their loads, swinging long racks of stingships out from their sides for deployment.

Before they were able to launch, powerful bolts of energy leaped out from empty space, so powerful that they completely destroyed the carriers and their cargoes of stingships on touch. Perhaps the Union pilots looked about in confusion for their unseen enemy, but their scanners reported only empty space. At the last instant indistinct shapes of enormous proportions began to register, only a moment before the carriers themselves became visible. The three immense ships went through the second line of de-

fense like mowers reaping a field, leaving nothing but Velmeran's assault force as he led it to the safety of open
space. The Methryn circled back to follow, accelerating
quickly to move ahead, while the Delvon and the Karvand
continued on. Their presence in the first field of battle
would decide matters there very quickly.

Once they were well away of the area of Vinthra and
the possibility of any danger, Velmeran cut acceleration to
give the Methryn a chance to overtake them. He waited as
she moved ahead and positioned herself before the packs,
matching speed for their final approach. The transport separated from the rest, heading for its own bay just ahead of
the big holding bays. The four packs moved apart, each
orienting on one of the Methryn's four flight decks as the
fighters fell back in single file for landing.

The welcome sight of home served as a signal to Velmeran that it was time to shut down, in spite of his best
efforts to remain alert. He had not eaten in ten hours now,
too long for a Kelvessan under any circumstances, who
could starve to death in only three days. He was able to
bring his ship in for an acceptable landing with only the
greatest effort, then sat back in his seat, wondering how he
was going to get himself out of the cockpit. Benthoran was
there as soon as the rack was in place, unstrapping him and
actually lifting him out of the cockpit to all but carry him
down the platform to the deck, leaning him against the
platform of the rack.

"Can you hold on here for a moment?" Benthoran
asked.

"Yes, of course," Velmeran insisted.

"Someone will be along to help you in a minute. You
are needed on the bridge."

Velmeran nodded, and promptly forgot all about it as
he wished for something to eat. Because he was not looking up, he did not see it coming. Four strong arms suddenly closed about him as he was hugged with crushing
force, so tightly that he squeaked in protest in spite of his
armor. He had no idea who might have hold of him; all he

could see was white armor, brown hair and a pointed ear. All Kelvessan had brown hair and pointed ears. The white armor was the clue, and it was not tall enough to be Mayelna. He could think of no one else who would spare him such obvious affection except . . . Consherra?

"Meran, you did it!" she exclaimed. Definitely Consherra.

"I know I did it. I was there."

She let go of him quickly, looking as if she had committed the worst of indiscretions. Remembering the container she carried in one hand, she pulled off the top and gave it to him. "Drink this."

Velmeran took the container and drank deeply. It contained a concentrated solution of sugars that Kelvessan could put to immediate use as a source of energy, as he had suspected.

"That is just to get you going again," Consherra explained. "I have more waiting. Just now you must get to the bridge in record time."

"What is it?" Velmeran asked as she began to lead him toward the lift.

"Someone wants to talk to you."

Consherra put them on a waiting lift, refusing to say another word except to explain that nothing was wrong. She distracted him from asking too many questions— which she would not answer anyway—by placing something to eat in every free hand he had. By the time the lift reached the bridge, he was beginning to feel not quite so hungry and a great deal stronger. Best of all, his mind was once again clear and his thoughts sharp.

As they entered the bridge, Velmeran saw that Mayelna was standing at the com station, both she and Valthyrra peering over Korleran's shoulder. All three glanced over when they saw that Consherra had returned with him. Mayelna hurried over to intercept the pair, drawing them up short.

"Listen to me well, Meran," she explained quickly. "Councilor Lake is on the com and he wants to talk to you.

Understand this. The ships have withdrawn their packs and the Vardon's memory cell is safely on board. We have had no losses, not a dent, scratch nor scoring. Your plan worked perfectly."

Velmeran nodded in understanding. With the taking of Vannkarn behind him, he must now play the part of the Starwolf extraordinaire, the young hero whose name made Sector Commanders swear and company executives turn pale with fright. He accepted that, because it was important to his plans. Mayelna led him to the communications console and Korleran surrendered her seat to him.

"Councilor Lake?" he said as Korleran helped him adjust the com mike.

"Commander Velmeran?" the Councilor asked in return.

"No, just pack leader," Velmeran corrected him.

"Excuse me. I confer titles where they are deserved," Lake explained. "I am so glad to be able to catch you at home. I do want to thank you for being so efficient. I went to take a quick look after you left. It looks a mess, but it is all superficial. I want to thank you for sparing my city."

"And you knew it," Velmeran said. "You ordered the evacuation of the three buildings that you knew we would destroy."

"So? The only intelligent move I made in this affair. I thought I was so smart, figuring out that you would be paying me a visit. Do you know, I had the dome shield rigged to collapse after a shot or two from your big ships?"

"Indeed? I like my way better."

"Of course it was better! I should have known that you would not kill a city to get at the thing, but how was I to know that you would come up the drain?" He paused for a moment. "Did you, by any chance, happen to run across Don?"

"Yes, we met."

"And you shot him?"

"I had my duty," the Starwolf explained. "He ran from me, and I shot him in the back. I do not know if he survived, but he did disappear while we were preoccupied with other matters. Either he crawled out the door, or someone came to collect him."

"I suppose that I will have to collect all the king's horses and all the king's men and go look for him," the Councilor mused, then grew serious. "You know, perhaps, that he set up the test date on our new weapon to trap you? Well, there is something else you should know. I dread having to tell you, but I do not want Don—if he is still alive—to use it as a weapon to hurt you sometime in the future.

"You see, we know that he killed Dveyella. Her body was intercepted and sent to me on a courier. Of course, I recognized her at once, and I knew that she was special to you. Now, before you send your fighters back to get me, I must tell you that I allowed no one to touch the body. I had it delivered into our sun, according to your own ritual, and attended the ceremony myself. I do hope that you can forgive me. Don may have already payed for it with his life."

"Such payment is of no value to me," Velmeran replied evenly. "Dveyella is avenged in a way that would mean something to her."

"I imagine so," the Councilor agreed hesitantly. "Then I do not think that we will ever meet again. Farewell, my young friend. I wish that you were on my side. No, I take that back. I wish that I was on your side."

"Farewell for now, Councilor," Velmeran replied. "You will hear from me from time to time."

"Ah, yes. That is exactly what I am afraid of," Lake muttered as his link began to fail.

Velmeran sighed and leaned back heavily in the chair as Korleran reached over him to return communications back to monitoring their own ships. She glanced down at him tolerantly. "Captain, I have work to do."

He opened his eyes to look up at her. "Can you get me up?"

"I can," Consherra said, and hooked a hand under each of his arms to haul him unceremoniously out of the seat. As soon as Velmeran was able to stand, he brushed her away impatiently.

"I can walk!" he insisted. "Why should I be any more tired than the pilots who flew under me?"

"Because you have been under the stress of responsibility for those pilots and their mission," Valthyrra replied. "I doubt that you have rested in days, not since the morning when you first tried to fly underwater. And perhaps not for days before that."

"Which, I suspect, is true," Mayelna added, turning him in the direction of the lift. "Your mission is complete, so rest while you can. We will be making a nine-hour jump to a system where we can straighten out our affairs in peace, and we will not need you until then. Consherra, will you take him to his cabin, un-can him and see that he gets the rest he needs?"

"Actually, I believe Consherra is due to go off duty herself," Valthyrra observed.

"I am?" she asked, pausing to look back. That was not what she believed. Then she understood, and brightened. "Thank you!"

Mayelna glanced up. "Are they. . ."

The camera pod made a shrugging motion. "I think so."

Consherra led Velmeran to the lift and sped them on their way. As soon as the lift was in motion, she began to remove his gloves, stacking them inside the helmet she carried. He had ceased to protest, for his strength was again fading fast. Valthyrra had been right. In a sense, he had been fighting this battle since Dveyella had died. Now he was tired, and there was only one cure for that—as reluctant as he was to admit it.

"I might just leave you in that suit and lean you against the wall," Consherra observed, reaching that same conclusion. "Meran, the only cure for this is a few hours of sleep."

"I know," he agreed weakly. "I do not think that I

could avoid it if I had to. But I do not like it . . . and I am afraid."

Consherra nodded. "I understand. It is not a pleasant thing, for all the good it does. I will stay with you, if you like. You do not have to be alone."

The lift slowed to a stop and the two stepped out. Then they paused and looked about, since they were not where they expected to be.

"This is not my corridor," Velmeran observed.

"No, it is mine," Consherra said, taking his arm to lead him on. "This is my cabin, over here. Valthyrra never misses a thing. No one is going to come looking for you here."

She started to lead the way, but when Velmeran hesitated she turned to glance back at him. She looked sad and defeated. "I will leave you alone, if that is what you want."

"I do not want to be alone," he said uncertainly. "I have had enough of being alone."

"This is for you to decide," she told him. "I wish that I might be the cure for your loneliness. I have been lonely myself, lately. But I will not try to be Dveyella and beg the love you had for her. Perhaps it is too soon."

"A day or a year, it would make no difference," Velmeran insisted. "I do not want someone to take Dveyella's place; that would be false. I do not love you, not the way you want. But I think that I do love you; I do know that you make me feel very calm and comfortable. I need time. Love me and I will love you in return, I can promise you that."

She nodded. "We will accept each other on our own terms, and I believe that we will work out a comfortable compromise. Will you come with me now?"

"I will," he said, taking the hand she offered. "Although I cannot imagine what pleasure you might find in my company just now."

Consherra smiled and drew him close. "As strange as it might seem, nothing would give me greater pleasure than to hold you in my arms and keep away your worries and fears while you sleep."

"I suspect that I would like that myself," he said, and submitted willingly to her kiss. Then, arm in arm, they turned and entered her cabin.

Farther down the hall, a vacuum cleaner lowered its camera pod and sighed with relief.

"Ah, our good Sector Commander returns from the dead!"

Donalt Trace peered about the room as best he could. He did not have much success, for he found himself lying facedown on a bed, his arms, legs and head immobilized by some type of framework. He did not have to see to know who it was; his uncle's cheerful tone was particularly grating. His back ached fiercely and he knew why, although he was not certain that he wanted to know the particulars. Councilor Lake moved into his field of vision, seating himself in a chair facing him.

"You look terrible," his uncle commented at last.

"How the hell am I supposed to look?" Trace demanded. "I was ambushed and shot by Starwolves."

"You were shot in the back while running for your life," Lake corrected him. "Do not be afraid to admit the truth. That was the only intelligent thing you did yesterday."

"Yesterday?" Trace asked in disbelief. "I must have caught it good, then. This is more than just burns from bolt flash?"

"A bit," the Councilor explained, leaning back casually. "Those Starwolf pistols carry a kick like our rifles, and you took a shot square in the middle of your backbone. Dr. Mervask worked on you fourteen hours yesterday, and that was just getting started. But you are likely to live now."

"Just tell me!" Trace hissed impatiently.

"Very well. It might shut you up. The good doctor put in a biosynthetic graft to replace the sixteen centimeters of spinal cord you lost, as well as eight artificial vertebrae. He had the devil of a time finding vertebrae your size, so he will have to replace those with new ones made special for you. Half the muscles in your back will be replaced by forced-growth clone types, as well as a piece of skin big enough to make a tent. You were fortunate in that your backbone actually stopped the bolt from cutting right through you. You were unfortunate in that your jacket caught fire and gave you more serious burns than you might have had."

"The old dress blues," Trace remarked. "Did the spinal grafts take?"

"Seemed to," the Councilor said. "The medical scanners insist that it will function as good as the original. The doctor says that your back is not likely to be the same—too much structural reconstruction. You will kick ass again, just not as hard."

"Good enough," Trace said, relieved. "What about the Starwolves?"

"Oh, they got what they wanted, poked a hole in the dome, and left. They leveled the Government Building, the Residence and Farstell Trade. They also completely destroyed the planetary defense power complex, and the sector fleet is gone—absolutely gone. All we have left are the carriers, which did not arrive in time. The Starwolves got clear with no loss or damage. Now that is planning!"

"Wait just a moment," Trace protested. "If they leveled the Government Building..."

"Do you recall passing a pair of guards and ordering them to follow?" Lake asked. "They were normal, short-legged humans and you quickly left them behind. They arrived just in time to sneak you out of the room, and they got you into a lift and to the levels below the building before the Starwolves blasted it."

Trace did not answer. Whatever drug he had been given to awaken him was no longer at its peak effectiveness; the pain suppressants that made him unaware of his ruined back were beginning to win out, clouding his thinking and deteriorating his awareness.

"What now?" he asked in weary resignation. He was hardly able to care about anything, except for a dim hatred of one Starwolf.

"Now?" the Councilor asked thoughtfully, crossing his arms. "Now we learn from our mistakes. For fifty thousand years we have fought them on our terms, and the best we have been able to achieve is an uneasy peace, mostly because we are too big to swallow whole. Now we are going to have to fight them on our terms if we are going to survive. I have already ordered construction of the first of our Fortresses."

Trace opened one very alert eye. "Do you mean that?"

"Of course I mean that! I never say things that I do not mean," Councilor Lake said impatiently. "In the last three weeks or so the Starwolves have wrecked enough of our ships to pay for the thing. We might as well spend our money on something they cannot tear up so easily. Of course, it will be two years before the thing is ready. Construction will be slow because we have most of the sector fleet to replace, as well as repairs to the city."

"So long?" Trace muttered as he began to surrender to the drugs.

"I am afraid so. But then, it will not be ready any sooner than you are, so don't worry about it," Lake said. Then noticing that his nephew was once again unconscious, he rose to leave. "Dream about it."

The group that gathered in the storage bay of one of the Methryn's smaller holding bays was indeed a little one, consisting only of the ships themselves, their Commanders, designates and helms. The center of attention was the immense gray block of the Vardon's memory cell, now secured in a special cradle. Consherra, assisted by the other two helms, was quietly assembling a large portable unit of computer equipment. Three probes, each with a ribbon of a different color tied about its long metal neck, hovered near. When everything was ready, Valthyrra called the others close so that she and Consherra could explain.

"There are two very important questions associated with this rather unimpressive block of metal," Valthyrra began. "The first question, of course, is the location of Terra. And the second is why the Union has never been able to access the information it contains. I do not expect to find the answer to the first any time soon, but I am going to try. Consherra will explain the second right now."

"We know that the Union has never been able to gain access to this unit," Consherra began quickly. "Since the memory cells of our ships contain vital information, their functions are our most carefully guarded secrets. Only two people on board any ship, the helm and the ship itself, know these secrets and can gain access to certain portions of the ship's computer. The core of the computer, the thinking portions, can only be opened in airdock.

"These memory cells have built-in safeguards to prevent access," she continued, picking up a thick-cabled lead from the portable unit beside her. "There are six receptacles at each end of the memory cell. Each receptacle accepts a fifty-two-prong lead, but only fifty of those prongs actually work. The other two prongs act as keys. Two of the fifty-two slots of each receptacle are lock-out devices. If prongs are inserted into these slots, the entire receptacle shuts down. The two lock-out slots are located at random among the total, and their location is different for each receptacle. You must know which prongs to remove to gain access, and all twelve receptacles must be operating to gain initial access. After that, only one lead must be functional to access the unit.

"Even then, you have to know the access code to phase the unit into the rest of your computer network. Even then, if the unit senses that it is not a part of a real ship's computer, it will shut itself down. The casing is shielded against X-ray, scanner probe and psychic divination, and physical tampering or disassembly of the unit triggers a self-destruct. And that is how we know that the Union never accessed it or tried to open it."

"I am going to try to access this unit," Valthyrra added as Consherra began to connect the leads. "I will tell you now that I will not be very successful. The first thing I will get as I open it will be the complete program that defined Theralda Vardon at the time of her destruction. That program will be at odds with my own in an open battle of electronic schizophrenia, causing the unit to remain a foreign object in my computer network. I will not get free access, but I do hope for a general overview. That might tell me if the information we seek is indeed inside this unit."

"What then?" Daelyn asked. "Even if it is there, you still will not have it."

"There is a new ship in the construction bay at Home Base," she answered. "Ordinarily new ships are given a general personality to serve as a foundation for building their own. Instead we will install this memory cell into that ship and simply bring the Vardon back to life in a new body. Mechanical regeneration, so to speak. Salamanders never had it so good."

"It used to be common practice," Gelvessa Karvand added, "in the early days of the war, that when a ship was heavily damaged—beyond reasonable repair—that its surviving memory cells would be transferred to a new ship."

"We are ready to try," Consherra said after locking in the final lead.

"Very well, then," Valthyrra replied, with just a trace of reluctance.

She settled her probe on a tabletop to prevent any accidents when she released control. She did not risk any damage from this, but if her own personality programming became locked in battle with that of the Vardon's, then she would have to shut down her computer core for the few moments she would need to rebuild her own identity. During that time the Methryn would be without guidance, and she was safely installed in a stable orbit to insure that nothing undesirable would happen during that time.

Valthyrra began the process of opening the memory cell, making her acquaintance with the unit through proper access codes. It recognized her and immediately fed her Theralda Vardon's personality program, and for the moment all she could do was to hold tightly to her own identity. If she became locked in a loop with that warring program, then she would have to cut contact. But it played out once and ceased, and the core of the cell lay open to her. She approached it cautiously, and was immediately engulfed in a flood of images, impressions and data. The instructions that would allow her minute examination of those files were in the Vardon's personality program, closed to her.

Those who watched could not see her struggle, although there was a vacant appearance to the probe's camera pod. That pod dipped slowly, sinking gradually as the seconds passed. Then it snapped back to full attention and glanced around at Consherra, who quickly shut down the computer link.

"Well?" Mayelna prompted impatiently.

"Well, I have good news and bad news," Valthyrra answered. "This is the Theralda's primary cell for her personal memories, and not a general data-storage cell. On the other hand, the location of Terra, important data that she may have consulted often, is probably inside this cell as well. We will not know until the Vardon is restored to life."

"And when will that be?" Commander Korlan asked.

"Twenty to thirty years from now."

The Starwolf fleet stayed only a day in that uninhabited system, since they wanted to return to their individual territories before news of the attack on Vannkarn could spread. They waited only long enough for the fighters to be stripped of their accessory cannons, serviced and returned to their own ships. During that time the ships and their Commanders discussed how they thought the rest of the Union would react to their raid. There were seventeen other sectors to be considered, seventeen other High Councilors and Sector Commanders, who had long assumed their inner worlds to be safe from these four-armed pirates.

There would be some reassessment of the standing and the power of the Starwolves on the part of the Union and the Starwolves themselves. The Union would be shaken to its core and that core would be angry and resentful. But it would also be frightened and apprehensive, unsure when and where the wolf ships would strike again. And they would strike again and again; the Starwolves had already decided that. The Union was going to be taught to fear the Starwolves, and above all the names of Velmeran and the Methryn.

Velmeran was on his way to the bridge just as the Methryn and her sister ships were making ready to leave orbit. He and his mother had seen Daelyn away only an hour before, an event that he recalled with sadness. He admired his sister greatly, for she was about the most interesting person he had ever met. That, she explained to his complete mystification, was because they were exactly alike. He did regret that she could not be with him for this final task. He did know that Consherra would want to be there, so he got off the lift at her corridor to collect her.

Consherra opened the door and stood staring at him in surprise. He was not in armor, but wore instead the closest thing the Starwolves had to a uniform. He was dressed in the solid black of a pilot, tunic and pants with boots tucked up under the cuffs, and a short cape fastened about the collar. His shaggy mane of thick brown hair was carefully brushed, laying neatly over his shoulders and falling into a smooth cascade halfway down his back. Combed to its proper length, his hair hung down over his eyes, which glittered within its shadow as he returned her stare. In spite of the lack of armor, he still looked very much the warrior —in spite of the inherently adolescent look of his features.

"Are you about to go up to the bridge?" he asked, almost eagerly. "I am on my way up to the bridge, and I do not want you to miss this."

"Yes, I am on my way there now," she replied uncertainly. "Miss what?"

"I have one more surprise for Valthyrra and the Commander," he replied cryptically. "You will have to wait and see."

"I will be patient then," she said, joining him as he returned to the lift. "Actually, I am pleased that you should remember me."

"Why should I not?" he asked. "We have not been alone together these past two days, but I have not forgotten you, and I never will. Are you certain of our love?"

"Are you?" she asked as they waited for the lift.

Velmeran frowned, glancing down shyly. "You were always open in your affections, and I was too innocent to realize that I was being courted. But who do you love? I am two people now. Do you see only Velmeran the warrior? He is strong and forceful and a very fascinating person, I do admit, but he is also false. He is the person I become when duty requires. But I want love during the time which is my own, from someone who knows and loves the real me. Do you understand what I am trying to say?"

"Of course I understand, but you are wrong," she insisted. "The two Velmerans you describe are one and the same, and I love them both."

They entered the lift, which had arrived a moment earlier, and Consherra quickly set the controls for the bridge. She turned back to him as soon as the door was shut. "To be truthful, you did surprise me. I held you in my arms four hours while you slept, and I assumed that we would become mates before you left me. I had the distinct impression that the thought did not even occur to you."

"Perhaps I am looking for more," Velmeran replied defensively, but his look argued that she was right. "Sex itself is easy enough for me to find just now. I have had five offers for duty mating since I returned from Vinthra, and I refused them all."

"What?" she asked incredulously. "Like it or not, you are Velmeran the Magnificent, and you have a certain responsibility to spread your well-ordered genes far and wide."

"Do you think that I am not aware of that? You are my mate, whether our union has been consummated or not. That is all I care about."

"Then what are you waiting for? You had the opportunity."

"I forgot! So what?" he demanded in return.

It was a good thing that the lift came to a stop at that moment, since it gave him a chance to escape. Consherra took her place at the helm console while Velmeran continued on to the upper bridge. The Methryn had already left orbit and now flew at the head of an arrowhead formation, flanked by her two sister ships as they accelerated casually to light speed. Velmeran saw that Valthyrra was watching him with particular interest; the formality of his appearance did not escape her notice. Mayelna's appearance was almost a mirror of his own except in white. Velmeran saw that his timing continued to be precise; it seemed that she had the same thought in mind.

"Ah, Meran. Half a moment," Mayelna said, glancing up briefly before returning to the com mike in the arm of her chair. "Three months it is, then?"

"Right," Commander Schyrrana replied. "Of course, you will need to come in two or three weeks before so that Velmeran can give it a good look and work up a plan. But he can do it."

Velmeran can do what? he had to wonder. He glanced at Valthyrra, but she only continued to stare at him in a most disconcerting manner.

"No problem," Mayelna promised. "We will see you then."

"No problem," Velmeran echoed sarcastically.

Mayelna glanced up at him. "Gelvessa Karvand has a

little task for you. Nothing on the order of what you just did. Is that all right with you?"

"Of course," he insisted. "That is my business."

She triggered her seat to roll back, out of the confines of her console, so that she could stand, moving up closely so that they could speak privately.

"Meran, are you happy?" she asked simply.

"Yes, I believe so," Velmeran agreed. "There is much for me to do. But I will take it piece by piece, and it does not frighten me."

"That is where we are different, you and I," she shrugged at her own helplessness. "Fate never whispers in my ear, the way it seems to take such good care of you. I have decided that, instead of fighting it, I should take advantage of my assets and give you command of this ship in such matters that are my own weakness."

She glanced over at Velmeran, as if for his approval, and he nodded.

"It has also occurred to me that this ship has gone entirely too long without a Commander-designate," she continued briskly.

"I understand," Velmeran replied gently. "That is why I am here."

"It is not as if Valthyrra has had any trouble deciding. . . . " Mayelna paused and turned to stare at him. "What do you mean you understand?"

"If Valthyrra wants me to command this ship some-day, then I would be happy to do it," he explained. "In fact, I have known for some time that I was being cultivated for that role. Add Consherra to the group, and the three of you are about as subtle as a herd of thark bison. I was fascinated to see which was going to endure longer, Valthyrra's patience or your own stubborn resolution. I also suspect that she knew that I knew."

"That seems obvious enough," Mayelna said, glancing suspiciously at the camera pod. "She is not at all surprised by this turn of events . . . just very self-satisfied."

"Of course I knew," Valthyrra insisted. "I knew that if

you did not go to him, then he would eventually come to you."

Mayelna turned to Velmeran. "Is that what you really want? In just a few short years I will be gone, and you will still be very young."

"Yes, it is what I want," he agreed. "I have found my purpose. I enjoy flying and I will miss the packs, but it is not enough. My purpose leads me here."

Mayelna nodded. "I understand that now. Back when you were seeking some meaning and purpose in your life, it was here all along. And you are very, very lucky, Meran. Few people ever find the true meaning and purpose of their lives except in retrospect. I made a mistake, and I am sorry for it. I tried to judge this matter for you, because I thought we were so much alike."

"We are not so different," Velmeran said. "Perhaps you were thinking only of what you wanted for me. If you had really looked into your heart, you would have known that I would make this same decision."

"I realize that now," she agreed. "The Aldessan do tell us that our futures lie in shadows, while our pasts are open to the plain light of day. I have been seeking the meaning and purpose of my own life, now that most of my years are behind me. You are the best part of my life, as it turns out. Not only do I leave the best part of myself behind, but something even better. And I am content."

Velmeran smiled shyly, and allowed her to take him gently in her arms. Valthyrra glanced away, as if to hide tears forming in the lenses of her cameras, while Consherra leaped from her seat and rushed from the bridge. The two Kelvessan were left staring in surprise.

"Well, there she goes again," Mayelna remarked. "Now what do you suppose got into those two?"

Velmeran smiled. "Too many wishes coming true at once, if I had to guess."

"Indeed? Well, the first rule to commanding this ship is to make it clear that only a certain amount of this behavior will be tolerated." She walked over to give the camera pod a sharp rap. "Get under way, you aged hulk! We have work to do."

"Right away, Commander," Valthyrra replied in an uncertain voice.

Still flying in close formation, the three carriers cut acceleration from their main drives, diverting that power into their star drives. The immense crystal engines began to glow from deep within, growing steadily brighter as they built to power, and exploded suddenly into life. As one the three ships moved into starflight, each one carried upon twin shafts of brilliant light.

MORE FROM QUESTAR®...

THE BEST IN SCIENCE FICTION AND FANTASY

___FORBIDDEN WORLD___   (E20-017, $2.95, U.S.A.)
by David R. Bischoff and Ted White   (E20-018, $3.75, Canada)
This is a novel about a distant world designed as a social experiment. Forbidden World recreates regency London, Rome in the time of the Caesars, and a matriarchal agrarian community in a distant part of space—with devastating results!

___THE HELMSMAN___   (E20-027, $2.95, U.S.A.)
by Merl Baldwin   (E20-026, $3.75, Canada)
A first novel that traces the rise of Wilf Brim, a brash young starship cadet and son of poor miners, as he tries to break the ranks of the aristocratic officers who make up the Imperial Fleet—and avenge the Cloud League's slaughter of his family.

___THE HAMMER AND THE HORN___   (E20-028, $2.95, U.S.A.)
by Michael Jan Friedman   (E20-029, $3.75, Canada)
Taking its inspiration from Norse mythology, this first novel tells the story of Vidar, who fled Asgard for Earth after Ragnarok, but who now must return to battle in order to save both worlds from destruction.

WARNER BOOKS
P.O. Box 690
New York, N.Y. 10019

Please send me the books I have checked. I enclose a check or money order (not cash), plus 50¢ per order and 50¢ per copy to cover postage and handling.* (Allow 4 weeks for delivery.)

_____ Please send me your free mail order catalog. (If ordering only the catalog, include a large self-addressed, stamped envelope.)

Name _____

Address _____

City _____

State _____ Zip _____

*N.Y. State and California residents add applicable sales tax.   136